SAVIOR

FIONA COLE

A FREEBIE FOR YOU!

Want a free book from me filled with suspense and steamy tension? Make sure you sign up for my newsletter and claim your free book!

Be the first to know about new releases by following me on BookBub.

To Karla.
#DreamTeam

PLAYLIST

Naked - James Arthur
Leave a Light On - Tom Walker
Howl - Florence + The Machine
Best of You - Foo Fighters
Come Out and Play - Billie Eilish
Saviour - George Ezra (ft. First Aid Kit)
I Won't Back Down - Dawn Landes
There's No Way - Lauv (ft. Julia Michaels)
Rise - Katy Perry
Let You Love Me - Rita Ora
Hurt You - The Weeknd & Gesaffelstein
What Kind of Man - Florence + The Machine
Is That Alright - Lady Gaga
Walk Me Home - P!nk
This Year's Love - David Gray

1

ALEXANDRA

A NIGHT WITH A VIRGIN: $10,000.

My stomach grumbled and I couldn't tell if it was from the nausea rolling through at the headline. Or from the hunger pains ripping through me.

I'd sat at this same computer at the library a week ago. I'd been searching for quick ways to make money and the suggestions started with using apps to save a buck on your groceries, which was useless since I didn't have a phone or money for groceries. After about thirty-two more clicks down a dark rabbit hole, I'd found something I could use for money. Me.

My sister had stripped and done God knows what in the back room, but I'd always promised I wouldn't sell myself for money. I'd rather starve, which was my current situation.

Apparently, I wouldn't rather starve because here I was considering selling my virginity just to lessen the pain. I reasoned that it was just a night. It was just once. I wasn't a prostitute. I was just a desperate girl trying to gain some traction in my life.

I'd seen the site and saw how much people were willing to pay. Then I'd read a comment about how much someone would pay for a virgin. My jaw hit the floor, my mind racing with the possibilities of what that kind of money could do. I could go to college. I could pay the rent. I could pay for electricity *and* groceries. My mouth had watered at the mere thought of something other than stale PB&J and ramen. So, I'd printed it off the screen to save the link and quickly ran to grab the paper before anyone saw it.

Folding it up, I stuck it in my pocket and carried it with me everywhere, constantly weighing the pros and cons.

Last night, after another late shift at the grocery store, I counted out the twenty dollars I had left over for the month and realized groceries weren't in the budget. My stomach had rumbled in protest and the paper had burned a hole in my pocket. I made a decision then and there.

I'd stolen some of my sister's makeup, highlighting my blue eyes and tousled my black hair, adding red lipstick for the Snow White look, and headed to the library. The camera on the computer wasn't great, but it worked. I uploaded it to the site and typed up the offer. All I had to do was hit enter.

"We're getting ready to close," the librarian called from the doorway.

I took one last deep breath, closed my eyes, and hit enter.

Done. It was done. My eyes glued to the chat box, waiting for a notification to pop up like someone would respond within the second, but nothing happened. My shoulders dropped and my heart sank. Maybe it was all for nothing. Maybe no one would want me anyway and I'd worried for no reason. The possibilities vanished like wishes in the wind.

Feeling defeated, I closed out of the browser and grabbed my bag. I stopped by the bathroom to fill up my water bottle with clean water before heading home. I didn't want to look in the mirror, not wanting to see what met my eyes, but I couldn't help myself.

Smudged eyeliner. Hallowed cheeks. Pale skin. Dull eyes.

I struggled to find the determination to persevere that usually lingered behind the blue eyes my mom claimed would captivate any man.

But it *was* still there. I had all the determination I could muster and it had to be enough. Lifting my chin, I clenched my jaw and stared, daring the girl in the mirror to deny we would make it. Before I could falter, I turned away and walked out, heading home.

My stomach rumbled again and I curled in on myself with each step. Thinking of the twenty dollars I had, I decided I could peel a few singles off to buy a couple packs of ramen.

The lights were on at home when I turned the corner into the trailer park. I took a deep breath to prepare myself for my sister before pushing the door open.

Smoke wafted past me, escaping into the night air and I cringed at the acrid smell. I hated the stench of pot. I also hated the disgusting man sitting next to my sister on the couch.

They were both hunched over, her kneeling on the floor leaning down to suck up a white powder through a paper, and him crushing the pills to make powder.

"I told you not to bring that shit here."

Both their heads jerked up. My sister's eyes were already glossy and unfocused, her body swaying from the motion of jerking upright. Oscar's were more clear as they scanned me up and down with a disgusting smirk that made my skin crawl.

"Didn't," he said. "Your sister is treating me tonight."

Leah smiled up at Oscar like he told her she was the prettiest girl in the world.

"Anything for you, babe," she slurred.

I cringed, my mind swirling with all the ways my sister could have gotten the drugs. She used to work, but now she couldn't keep a job—always too high or drunk to make it to work consistently.

"Where'd you get the money, Leah?"

She looked down at the table and began making more lines, shrugging as she flippantly replied, "Found it lying around."

Bullshit. There was never any money just lying around. My heart stuttered and all the air left my lungs. *She wouldn't have.* I tried to reason with myself as I ran down the hall, fire burning behind my eyes. My door hammered against the wall and I rushed to my dresser, falling to my knees. I ripped the drawer open, almost pulling it from its tracks, and searched through the pants folded inside.

Nothing. There was nothing in there.

Not a bill to peel off for ramen.

No money to get me to and from work.

Nothing to ease the knives cutting away at my stomach.

Tears slipped down my cheeks until drops darkened the denim covering my thighs.

How could she?

It was all I could think until the pain shifted—morphed into a fiery rage threatening to burn the cheap trailer down. I clenched my jaw and roughly wiped the tears from my cheeks and stood. I tried to take a deep breath to calm myself and find a way to stay in my room, but the flames grew until they burned my throat and I was going to explode.

Clenching my fists, I stomped down the hall. Leah and Oscar were too lost in their haze, their bodies swaying to the music coming from Oscar's phone, to pay attention to me. I rounded the table until I stood in front of Leah and she still didn't look up at me. My anger grew until it had a life of its own—until it controlled my muscles and vocal cords.

I shoved her shoulder hard, slamming her against the couch,

but she bounced back and even giggled. The lack of satisfaction roared through me.

"How could you?" I screamed. "How fucking could you? That was *my* money. *My* money to get to work." Her eyes widened and she cowered back against the cushions finally realizing it wasn't a joke. I'd never lost my cool before. "You fucking bitch. You lazy bitch. I hate you."

I saw Oscar moving out the corner of my eye, but I was too consumed by my anger to pay attention. At least until he shoved me back. I stumbled but managed to stop my fall with my hand on the wall.

"Don't fucking talk to her like that," he yelled, stumbling. The shove had knocked him off balance.

"Fuck you, Oscar. You're a disgusting pig."

"Well, you're a bitch with a stick up her ass."

His angry sneer softened before twisting into a disgusting smirk. The fire pushing me earlier ebbed at his change in mood, sending alarm bells ringing. I edged my way around the table, keeping my back to the wall and my eyes on him.

"Maybe you just need to loosen up. Maybe you need a little Molly to cheer you up."

Faster than I thought possible with all the drugs in his system, he snatched up a pill and lunged for me. I tried to turn and run down the hall, but he grabbed the back of my jacket and jerked, knocking me off my feet. Air whooshed out of my lungs when I hit the ground. He took the moment to grab my ankle and flip me before straddling my hips.

My stomach threatened to revolt and throw up the water sloshing around, but decided to hold on to what little was in there. Oscar smiled down at me, his teeth yellow and not all there as he held up a white pill.

No. No, no, no, no.

I tried to sit up and hit him, but he pressed my shoulders to the ground, his bony fingers digging into the soft spot under my clavicle. His rancid breath reached me from above and renewed my energy. I slapped my hands wherever I could hit—formed fists and tried to connect with his face. I used all the strength in my legs to try and lift him off me, but for as scrawny and emaciated as he looked, he was heavy and stronger than me.

"Come on, Alexandra. It's just a little Molly. It'll make you feel so good and I'll be here to help you through all that pleasure."

My stomach cramped again but I forced it down. I needed to focus to get out of this. Looking around the room, I searched for a weapon—anything within reach to knock him out. My sister sat behind the table, making lines like she didn't even notice her boyfriend pinning me to the ground.

"Leah," I yelled. "Leah, please."

Her head lifted slowly and when her eyes met mine, they were empty. It took a full ten seconds before they focused on me, but they were still vacant as a small smile tipped her wide lips. "Oh, hey Alex."

"She's too fucked up to help you." Oscar's laugh brought my attention back to him. "I never thought about having you because you were such a prude, but with a little help, maybe I can have both sisters at once."

He leaned down to bring the white pill to my mouth and my moment hit. With a cry filled with all my fury, I slammed my fist into his cheek. It didn't knock him out like I hoped, but it did throw him off balance enough for me to force him off me. I scrambled to my feet and backed away.

"You fucking bitch," he wailed from the floor. He was crouched on his knees holding his hand to his face, his eyes screwed shut.

I stepped forward and kicked him in the thigh before backing away quickly. He shouted again, his other hand going to grip his leg. I hadn't kicked him too hard, just enough to ease the strain on my muscles and make a point.

"Don't you ever fucking touch me again or I'll fucking kill you." I wasn't sure how true it was, but in that moment, with my blood on fire and my heart pounding in my chest, I would.

I backed down the hall, never taking my eyes off him and locked my door as soon as I was in my room. Snatching a pillow and blanket from my bed, I darted back to the door, pressing my back to the wood. I didn't want to be an easy victim in my bed if he decided to pick the shitty lock keeping him out. I stripped out of my jacket but kept my tennis shoes on in case I needed to run.

Then I fluffed the cheap pillow and pulled the blanket over me, my back still pressed to the only thing between me and the raging dickhole outside.

Not long after I'd settled, I could hear their moans and grunts and my stomach grumbled. Curling in on myself to stop the cramping pain, I plugged my ears and hoped that maybe when I went to the library tomorrow a message would be waiting for me.

2

ERIK

"SORRY TO INTERRUPT, BOSS."

My eyes moved past the breasts bouncing in my face to see Jared covering his eyes as he looked in the opposite direction. The blonde who I was currently fucking turned to look over her shoulder, a coy smile tipping her lips.

"Come to join in?" she asked Jared before turning to lock her eyes on mine. "You know I'm an adventurous type." She slid up and down my cock again before leaning down to whisper in my ear, "Especially for you."

Tempting, but Jared's projects always came first. Always. I gripped her hips to hold her in place, ignoring her pout, and directed my order to Jared. "Continue."

"There's a matter that I think you'd want to be a part of."

"Thank you. I'll be right there."

Jared left the room as soon as the words left my mouth. He'd been with me for a while, so he was used to my activities. It wasn't like he could see anything with the way her skirt draped over where I was buried inside her.

I lifted her off my softening cock and set her on the couch next to me, ignoring the whining protest forming on her lips. Tucking myself back into my pants, I stood, preparing to leave. Her full red lip was stuck out like a pouty child, which contradicted the full breasts spilling out the top of her dress.

"Seriously?" she finally said, her voice shrill and grating.

It was rude to stop mid-fuck and leave her there, but I'd already given her an orgasm before I'd even entered her. Besides, she was just another woman to lose myself inside of for a moment in time. Nothing to keep me from what took priority over everything.

"I have a matter that requires my attention. I appreciate you stopping by for dinner, but I need to go."

Her jaw hanging open was the last thing I saw before I stepped into the hall. My secretary looked up from where she was packing her belongings into her bag to go home for the day.

"Please make sure Miss Stutz gets out safely to a cab."

Only a slight twinge of regret pinched my chest at making Laura stay, but I couldn't waste any more time.

Jared's office was two doors down from mine. I walked into the generic room with a desk, computer, and chair. Nothing extra besides a diploma on the wall indicating that it was actually inhabited by a person. I moved to the other door on the right and held my thumb over the scanner before hearing a click. This was Jared's real office.

On paper, his job title was an IT analyst, but in reality, he was a hacker I employed personally. We'd connected a couple years ago by accident when our paths crossed. Both of us were trying to stop a sale of women and I'd been damn lucky he happened to be there. After that night, we talked and I realized he was much better than me at filtering his way through the dark web, so I made him an offer he couldn't turn down.

I stepped into the second room. This one contained a couch, a mini-fridge, and a table with a lamp and a photo of his family against the wall. Across from that was a wall of six monitors, two keyboards, and probably the fanciest office chair I'd ever seen. I'd given him free rein on how he wanted to utilize the space with no budget in mind. I think he put most of the money toward that damn chair.

"What do you have?"

Jared briefly glanced my way over his shoulder, the light from the monitors illuminating his face. I'd offered a room with windows, but he claimed he didn't want the glare.

"This popped up late last night," he said, gesturing to the computer directly in front of him. "I responded as soon as I saw it, but I just got an answer now."

I leaned over his shoulder and read the headline: "A night with a virgin: $10,000." Below that was a picture of a girl that knocked the wind from my chest. She was gorgeous. A living version of Snow White. She had porcelain skin that made her heavily shadowed eyes stand out even more. Her eyes—Jesus—they were like silver. Such a faint blue tinged the edge of the pupil and faded to gray on the outside. And to top it all off were her full lips painted a sinful red to match the seductive smirk.

But her eyes held the truth. They didn't hold the same come hither look, even though she tried. I could see the nerves and fear behind them. I questioned my sanity as I stared and felt like she was reaching out through the screen and begging for help.

"She's gonna be eaten up and spit out," Jared said with disgust. "If I hadn't caught it when I had, she'd already be sold and last less than a week with how much they'd use her."

My stomach revolted at the vision he painted. I squeezed my eyes shut tight trying to erase the images that haunted my nightmares. I needed to focus.

I looked down at the screen to see the exchange Jared had begun.

Mr_E (11:23pm): I'm interested
snow_white_783 (6:14pm): Okay.

I looked down at my watch to see that ten minutes had passed. Hopefully we hadn't lost her.

"Did you track the IP address?"

"A local library." At my furrowed brow, he explained, "Harder to track a person in a public area."

"Cameras?" I asked.

"Already looked and they didn't have anything suspicious that I could pick up on."

"Let me respond," I said, gesturing for him to pass the keyboard.

He slid it across the desk and I hunched to begin typing.

Mr_E (6:25pm): Do you have a specific place you'd like to meet?
snow_white_783 (6:25pm): Budget Inn on Eighth St.

My hand rubbed down my face, picturing the shitty part of town the hotel was located in. No one would ask questions if they heard a woman screaming for help as she was dragged to a car. Taking a deep breath, I thought of my next question. Maybe I could get more information on who was in charge of the sale. The leaders were always the bigger goal when saving the women. We needed to cut off as many heads as we could.

Mr_E (6:28pm): Who should I pay?

snow_white_783 (6:28pm): Me.

Mr_E (6:28pm): Will you be in there the entire time I'm with the girl?

There was a long pause as I waited for the response and I worried I'd lost my chance to another client.

snow_white_783 (6:31pm): I'm the girl in the photo. I'll be the only one in the room.

Mr_E (6:31pm): Will your pimp be okay with me paying without direct contact?

snow_white_783 (6:32pm): I don't have a pimp.

Mr_E (6:32pm): Then who is in charge of the sale? Whatever you want to call him.

snow_white_783 (6:33pm): It's just me. I'm in charge of it.

"What the fuck?" Jared breathed next to me.

"She's doing this alone? She's doing this alone." Maybe repeating it would have it make more sense.

"What the fuck?" Jared said again, apparently needing to repeat his shock too.

"Why? Why would she put herself in this kind of danger?" I couldn't fathom why she would do that. My mind spun around the fact that she had optionally gone onto this site and chosen to sell herself.

"People get desperate."

"That's a shit excuse." I jerked back from the laptop needing a minute to think. I paced the small distance to the wall and back again, trying to wrap my head around it. "Her life would be over. She'd die. And she's doing it *voluntarily*." I was almost shouting by the end.

Jared held his hands up. "Don't have to tell me, Erik."

"We need to set this up and get her taken down from here before someone else pulls her in."

"Already on it. As soon as we set it up, she'll be hidden from other viewers like she wasn't even there."

Mr_E (6:35pm): When?
snow_white_783 (6:35pm): Tomorrow night? 8pm?
Mr_E (6:36pm): Done.

"Delete it," I commanded as soon as I hit enter.

Jared's fingers moved quickly across the board until the conversation and her profile no longer existed. "This is a little different than the others since we're not doing an extraction. Do you still want me to call MacCabe in?" When I didn't speak, his fingers stopped moving and he turned to look up at me. "Erik?"

"No," I said, coming to a decision. "I'll go."

"What?" he practically screeched.

I understood his shock. I usually handed them off to a security company, occasionally joining in. But like he'd said, this was different.

It would be the only thing that was different. Once I retrieved her it would go like all the others: make sure she was back with her family—if she had one—and help with any medical fees to get her back on her feet.

Anything to help blot the horrors of my past.

"I'll go to the meeting and take care of it."

"Do you remember the last time you went to collect?"

"It's been a few years, but it's hard to forget," I answered sarcastically.

"Then why are you going?"

"This is different."

Jared sighed, giving up, knowing he would get nowhere now that I'd made a decision to go.

"Just be careful. I don't want to have to save your ass twice."

Something urged me to be the one to retrieve her, maybe the look in her eyes. I didn't know what it was exactly, but I didn't question it. I followed my gut.

The one time I hadn't, it had cost me my sister.

3

ALEXANDRA

I STOLE two dollars from my cash drawer today at work and dealt with being reprimanded for being short. I'd be able to put it back tomorrow once tonight was over. I just needed a way to get to the hotel and walking wasn't an option. Especially in the little black dress I'd borrowed from Leah. She was a few inches shorter than me, so it barely covered an inch past my bottom and kept riding up.

Rummaging through my bag, I made sure I had everything. A change of clothes because I'd probably want to burn this dress and everything on me before it was all over, and condoms because I wasn't going to leave that to chance. Add that to the list of things I'd stolen from the store and needed to pay for tomorrow.

That was all that was in the bag. I didn't have much else or could think of anything else to bring with me. I didn't need much. Just my body.

I zipped up my bag and lifted it to my shoulder. Looking at my reflection one more time, I smoothed my hands over the stretchy black material covering my curves. My eyes were a stark contrast against the heavy eyeliner, making them look almost silver. My lips were painted a deep red so I looked like the Snow White I used in my username. I wore the makeup like armor, protecting me from the reality of what I was doing.

When I got to the hotel, I was glad for the armor—a mask to help me flirt with the clerk at the front desk. I could be someone else with it on. Someone who leaned over the desk and dragged her finger along her bottom lip as I pouted to the scrawny kid, asking him to let me pay once the night was over. The hotel wasn't nice and had a pay by the hour option, so I was sure he knew exactly where the money would be coming from in the morning.

My mask let me pretend I was a girl who'd done this before and knew what I was doing. My mask let me pretend I wasn't shaking from the inside out with nerves about making a mistake.

Now, looking around the room, the feeling that this was a mistake hit me like a sledgehammer.

I'd spent the night wondering who I'd open the door to. Would it be an old man who had an affinity for young virgins? Would he be attractive? Would he be dangerous? Would he hurt me?

I shook away the questions. It was too late. The clock said it was already five past eight and there was no turning back. I'd be fine. It was just a hymen. Even if the guy was rough and gross, it was only a night. One night to get me through the rest of my life.

Watching the minutes tick by, I wondered if I got the time mixed up. I tried to double check this morning at the library, but the chat was gone—my whole ad was gone. I assumed the website removed everything once it had all been set up. So, I went from memory, but the closer it got to eight-thirty, the more I questioned it.

I jumped and my heart skipped a beat when a hard knock came at the door.

This was it.

I was doing this.

I could do this.

No more stealing money. No more laying in bed praying to fall asleep so I could ignore the hunger. No more sleeping in front of my door to keep any predators out.

No. I just needed to walk across the room, open the door, and give myself to one predator to save me from all the others.

I closed my eyes, pictured my future, and took a deep breath. Letting it out slowly, I released as much fear as I could and walked over.

With a trembling hand, I opened the door and froze at what greeted me on the other side.

The first thing my eyes collided with was a broad chest encased in a black cotton shirt and a black leather jacket. I slowly scanned up to a square jaw dusted with stubble, surrounding lips pinched closed. The bill of his black baseball cap covered his eyes. At least until he looked up, the heated emerald glaring down at me sucked all the air from my body, knocking me back a step.

He was beautiful—easily the most attractive man I'd ever seen, like a model. But the heat wasn't all attraction. The heat mixed with an anger that couldn't be hidden. An anger that made fear rise in me that not even my mask could cover.

His eyes scanned me from top to bottom and back up again. My first instinct was to slam the door in his face, lock it and pray for a miracle that he left. But I reminded myself of my future. I could do this. Steeling my spine, I gripped the door and held strong to sticking with the plan.

"M—Mr. E?" My voice hadn't gotten the memo that we were strong. No, it stuttered out, giving away the tremors rattling my insides.

"Snow White." His voice was soft but deep and somehow reached in my chest and squeezed my lungs tighter.

I held strong to the door and kept the entryway blocked like I'd be able to stop him. Fake it until you make it. "Do you have the money?"

His shoulders bunched before he leaned off to the left and grabbed a black duffel bag and held it out to me.

I stepped back and opened the door wider. "Come in."

He walked into the room, towering over me even in my heels, taking up more space than he should. Like the aura around him filled any empty spot, not leaving enough for me. He dropped the bag by the table and looked around. I remained by the door and never turned my back on him. Holding my breath, I waited for him to turn and claim what he came for. Instead, he faced away from me, looking around the typical cheap motel.

If he had wanted better, then he should have paid himself.

He turned to face me and I took a few steps toward him away from my exit. Keeping my face neutral, I took him in. He was gorgeous like a rugged model, but I'd learned from a young age that looks could hide a monster inside. He may not be an overweight older man, but that didn't mean he wouldn't hurt me. I pulled my shoulders back, forcing confidence as I held his stare. It felt like a duel as we stood across from each other, each of us waiting to make the first move. But I was tired of waiting. I didn't want to drag this out any longer.

Moving my eyes to his chest—avoiding the intensity in his eyes—I reached my hands to the straps of my dress and began working it down my arms. His body stiffened and I focused on the way his arms flexed against the leather and controlling my breathing. I focused on being grateful that he wasn't an old man who would crush me under his weight. But despite his attractiveness, I couldn't hide from the truth that he was emanating an air of danger. Like he was a man barely holding onto his control.

Tugging the dress past my breasts, I ignored the fear of what would become of me when that control snapped. I'd just hooked my thumbs in the material to begin tugging it down my hips when his words cracked like a whip in the quiet room.

"Stop."

My body froze and I blinked, trying to process what he was saying. I took a chance at looking up and found his eyes closed, his jaw clenched and his nostrils flared over heavy breaths. None of it made sense. "W—what?" Seconds ticked by and his eyes stayed closed. My heart thundered and I felt more naked than I would have in nothing. I tugged the dress up to cover myself and held it to me like a shield.

"Are you fucking stupid?"

His words were low and growled like a restrained beast. They crept across the space between us and seeped into the cracks in my armor. Doubt pushed through my barriers, hurting me more than it should. Had I done something wrong?

His eyes slid open and pinned me to the spot. "To let me come in here and then you start stripping?"

"D—did you want to take my clothes off?" I guessed.

He barked a laugh that sounded unused and filled with anything but humor. "No. Jesus Christ." His fists unclenched and one went up to rub at his jaw. "Did you think at all? Did you use any common sense at all when you began this?"

My anger rose, pushing out the pain his words had caused and filling in the fissures he'd created. My armor solidified in place. "I didn't come here to be insulted. As you know I've never done this before."

"No, you came here to get fucked. However I want, right?"

A sneer stretched his lips as he took two long strides to reach me. I backed up, but I didn't have far to go until I hit the wall. Two more steps and he crowded my space, blocking out the dim light coming from the only lamp across the room.

"The things I could do to you."

The words whispered across my skin, making goose bumps prickle down my spine. I pressed against the wall and swallowed hard. No amount of makeup or anger was hiding the fear taking over my body. My eyes flicked to the door, but I wouldn't make it. Maybe if I kneed him in the balls. Maybe I'd buy enough time to grab the money and run. Maybe I'd make it out of this alive.

"There it is. There's the fear that should have stopped you from this dumb mistake."

"It wasn't dumb," I tried to defend. It was weak and we both knew it was a lie. I knew it was dumb, but I was desperate. But defending my choice gave me something else to focus on besides fear.

His hands snapped out and gripped my bare arms. They almost encircled my bicep completely as he yanked me from the wall, closer to his face, and shook me. Not hard, but enough to pull a yelp from me. He bared his teeth like an animal, and growled, "Of course it was dumb. If I was anyone else from that site, I would ruin you. Was that what you wanted?"

"N—no."

I was on my toes, a swirl of fear and anger mixing like a pot of boiling water getting ready to bubble over. I had stuttered my answer, but it came out hard, tired of his judgment and intimidation.

"What would you have done? What if I wanted to fuck your ass? Your throat? What if I wanted to stick every finger inside you until you screamed?"

"Stop. Stop."

"Do you want to be kidnapped?" he shouted, shaking me again. "Sold? Drugged and raped every way possible against your will until you die, chained to a bed alone?"

Fire burned behind my eyes and I squeezed them shut, hating the few tears that leaked out. Each option lashed at me. Each option I'd refused to think of because I'd been desperate. Each option crushing me under fear and rage because I didn't know if that was still my fate or not.

"You're so fucking stupid," he shouted in my face.

I dug my fingers in his chest and pushed against an immovable wall, but it helped. It helped me feel some control. I wasn't just being shaken like a rag doll and questioned by someone who probably didn't know what hunger was.

"Stop calling me that." He wanted to growl at me, then I could growl back.

"Then don't make stupid choices."

"I'm tired of starving," I yelled in his face, feeling the most minor spark of satisfaction at him pulling back, even if it was only an inch. "I'm hungry and tired and desperate. So fuck you and get out."

For the first time since I opened the door, his jaw relaxed. His brows were still furrowed over his eyes that still seared my skin when he looked at me. But his grip on my arms loosened and my feet fully touched the floor. It was as if each muscle slowly released until he'd let go of me completely and backed away a foot. Oxygen flooded the space and I inhaled as deep as I could. He never stopped looking at me, like he was worried I'd bolt or attack if he gave me his back.

"Do you have family I can take you to?"

My eyebrows rose to my hairline, unprepared for the change in topic—unprepared for his soft tone. I tried to keep up and form a coherent response. "What?"

"A family. Someone I can take you to, to get you away from here."

"Why?"

"I'm trying to help you."

I scoffed. "Help me? Really?"

"Have I pinned you to the bed yet and taken what you so

willingly offered?" he snapped, his irritation back, and I shook my head. "And I won't. I came across your post and didn't want anyone else to find it. Someone who would take and take until there was nothing left."

I swallowed and couldn't stop my mind from wondering why he'd been on the site in the first place if he was a good guy.

"Do you have a family?" he asked again.

I dropped my eyes. "No. I have no one."

His Adam's apple bobbed and his shoulders dropped. I watched his hands move up to pull his hat off and run his fingers through his short, dark hair before putting the cap back on. He searched the room like it'd have answers for what to do next. Hopefully, he'd just give up and go, leaving the money behind. He was silent for so long, but I didn't know what to do to fill it, so I continued to hold my dress up and wait.

He eventually faced me again and stood to his full height. I matched his posture, preparing for whatever he was going to say next.

"I want you to leave with me."

My eyes bulged and I reeled back. "What?" My voice was shrill. Why would he want me to come with him? Was he kidnapping me like he'd mentioned others would? Had he decided to take advantage of the situation now that he was here? My chest rose and fell faster and faster with each thought. I held my hands up in front of me like I could fend him off. "No. Please. I'm sorry. You can go and take the money. You're right, this was a mistake. Please just don't...don't..." My voice trailed off, unable to voice the possibilities.

"Stop." He made an effort to soften his features. "I'm not going to kidnap you. I'm...I'm just trying to help you." It looked painful for him to say. "You say you're hungry and desperate, well I'm trying to give you another option that doesn't require you to sell your virginity. I'll give you five thousand to come with me."

Five thousand dollars, just to leave with him? The thought alone had the air rushing from my body. "Whe—where would you take me?"

Was it stupid to even consider? Probably, but my curiosity rose and the sandwich I'd stolen from the market earlier wasn't enough. The thought of real food had my mouth watering and my standards lowering.

"I have an apartment in the city."

"Are you still wanting my virginity?"

He cringed and shook his head.

"I just need to know what to expect."

"Expect dinner and a warm bed. Alone."

And five thousand dollars.

"I don't understand." The night was spiraling out of my control and I was struggling to keep up.

"It's not hard. I'm offering you a safe haven tonight and help tomorrow."

He made it seem so easy. I looked over to the bed, still made with its cheap comforter covered in God knows what. My options were to sleep there or to return back to the trailer and face Leah and Oscar again.

Or I could go with the green-eyed stranger who could have easily done any of the things he'd mentioned, but hadn't.

Maybe I was as stupid as he claimed, but like I'd said, I was desperate. "Okay."

He sighed, his shoulders dropping the tension as he'd waited for my answer. "Pull your dress up and let's go."

I turned sideways, still unsure of turning my back on him and tugged my dress over my shoulders.

"I still need to pay for the room," I explained, grabbing my bag and following him to the door.

"Already done," he explained, not bothering to turn around.

The cool night air brushed across my bare skin. After the

23

onslaught of emotions and fear that had consumed me in the hotel, the fresh air washed over me like a freedom I wasn't sure I'd get again.

He walked to the end of the lot and the lights flashed on a sleek black car. With my hand on the passenger door, I hesitated. Closing my eyes, I said a quick prayer I wasn't wrong—that getting in the car wasn't a mistake.

My mind whispered the reminder that he'd been on that site for a reason I wasn't sure of yet. But my stomach growled and the promise of an actual dinner had me pushing the whispered warning aside and getting in.

4

ERIK

WHAT THE HELL was I doing?

The question rattled in my brain with each step I took toward the car, the girl's heels clicking behind me. By the time we both sat in the small space and the engine purred to life, I still was no closer to figuring out the answer. Glancing out of my peripheral, I watched her tug the too short dress down unsuccessfully to cover her long legs and then shift the bag to do the job.

Neither worked.

My hands squeezed the wheel, hearing the leather creak under the pressure as I forced myself to look away. Realistically, I knew she had to be at least eighteen, but she looked so much younger even under all that makeup. It was the innocence in her silvery eyes that still managed to peek through the hard edge life had given her. My cock had failed to take note of her age when she'd begun stripping out of her clothes. Hell, my cock had failed to be soft at any point after I'd walked into the room. Her innocence had been like a fist squeezing my chest, pushing all the blood down to my groin.

I'd had to clench my fists to keep them at my sides when she'd

25

tugged the material past her breasts. They were encased in a black bra that looked two sizes too small, the plump flesh spilling out so much even the darker edge of her nipple could be seen.

I ground my molars and squeezed my eyes shut to try and blot out the image before backing out. I'd made it about twenty feet when she shifted the bag, pulling my eyes back over—again.

Irritation with myself and my weakness—feeling like a predator—I unintentionally snapped at her. "Do you have anything other than that scrap of material to wear?"

She shrunk in the seat and I bit back my growl. I'd done nothing but scare her all night. But I wasn't sorry for it. She may have been dealt a shit hand to put that edge on her, but she was still young and so naive about the world. It was better I scared her than her winding up dead or worse.

"I have some shorts and a shirt in my bag."

"That's it?"

"I wasn't exactly planning on staying long at the hotel," she snapped back. Good. It boosted my hopes for her when she stiffened her spine and didn't take my shit.

"Do you have more clothes? Somewhere I can take you to get them?"

She bit her lip and stared down at the bag, seeming to think over her answer.

"Yes. I have a place to keep my things."

"Where?"

With a deep breath, she began telling me directions. Her soft-spoken lefts and rights were the only words that filled the car as we worked our way just out of the city and into the shittier part of town.

"Turn here."

She pointed to a gravel road, only partially illuminated by a flickering light. Once I'd made the turn, a trailer park came into view. The first home had a group of men off to the side smoking, who watched my car drive by like it was payday for them. I made a note to have her be quick to avoid any altercations.

My tires crunched over the stones, each scrape sounding like a warning and making me want to reverse out of here and just buy her a new wardrobe.

She finally directed me to the left and my lights illuminated the avocado green trailer. A crate was turned upside down to be used to reach the rotted wooden step in front of the door.

She sighed, her shoulders and head caving in on itself as her hands opened and closed on her lap. "You okay?"

"Just stay here. My sister and her boyfriend are home."

Her *what?* I took a deep breath and closed my eyes trying to convince myself I wasn't being played—trying to convince myself that I wasn't taking in a stray that wasn't really a stray. Maybe she saw me and thought I was a meal ticket to something better than a quick romp for ten-grand. The click of the door opening snapped me out of my pessimism and I snatched her bicep to hold her in place.

"I thought you didn't have anyone to go to," I managed to grind out between my clenched teeth.

She looked down at my hand before glaring at me and easing back into the seat.

"Because I don't have anyone to go to. She may be my sister, but she is by no means someone to rely on. If anything it's the other way around."

I scanned her face looking for any hint of a lie before finally releasing my grip.

She went to move out of the car again, but stopped, not bothering to turn and look at me when she said, "Listen, maybe this is a mistake. Thank you for the ride, but..." She trailed off.

She didn't need to explain. We both knew this was an unconventional situation that had both of us on edge. But maybe I was just as desperate as her to not let her back out into the world alone without knowing she was safe.

I opened my mouth to let her know it wasn't a mistake when a crash came from the trailer. My body tightened going on high alert. But she just let out another sigh before barely turning her head back and muttering another thank you and left.

Yeah fucking right. I opened my own door and slammed it just as she took her first step onto the crate. She turned back, my headlights shining a light on the confusion marring her face.

"What are you doing?"

I didn't say anything because I wasn't the slightest bit sure. A weight sat heavy on my chest and urged me to not leave her alone. I'd hoped I'd have an answer in the few steps it took for me to reach her. I didn't. So when I stood in front of her, her perch on the crate bringing her to my eye-level, I just stared in silence. Her eyebrows rose like she was waiting for a response I still didn't have.

Instead, I reached past her to grab the handle and pushed the door open. "Just go."

She pursed her lips before finally doing as told.

When we entered, she dropped her bag and took off the ridiculously high shoes, dropping five inches, her head now at my chin. I looked past her and took in the clean, but rundown place. Stains marred the walls and ceilings from leaks. The carpet was faded and flat. The furniture was sparse. But what little filled the space was clean and organized.

I'd expected to find her sister when we entered, but the room was also empty and no sound came from anywhere in the house.

"You can go now."

I looked around again and hated the way my gut churned. Everything inside me was telling me not to leave her there, but I couldn't exactly kidnap her.

"Let me at least feed you," I said, buying more time.

A slew of groans and moaning came from down the hall and she cringed, a flush working its way up her neck. I could only imagine that was the sister and boyfriend. "I'll find something to eat here."

I cocked a brow, not believing her. She lifted her stubborn chin, not admitting what we both knew. There was no food here. She'd already confessed to how much she'd struggled. Just because she wouldn't admit it now, didn't mean I wasn't going to make her face it. I strode past her, my long strides taking seconds to bring me to the kitchen.

"Hey," she shouted behind me.

I ignored her and opened cabinets and the refrigerator. Both were barren. Only a few dishes littered the shelves.

I turned and faced where she stood at the entryway of the kitchen with her hands on her hips. "Really? What food will you find later?"

A door slamming open stopped her from responding. A wisp of a girl came stumbling from down the hall, laughing and barely holding herself up against the wall. Her long black hair tangled around her face as she fell to the floor, still laughing. What I assumed was the boyfriend came next with only a pair of jeans barely clinging to his waist. His upper body was pale and scrawny. Seeing the track marks on his arm, I imagined most of his money went to drugs rather than food.

"The other sister is home," the guy said when he saw the girl standing there. He came up behind her and slapped her ass before stumbling back a bit and laughing. My blood roared through my veins and I clenched my fists as I watched her stiffen and step away. "Ready to remove that stick from your ass and replace it with something more fun?" he asked, grabbing his crotch. "Leah's too high for another round, but for you, I could be ready in seconds. Especially if you let me fuck those sweet lips."

"Fuck you, Oscar," she growled.

"Oh, I intend to fuck you." He reached out to grab her, but I stepped out of the shadows of the kitchen and gripped his wrist before he came close.

"Don't," I growled.

"Who the fuck are you?" Oscar sneered.

"Tell your boyfriend to get the fuck off Oscar," the sister—Leah—whined as she struggled to get up from the floor.

"He's not my boyfriend."

"Well, then do you mind if I have a go at him?" Leah said, leering at me with glassy eyes. I could see one was bruised now that she'd brushed some of her hair out of her face. "Oscar can fuck you and I'll play with the new guy."

"Don't be a slut, Leah," Oscar shouted, ripping his hand out of my grip and shoving Leah back.

The girl gasped as she watched Leah stumble back. But Leah caught herself and laughed as she flipped her hair back and stood upright. She was too high to care.

But the girl standing next to me vibrated with rage as she finally got a good look at her sister's face. I watched, as if in slow motion, her whole body pulled tight with tension. Her shoulders slid back and her fists tightened as she slowly turned her head to look at Oscar.

"I'll fucking kill you," she whispered before exploding.

She landed one solid blow to Oscar's face before I was able to wrap my arm around her waist and pull her back into my chest. She squirmed and twisted and lashed out with every limb she had trying to reach him as she screamed obscenities and threats that had me cringing.

"How dare you touch her. You disgusting motherfucker. I will cut off your dick and shove it up your ass before I make you eat your own shit. I will fucking *murder* you. Don't you ever touch her again."

Oscar removed his hands from his swelling eye and glared at

the hellion in my arms, his own body preparing to attack. As much as I'd love to let this woman loose on Oscar, I'd rather not have to deal with the aftermath. I pinned her arms by her side and held her tight, growling in her ear, "We're leaving."

"No," she yelled. "I can't leave her with him."

Oscar took a step toward us and I shoved the girl behind me and used my other arm to pin him to the wall, digging my thumb into the soft tissue below his collarbone. "Get out." I gave my most menacing tone, using every inch of height and pound of muscle to intimidate him.

"No," Leah whined behind me. "Don't hurt him."

"You can't tell me what to do," Oscar challenged. "She wants me here."

I moved my hand to his throat and squeezed, finding satisfaction when his eyes bulged and his hands moved to rip at my fingers. "If I ever find out you hit her again, I'll rip your limbs from your body and beat you with them until you bleed out and die." I knew I couldn't keep him away if her sister wanted him here, but I could put the fear of God in him.

"Whatever," he choked out but managed a nod too.

I let him go and he fell to his knees, gasping for air. Leah came over and cradled his face, whimpering.

"Let's go," I said, looking away from the drugged couple.

I gripped the girl's arm and dragged her out of the house despite how much she fought me. I ignored her shrieked protests because nothing was going to keep me from removing her from that mess inside. When she began slapping at my arms, my patience snapped and I swung her around until her back was pressed to the passenger side of the car.

"I said I didn't want to leave her," she growled up at me, shoving hard.

I gripped her hands and pinned them by her head, using my hips to pin her legs. I should have been ashamed of the way heat flooded my cock when it pressed to her soft curves. Ignoring my reaction, I sneered, "What are you going to do? Did you have a revelation that shit will change for you? Did you figure out how to make your life better than the reality in there?"

Her chin came up high as she tried to burn me down with her eyes. "I'll be safer next time I try to make money. I can figure something out that will work. I can't just leave her to suffer. I was going to at least give her a chance by leaving her some of the money."

"Did you really think she'd buy food? Are you that naive?"

"I had to try. I could at least leave with a clean conscience, knowing I didn't abandon her like you're making me do now."

"How much?"

"What?"

"How much would you have given her from the money?"

She swallowed as she studied my face, probably trying to figure out why I wanted to know. "One thousand."

I stepped back and pulled my wallet out. She stayed pressed to the car and watched as I peeled off a wad of bills and stormed back to the house. I stepped just inside to drop the bills and got the fuck out.

"Your duty is done. Now get in the fucking car," I said, pointing at her as I walked past to the driver's side. "I'm hungry."

She stared with wide eyes, but when I glared over the roof, she gave a single nod and got in.

Thank God. I didn't want to explain why I needed her to get in.

Because I couldn't. I just knew I did.

5

ALEXANDRA

I BARELY SAW the streets pass by as I stared out the window. My mind was a tangled mess and I used the drive to try and place it in some order. I tried to organize the events and predict the outcome. I wanted to ask questions, but every time I glanced over, I took in the way his fist squeezed the steering wheel and I lost my nerve. Instead, I kept my mouth busy by chewing on my nails.

I'd moved on to nail number three by the time the city disappeared behind the walls of the parking garage. When he parked, I didn't move. I didn't know what to do. None of this was normal and I had no idea the protocol for going home with a stranger. One you planned to sleep with or not. At least if I had planned to sleep with him, I could make an educated guess on how to act.

But apparently, I wasn't losing my virginity tonight. I swallowed a laugh at how the night had changed. Had it only been a few hours ago I'd opened the door to him, expecting—hoping—for a wham-bam, thank-you-ma'am? I felt like a whole new human by this point.

Finally, I couldn't take the silence in the car anymore and I was too terrified about what I'd find if I looked over at him, so I reached for the handle but froze at his voice.

"What's your name?" He breathed a laugh. "The whole time in the trailer, I kept almost calling your name to realize I don't know it."

I shifted back in my seat and turned to look at him cautiously, like him knowing my name was the real danger. I was about to let this man take me up to his apartment and hopefully not lock me in a room forever, and I was worried about telling him my name. I needed to readjust my thought process.

"Alexandra."

He gave a single nod. "Nice to meet you, Alexandra. I'm Erik." He stretched his hand out and I had to fully let go of the handle and reach across to slip my hand in his. He'd touched me many times tonight. When he'd gripped my shoulders and shaken me. When he'd held my back to his body as I tried to attack Oscar. When he'd pinned me to the car. But this was the first touch he offered. It was the first touch I took. The rough calluses abraded my softer palm. His hand engulfed my smaller one, the warmth slowly working its way from where we touched to up my arm.

"Hi, Erik."

He didn't jerk back and neither did I. We sat for maybe five seconds, but a monumental shift happened. Like just introducing ourselves erased the last few hours and gave us a chance to start anew. Fresh.

The moment was broken when he nodded and he pulled his hand back like he'd been burned from holding on too long and got out. I followed, reaching the elevators as they opened. He scanned a card on a panel inside and hit the twenty-three. Almost the top floor. My heart raced as the doors slid closed. We'd been alone almost all night, but each door that shut on us seemed to add another barrier between me and the world. I didn't know what that meant for me, I just prayed I hadn't jumped out of the frying pan into the fire.

The doors slid open to a small open hallway that only held two doors. We entered the one on the left and I had to hold back my gasp when we cleared the foyer and he stepped aside revealing the view of Cincinnati. I may have had ten barriers between me and four hours ago, but here—standing in his living room with nothing but a wall of windows in front of me—I felt nothing but wide open.

"I've never seen so many windows in an apartment before."

"It's a corner unit, so it adds to the effect."

The living room was open to both floors. The second floor had a balcony that overlooked the living room and the windows extended from the first floor all the way to the second. It was beautiful. Cincinnati's sparkling lights winked at me in a way I'd never seen when I'd always been on the ground looking up. You could see everything from here. The Great American Tower with the woven metal lighting up like a tiara. The stadium with the river a dark streak behind it. The Roebling Bridge.

The man—Erik—came to stand by me and stared at the wonder beyond. He stood at least two feet away, but his presence emanated from him, taking up more space than anyone should be allowed. No wonder he had such a large open space. He looked like just a man but felt like so much more.

"It's beautiful."

"It reminds me why I love the city so much."

We both stood still and took in the sight until a buzzing from the counter pulled his attention away. He went to check the phone vibrating across the kitchen bar and as though the sound jarred something free in me, I became aware of my situation. A manic laugh almost bubbled up as I stood there in a stranger's apartment in nothing but black stilettos, a too-short black dress, and a purse he'd managed to grab before dragging me out. Too bad he couldn't have grabbed my duffle bag. That held at least a toothbrush and a change of clothes.

"I'll show you around."

Nodding, I stumbled a few feet before deciding to discard the shoes. He watched my every step like I was prey that could run at any moment. I was an easy prey for him, I had nowhere else to run. I held his stare, having to tip my chin back when I stood next to him, waiting for him to make the next move. I wasn't a short girl at five-seven, but next to him, I felt like a child. After another moment of scrutiny that had me fighting not to squirm, he finally got on with the tour.

"This is obviously the kitchen. Help yourself to anything inside. There's beer in the fridge and wine right here." He gestured to the squares built into the wall by the fridge before stopping and cocking his head to the side. "Can you drink?"

"Um, no."

That answer brought him back to facing me, his hands in his pockets, his shoulders back like he was bracing himself. "How old are you?"

"Nineteen."

Erik gave a single nod and his shoulders relaxed. "At least you're of legal age," he muttered before pointing across the room and speaking louder. "That's obviously the dining room and if you'll follow me, I'll show you upstairs and to your room.

The stairs didn't have a railing and I kept myself pressed to the wall, imagining one wrong move would send me over the edge. Thankfully when we reached the top, a half wall guarded the second floor. My toes sank into a plush carpet with each step I took down the hallway.

"This is my home office," he said, pointing to the first door. He moved a bit further before opening the second door. "This room is where you can stay tonight. The last two doors are the media room and my room."

I glanced around and took in the bland, but beautiful furnishings. It looked exactly like a hotel suite with minimal decorations and muted gray colors.

"That is your bathroom." He pointed to an open door. "It also opens to the hallway."

I stood in the middle of the luxurious space, my eyes looking over every inch, overwhelmed by the night. A knot was rising up my throat and I worried that if I opened my mouth, my stress would come spewing out.

"You can shower and I'll order some dinner. Is there anything you don't like or any allergies you may have?"

"No," I choked out. When he turned to leave, I swallowed hard and forced my vocal cords to work. "I didn't get a chance to grab anything."

He looked over his shoulder and scanned me from head to toe. "I'll be right back."

My feet remained rooted in the same spot, sinking into the carpet, afraid to move and dirty the pristine room. He returned a moment later and handed me clothes. "Thank you."

Another nod and then he was gone.

I showered quickly, not wanting to appear like a glutton. I didn't want to look like I was taking advantage of his hospitality. I did my best to wash away the night, but it clung to me. In this opulent glass shower, my whole life clung to me, like a dirty cloak reminding me how out of place I was. I didn't belong here.

When I stepped out of the room, whether I belonged or not didn't matter. The aroma of food hit me and my stomach protested any thought of not being here. I self-consciously tugged at the black boxer briefs he'd given me as I walked down the hall. I'd had to roll them a few times to fit my waist, but it made them shorter, almost disappearing under the white undershirt that smelled of lemon and sandalwood. I wondered if the scent came from his detergent or maybe just the man himself.

"Are you coming?" he asked without looking up from serving heaps of pasta on pristine white plates.

I jerked softly at the question, not realizing he'd noticed me hesitating at the top of the stairs.

"I'd prefer you to eat with me so I can ask a few questions."

Heat crept in my cheeks, embarrassed that I'd come off as rude or ungrateful. Swallowing, I kept my shoulder pressed to the wall and made my way down the stairs. He glanced over his shoulder, his eyes dropping to my bare legs, lingering, making me feel more naked than I was.

"Please, have a seat." He gestured to the cream chair across from his. "I didn't know what you'd like, so I put a little of everything."

My brows rose to my hairline as I looked down at the three kinds of pasta, chicken, asparagus, mashed potatoes, and meatballs. It barely fit on the plate. "Thank you."

"What can I get you to drink?"

"Water is fine."

He came back with a pitcher of water and filled both glasses, but drank from his beer bottle before even touching his water. We ate in silence for a while and I did my best to not shove the food in my mouth like an animal. When was the last time I'd had a meal with protein and vegetables? Before my mom died. And even then, we'd scrimped and had to watch what we spent on groceries.

"Where's your family?" he asked, finally breaking the silence. "Other than your sister."

I swallowed my bite and peeked up from under my lashes. I'd been scared to look up and see what I'd find in his eyes, so I kept mine glued to my plate.

"Dead."

His beer paused halfway to his mouth. "I'm sorry to hear that. Even extended family?"

"I'm not really sure," I said, shrugging. "My parents separated when we were young and my father took us back to Ireland. He died when I was ten and we used what little money was left to us to be sent back to our mom. We didn't have anyone in Ireland besides some of my dad's friends. If we had aunts and uncles, we never knew about it." Taking a breath, I decided to get the whole story out in one go rather than having him drag it out question by question. "My mom died two years ago of a drug overdose. Leah was just old enough to claim me."

"How old was she?"

"She had just turned eighteen the week before. We're Irish twins." His brows furrowed and I explained. "Born less than twelve months apart."

"That must have been hard."

Another shrug. Our life was what it was. The years in Ireland had been the best of our lives, but never what I'd consider easy. "We made do. She ended up getting a job at the club close by but eventually fell into the same habit as my mom. Which led her to Oscar."

"He seemed like a real winner."

"Yeah," I laughed, my lip curling in disgust.

He sat back and took a long pull of his beer, finishing it off. I struggled not to squirm under his scrutiny, forcing myself to sit still and wait for him to speak again.

"What are your skills?"

It was rarely with innocent intentions when a man asked me about my *skills*. I sat up straighter and my eyes widened, alarmed at what he wanted.

"Not that," he explained. "What would be on your resume? Your last job? Any education? Things like that."

Breathing a sigh of relief, I thought about the dismal list of skills I could give him. "I am currently working at a grocery store. When they need help, I also pull late shifts at the diner close to us. Transportation is expensive, so I try to stick close to home."

"Any schooling?"

"Um." I hesitated, looking down at my thumbs fumbling in my lap. "I've graduated high school."

"Any college?"

"No." I forced myself to look up. "I wanted to go to college for a business degree. I figured it was generic enough for anything. But I've watched a lot of YouTube videos and read a lot about website design and coding. I thought maybe I could do online work at the library, but I overestimated the cheap computers they have."

Another long stare as he spun the empty bottle on the table, the ringing scrape the only noise in the room. I couldn't tell if I wanted him to tell me what he was thinking or let me finish my meal and go to bed.

"You can come work for me tomorrow. I own an IT company."

I should have had more intelligent words to say. I should have had better questions. Instead, I said the most prevalent thing rattling through the chaos. "What?"

"I know you're limited on options. So, for tomorrow at least, you can come work for me."

"And after that?"

His face scrunched and he hesitated. "Honestly, I don't know. I've never done this before, so I'm kind of winging it. What I do know is you seem to want to learn and are willing to work for it. We'll figure out the rest tomorrow. But for now, it's late and I'm sure you're tired."

I nodded slowly, unsure if this was good luck or if I was looking at it with rose-colored glasses. "Okay."

"Good. Why don't you head to bed and be ready to leave by

seven. I'll have your five thousand waiting for you if you're still here in the morning."

"Okay."

"There are toiletries under the sink in the bathroom. Use what you need."

"Okay." God, I sounded like a broken record. An idiot only capable of one-word responses. Before I could make a bigger fool of myself, I stood and brought my dishes to the sink. I was getting ready to wash them when he stopped me.

"Don't worry about it. My cleaning lady can get it in the morning," he said right behind me.

My heart stuttered, not having noticed that he'd moved into the kitchen. I set the dishes off to the side and turned, getting ready to bolt to the room, but found myself rooted to the spot under his stare. Only a small space in the galley style kitchen separated us from where I was at the sink and where he leaned against the island.

Something about the dark backdrop with glittering lights sparkling behind him made me stop. For the first time all night, I noticed him. Not as a man who would take my virginity. Not as the man dragging me around and insulting my intelligence. But as a man. A man who was offering me sanctum for a night. A man who was giving me more than any man had in years.

Looking at him like that, dropped my doubts and he looked different. The room no longer felt small because of how intimidated I was of him, but because of the heat slowly rising around me, creating a thick tension. He must have felt it too because we both stood frozen between the two sections of marble and stared like we were seeing each other for the first time.

Heat rose up my cheeks and I tugged at the briefs he'd given me. His gaze dropped to the movement but lingered before slowly—achingly slowly—scanning up my body. What would it have been like if he had taken my virginity? Staring at his large

41

body, obviously muscular beneath his clothes, I couldn't help but imagine him over me. The picture had me rubbing my thighs together to ease the heartbeat growing between them.

I kept track of his eyes, waiting for them to meet mine again. When they did, the throb increased and for the first time ever, I felt desire for a man—a real man in front of me. Not a fictional one, or one I made up, but a real man. My tongue slicked across my lips and I considered what to do next. The night had been so crazy and it was so late and maybe the adrenaline rollercoaster was pushing me to make rash decisions. Maybe I needed comfort to cope with everything. I didn't know why, but I stepped forward, moving to close the small distance between us.

And he cleared his throat, jerking his gaze from mine, halting my movement like a bucket of cold water. "It's late."

"Yeah," I breathed, embarrassment heating my skin.

"I'll see you in the morning." He looked back but there was nothing there. Maybe I'd imagined it. Maybe it was all a desperate reach to feel like he was a hero. I'd wanted it so much that the desire had flooded out the seeds of doubt about why he had been on the site in the first place. It all felt like too much and after the day, I didn't know anymore.

It was late. Maybe sleep would clear my head. "Thank you for dinner."

"No problem. Have a good night, Alexandra."

"You too, Erik."

I didn't look back as I walked up the stairs, even though I wanted to confirm if the heat at my back was his stare or only my imagination. I even took my time down the short hall wondering if I'd see him again before sleep. I lingered at the door, my eyes on the stairs. I'd all but given up when I heard him check his voice-mail. It was wrong to eavesdrop. He probably assumed he had privacy and I should give it to him. But he was a strange man who found me from an ad selling my virginity. I figured the more I knew the better. I'd be able to make the right decisions with more knowledge.

"Erik," a female voice said through the speaker. "I miss you. I hate that I haven't heard from you after our trip together and I don't understand. Or maybe I do. I was walking down the street when I saw you at lunch with a young woman. She looked like a kid, and maybe that's what you're in to, but you could at least let me know. I could—"

The message was cut off. But it was too late. I'd heard it and the doubt in my mind about his intentions grew. Everything from the kitchen vanished and the wall of questions rebuilt itself one brick at a time.

Footsteps crossed the living room getting closer to the stairs. I quickly backed into my room and closed the door without a sound, making sure all the locks were turned. Stepping back, I stared, half expecting the handle to try and turn. Half expecting him to come after me and demand I repay his hospitality. I stood there for a few more minutes before backing up until my knees hit the bed. Even when I sat, I didn't move my gaze from the door.

When my eyes began to burn from the effort to stay open for so long, I forewent the welcoming bed and grabbed the blanket and pillow and made myself comfortable in front of the door. Just like at home, I was unsure of my safety and did everything I could to protect myself.

A sexy stranger wasn't coming to save me.

A miracle wasn't happening.

It was just me.

I had to be my own savior.

6

ERIK

STARING at the black liquid slowly draining into the cup, I willed it to go faster. I needed an energy boost before I had to face the girl—Alexandra—again. I'd lain awake most of the night trying to figure out every possible scenario for today. None of them had eased the pounding behind my eyes enough to sleep. Add in the erection that refused to subside after the whole kitchen stare down and I'd been wired for hours. It wasn't until I finally caved and reached my hand under the sheet and stroked myself that I was able to relax enough.

I hadn't allowed myself to think of her when I first gripped my cock. She was a child in a vulnerable situation and no matter how much I tried to repeat it to myself and imagine the blonde with bouncing tits from earlier in the week it didn't work. My mind strayed to crystalline blue eyes staring up at me like I was the answer. When I closed my eyes and tried to focus solely on my impending orgasm, it was remembering her tongue slicking across her lips that had me grinding my teeth to hold back my moans as I came.

Rubbing a hand across my face, I growled out my frustration.

"Rough night?"

I jerked around to find her standing in the middle of the living room back in her little black dress. Her hands were clenched together in front of her and she looked like a little girl playing dress-up now that she was missing the makeup and shoes. Her lips rolled between her teeth and she raised her dark brows.

She'd asked me a question and there I was ogling her.

"It was okay."

She inched her way toward the island like she was worried I'd attack.

"Did you sleep okay?"

"Yeah. Thank you."

"Would you like coffee?" I almost shouted for joy when the machine was done with my cup.

"Sure."

"How do you take it?"

"Umm... I don't know. I've only had it when it was free. I think I added a creamer packet to it and a packet of sugar."

My hands paused over the buttons taking in her words, cringing at how poor she must be. Most people managed to splurge every now and then, could scrounge up a dollar for gas station coffee, but then I remembered her barren cupboards. "Did you like the flavor of it?"

"It was a little bitter."

"I'll come up with something for you." I pushed the button for the coffee to brew and turned. "Here are some clothes for you to wear today for work. I forgot I had these in a drawer, but you can borrow them until we can get you clothes of your own. Also, the five thousand as promised."

She grabbed the items I pointed to on the island but didn't move to go put them away. "I have clothes and you don't have to take me to work. I can head home now. Besides, I have a shift at the grocery store this evening."

No. The word rattled through me and I somehow managed to hold back the command. However, I was unable to soften my words, my irritation at even the thought colored my tone. "You're not going back there."

Apparently, that hadn't been any better than the original no I'd wanted to say because her eyes widened and she took a step back.

"What?"

This time I took a deep breath before responding, making an effort to sound calmer than I felt. "If you go back, she will expect more money. Especially since she knows you can get it. Just...stay until we can figure this out."

"Figure what out?"

"I...I-" I stuttered. I was a man sure of my decisions and yet I was questioning everything I said to her. I was stumbling through this mess I made, desperate to keep her from running back to that site, praying she didn't bolt with the five thousand I'd already given her. I needed to give her a reason to stay, that was what I needed to figure out.

Then it hit me. She needed money and I needed to keep an eye on her to keep her from making stupid decisions. Pulling my shoulders back, I stood tall and hoped the authoritative stance hid my nerves that she'd turn me down.

"You can't go back to that trailer, and there's no easy solution that can keep you from being dragged back to where you were. At least not one you can get without my help."

"I-I don't understand."

"Stay with me for a month and at the end of that time, I will give you ten thousand dollars." Her jaw dropped and eyes widened, but before she could talk, I had to make my own stipulations. "If you decide you don't want this offer, you can take your five thousand and leave today. If you stay, you give me the five thousand back in return for the ten at the end of the month.

And there are rules. You don't ever go to that site again. If you're here, then I don't want to find out you're trying to get more money in dangerous ways." I ticked each rule off on my fingers. "You quit your job at the grocery store. While you're staying here, there will be no guests and you must check in with me before leaving."

"You're making me sound like a prisoner."

"Are you telling me you have friends and parties to go to?"

She looked away. "No."

"Then it shouldn't be an issue."

She didn't say anything, but I could see the questions swirling behind her eyes and, as I spent more time with her, I picked up on her tells. Like the way she chewed on the corner of her lip when she was thinking. Or how her hands clasped too tightly in front of her lap when she was anxious. She did both now.

"If you break any of these rules, then you can leave without anything. I'm not going to expect anything except maybe some office work." I softened my severe tone. "I won't hurt you."

I almost explained to her about how I'd found her—about how I rescued victims of sex trafficking and would never hurt a woman, but I didn't. Maybe because I wasn't ready for more questions. Or maybe I didn't want her to assume I brought them all back here with me like it was a scheme.

She felt different and I didn't even know how to explain it to myself, let alone her.

"Okay," she finally said.

"Good. Go get changed and we'll head out."

WE WALKED INTO THE BUILDING, her heels ringing like gunshots through the marble lobby. I'd had slacks and a blouse for her, but no shoes, which left her in her sky-high stilettos from last night. She fidgeted next to me in the elevator and I struggled not to reach out and lay my hand over hers.

The elevator doors opened, saving me from the urge. I bolted, expecting her to follow me around the corner to my company's main lobby and Laura's desk.

"Good morning, Mr. Brandt."

"Good morning, Laura." It was a natural move to rest my hand on Alexandra's back as I introduced her. She stiffened, but I didn't pull away. "Alexandra, this is my secretary, Laura Combs."

"Nice to meet you, Ms. Combs."

She stepped away from my touch, reaching to shake Laura's hand, a smile spreading across her face.

White noise flooded my hearing and everything stopped. I'd seen her pissed and scared and upset, but I'd never seen her smile. She was a beautiful young woman, there was no denying it. But Jesus, when she smiled, she was exceptional. The faintest dimples appeared just under the well-defined apples of her cheeks.

But it was her eyes that had me frozen. They sparked to life for the first time since I'd met her and the urge to make that spark happen again and again thrummed through me.

"I wish you stared at me like that when you saw me," a deep voice called from my right.

Alexandra jerked her eyes to the newcomer who'd called me out for staring at her. I quickly looked away, doing my best to keep my face neutral. Not that it would matter. My business partner and best friend, Ian, could read me like a book. But a man had to try.

Ignoring his comment, I said, "Well look what the cat dragged in." He came over and we did the brotherly back pat. "How was New York?"

"Good. Uneventful. Meetings went fine. Which I'll tell you about later." He smirked and cocked a dark brow. A mischievous look I knew so well, glinted behind his gray eyes. "But first, tell me about this beautiful woman. I'm gone less than a week and we're hiring supermodels."

I rolled my eyes. Ian was laying it on thick. "This is our new intern we're trying out."

"I thought we filled that slot. And don't they usually work downstairs with Hanna?" The smirk didn't leave his face. He'd already seen me entranced with her and I just needed to buckle down and endure as he had his fun at my expense.

"I'm opening another one. And she'll learn what she needs on this floor with Laura."

"Is she even 18?" he asked, looking her up and down.

"Yes," I practically growled.

"Interesting." He dragged the word out and a moment of silence fell between all of us as we waited for Ian's next move. But apparently, he was done torturing me. He gave a real smile and turned to Alexandra. "Well, welcome to Bergamo and Brandt."

She shook his hand but pulled back quickly and I wanted to throw my arms up in victory. Ian was a playboy. We each had our exploits, but he had the outgoing personality that drew women in.

"Hey, Ian. Welcome back," Jared called from his office door.

I held my breath wondering what he would say when he realized the girl we found was now standing in the office to work.

"Hey, Erik. I wanted to touch base with you about the case before you get..." Jared trailed off as he came out of his office and saw Alexandra. She shrunk back a little at his staring, but he collected himself quickly and focused his attention back on me. "Before you get to work," he finished.

"Yeah, let me just leave Alexandra with Laura. By the way, Alexandra, this is Jared. He's an analyst here."

"Nice to meet you," she said softly, only giving a wave.

49

"She'll be working with Laura today." I turned my attention to Laura. "Would you mind showing her around and explaining what we do? She can help you with office tasks and whatever else you need." Walking to my office, I jerked my head for Jared to follow. "Let me know if you need anything," I said before closing the door.

I'd just sat on my couch when the door flew open again and Ian strolled in.

"Before you girls get to chatting, I wanted to remind you about London next week."

"I remember." We were opening a small office in London to expand to new interests and reach more opportunities. "Do you need anything from me before your trip?"

"No, I have all the files. I should be there only for a month or so, but I'll let you know if anything changes."

"Okay."

Instead of leaving, he plopped himself in one of the lounge chairs across from me. "Now that that's out of the way, you want to tell me what you're doing with jailbait out there? I didn't know we could hire people we wanted to sleep with."

"I don't want to sleep with her," I growled at him.

"Okay," he said with heavy sarcasm.

"He did go get her personally," Jared chimed in, pulling my glare to him.

Ian pressed his hand to his chest and gasped like a damsel in distress. "What?"

Dragging a hand through my hair and over my face, I gave the rundown of the previous few days. Explaining how we found her and how I ended up bringing her home with me.

"What are you going to do now?"

I was getting annoyed with the questions.

"I don't know. And please stop fucking asking."

Both men sat across from me and stared with wide eyes. I

always had a plan before I took action. This time threw me for a loop and no one in the room was used to me not knowing what the hell the next step was. The only thing I knew for sure was that I had her for a month. What I did with her during that month, I had no fucking clue.

Jared sat forward. "May I suggest a plan?'

At the moment, I would have taken advice from a psychic on a street corner.

I nodded and the more he spoke, the more I liked.

I just needed to get Alexandra on board.

7

ERIK

"How old are you?" Alexandra asked from the passenger seat.

"Thirty-one."

"That's kind of amazing that you already own your own successful IT company and you're already looking to branch overseas. Will you be moving to London?"

"No. We're not quite sure what we are going to do. If Ian will go or if we'll hire a business manager while we visit."

"Did you always want to work in IT?"

I laughed. "No, actually. Ian and I played baseball growing up. He got picked up for college, but I had a pretty bad tear in my shoulder that required surgery my senior year."

"Do you still play?"

"Sometimes."

"Do you miss it?"

"Not really."

She'd been an endless fountain of questions since we'd left work. She'd begun her interrogation slowly when I'd seen her on her lunch break, asking only a few questions here and there. Each time I saw her as the day went on, she talked more, like being around other people—being able to focus on something other than the current situation had allowed her to relax. I assumed this was more of her everyday personality and I was surprised by how happy she seemed.

Nothing about what she told me about her life led me to imagine the girl currently rattling off her day in the seat next to me. She had a resilience I'd never seen before. At least not in the last five years.

The last girl I knew that was that positive had been snuffed out like a candle in the wind. And I missed her every day.

Thankfully the apartment came into view, halting that train of thought. Rather than pull into the garage, I stopped at the front doors.

"Are you not parking in the garage?"

"No. I'm dropping you off. I've already called the front desk and they have a key waiting for you. There should be enough cash on the counter to order whatever you want for dinner."

She stared, wide-eyed and blinking. "You're not coming in?" she asked, her voice almost childlike.

No. I needed to get out of there. Watching her be closed off and reserved was one thing. It made her look vulnerable and scared. But the chipper young woman I'd watched throughout the day, watching her smiles and easy interaction with everyone, was an entirely different beast I wasn't ready to battle.

"No. I have dinner plans and probably won't be home until late."

"Oh." Her eyes dropped and she nodded.

I could only imagine she assumed I had a date and I didn't say anything to correct her. Throughout the day, her smiles had been increasingly directed at me. She began giving me soft looks that lingered rather than the hesitant nods and blank stares. I needed to squash any vision she may—or may not—be concocting in her head about me. It was better safe than sorry.

"Okay. I'll see you tomorrow."

When she got out, I watched the black pants stretch over her round bottom. She looked thinner than she should which I can imagine was due to the lack of food. But she hadn't lost any of her ass. I bit my lip, holding back the moan as I imagined her full ass only getting more plump and firm. The car door slammed, pulling me out of my daydream. Maybe I really needed her to think of me as an ass so she stayed away from me and removed any temptation.

I didn't watch her walk into the building, not needing another reason to watch her bottom sway with each step. Instead, I counted to ten before pulling out into rush-hour traffic, leaving the city.

Fifteen minutes later I pulled up to a typical, two-story, suburban home. I'd wanted to buy my parents a better place when I began making more than enough money, but they refused to leave the memories the house held. It was all they had left.

"Hey, man. Long time, no see," Ian greeted me when I walked in. Ian came to a lot of family dinners, even as adults. I'd known him since grade-school and his parents had traveled a lot, leaving him to fend for himself. Which my mom would never have allowed, so he became her second son.

"Who invited you?" I joked.

"I'm always invited. Your mom loves me more than you anyway."

"Ha! Bullshit."

"Language," my mom reprimanded, coming around the corner to give me a hug.

"Sorry, Mom." I bent down to wrap my arms around her short frame.

"Come sit down. Dinner is almost ready and your father and sister are already at the table."

"Hey, Dad," I greeted, taking the seat next to him.

Ian took his usual spot next to my sister, Hanna. He wrapped his arms affectionately around her shoulders and pulled her in for a rough hug and a kiss to the top of her head. "Missed your sassiness last week."

His actions were brotherly, but Hanna blushed and smiled. "Missed you, too."

I didn't love the idea of my sister crushing on my best friend, but to see her smiling at anything—let alone a man—was more than enough reason to deal with her crush. The thick gold bands she always wore around her wrists rattled as she brushed her hair behind her ear.

"How was work?" Mom asked, placing the final dish on the table.

"Boring," Hanna answered first.

I glared at her across the table, not liking her calling my company boring.

But the glare quickly shifted to Ian when he opened his fat mouth. "It wasn't boring for Erik, that's for sure."

"What happened?" Hanna asked.

"He hired a new girl today."

"I didn't know we were hiring."

"We weren't," I answered Hanna before Ian could say more. I needed to nip this conversation in the bud. "Something came up and she needed a job."

"What came up?" Dad asked, not accepting the short answer.

I glared harder at Ian for bringing it all up, but he just smiled back, not a regret to be had.

"She was in trouble and had nowhere else to go. I'm just helping her get on her feet."

Everyone at the table knew what I did. Everyone knew why.

I glanced over to Hanna to make sure she was okay to find her shoulders slouched. I hated imagining what horrors were rolling through her mind as she stared at the chicken on her plate. Ian, realizing the can of worms he opened, rubbed her shoulder. But Hanna was resilient. Not as much as Sofia, but she was strong.

She lifted her chin and swallowed before asking, "Is...Is she okay?"

"Yeah," I rushed to reassure her. I took a moment before explaining, not wanting to share Alexandra's story. It wasn't mine to tell. "This was different. I got to her before anyone else could."

Hanna exhaled hard. "Good. Good."

"Wait," Mom cut in. "Erik, *you* went to get her?"

"Mom—"

"No. I thought you hired people?" Her words were an accusation and a plea for me to tell her I hadn't gone. "You promised you wouldn't go again. You almost died the last time."

"This wasn't the same. I knew ahead of time that no one would be there but her. I was safe."

"Just like you were safe before." Tears glossed her eyes. "Do I have to lose another child?"

A silence descended over the table. Everyone remembering the one person not here who should have been. Everyone taking a moment to feel the empty place in our hearts and our home. I rushed to reassure her, needing to pull us back from the edge of the black hole we walked on.

"Mom, you know I wouldn't be reckless. I promised. This case was different."

I looked across the table to Ian, pleading for help to move the conversation away from dangerous topics.

"He has a crush on this one," Ian supplied helpfully, immediately making me regret asking for his help.

"I don't," I defended. "She's only nineteen and vulnerable with nowhere else to go. I wouldn't take advantage of her situation. I'm just trying to help."

"Age is just a number, and she seemed pretty strong to me," he pushed.

"Shut up, Ian."

"You won't mind if I step in then?"

"Stay away from her," I growled.

Ian winked at Hanna and she laughed at his taunts, the bubble of sadness broken for now.

Shaking my head at the lack of support from my sister, I went back to eating my chicken. Anything to avoid any more talk of Alexandra. Because Ian was right. I *was* attracted to her, but I couldn't act on it. She may have been as strong as Ian predicted, but I could tell she needed more than a quick fuck and I didn't have that to give.

Don't even get me started on the virginity.

"Well, next time bring the young woman to dinner," my mom reprimanded. "And if she has no one, then she can always come here."

It was a viable option to let her stay at my parents. They had the room and cared. But my mind shut it down. I needed to keep her close.

"That's okay, Mom. I don't want to add any stress on you."

"It's no stress at all. I'd love to take care of someone now that all my children have abandoned me."

"Fifteen minutes away is hardly abandoning you," Hanna defended.

"She'll need rides to work, it's easier to have her close."

"She can stay with me," Hanna suggested. "My apartment is only a few floors below yours. You could just pick her up from there. Or I could take her."

"There's an idea. Isn't that a perfect idea, Erik?" Ian taunted.

"No," I growled from my clenched jaw. "It's not because Hanna lives in a one bedroom apartment. Where would she sleep? The couch? Why bother when I have the extra rooms?"

"What about an apartment in your building? You've set other survivors up with a place to live," my dad suggested.

I took a deep breath, not liking any of the options. I just wanted to keep her close to me and didn't want to have anyone probe too deeply into why. Because I didn't know.

"I'll have to look into availability and see if she'd be open to it," I conceded. It satisfied everyone—thank God— and we moved on to other mundane topics for the rest of dinner.

"You know, I'll never forget the day I got the call you were in the hospital," Ian said.

We were sitting in the back sunroom, drinking beer while Mom and Hanna washed dishes and Dad watched the football game.

I cringed at his words and brought the bottle to my lips rather than say anything. I didn't know what to say. Our family had lost so much and I'd almost added to it.

"But not even that was as bad as walking into your room and seeing what had happened to you. You're my brother and I almost lost you."

Swallowing past the lump in my throat, I tried to make light of the conversation. "I'm harder to kill than that."

"I don't know about that. But I do know you're damn lucky Jared found you."

The first year I began rescuing girls from sex trafficking, I'd made a name for myself. I'd been cocky and almost wanted them to know I was coming. I'd even used the name Robin Hood, thinking I was clever because I was taking from those in power and helping others in need. I'd made it so people in the business knew who to watch for on the web.

I'd pissed off some powerful people the first year I began rescuing women from sex-trafficking. One night a few years ago, I'd been caught by the wrong man. He'd known I was coming and planted a trap. I fell right into their hands and they beat the shit out of me. I would have died if not for Jared. He'd been following the same sale and found me left for dead out back. He'd taken me to the hospital and I'd barely made it back to the land of the living.

"I know. And I learned from my mistakes. I now hire MacCabe's team to do the extractions."

"Do you? Then why did you go get her after you promised your family you wouldn't go out anymore?"

"It was different." I sounded like a broken record even to my own ears.

"DeVries is still out there. But not even just him. There are tons of people who would love to see you dead."

Marco DeVries was the man who set me up. There wasn't anything special about him. I didn't target him specifically. I didn't search for him or look for revenge. That wasn't my goal. My goal was to save as many women as I could no matter who they were from. I'd learned the hard way to just keep my head down and get the job done the most efficient way possible.

"I'm more careful now. I dropped Robin Hood and I don't make as big of a splash with Mr. E."

"But it could happen again."

"It could, but I'm doing my best to keep it quiet. You know why this is so important to me."

"I know. It's important to all of us. Just don't get so caught up in avenging one dead family member to wind up leaving us to mourn another."

"I have no intentions of dying."

"We never do." Ian finished off his beer. "Just be careful, man. Like I said, you're my brother."

"Unfortunately," I muttered, trying to lighten the mood again. This time Ian took the bait. He punched my arm almost making me drop my beer.

"The better-looking brother."

"Yeah right."

"Hey, maybe Alexandra will want me over you."

I glared at him, but he was laughing, ruining the effect.

"You're so easy."

I hoped no one else saw through me as easily as Ian did. Not that it mattered, because no way was I giving in to anything with Alexandra.

8

ALEXANDRA

ERIK HADN'T COME home before I fell asleep. I stayed on the couch for a while hoping to see him, until I eventually went to the bedroom, but I'd lain awake past midnight.

His date must have been a good one.

Seeing him interact with his friends and hearing them talk about him painted him in a different light. One that had me lowering my guard. I didn't even think about laying in front of the door this time. I'd sunk into the luxurious bed, letting the down comforter keep me warm. I couldn't recall the last time I'd felt that kind of comfort.

When we'd left the office I'd been excited about getting to know him, hoping to understand the connection between the man who pinned me to the wall and laid out a terrifying future I could have to the one who smiled at his secretary and made jokes with his friends.

I wanted to get to know the latter man more.

Then he'd dropped me off at the apartment with terse instructions and left. My heart had sunk to my stomach and I'd felt foolish—naive. So, I'd gone up, changed back into the clothes he'd given me the night before and ordered a pizza, relishing every bite of the salty, greasy, heaven. Then I'd watched TV—actual cable TV. I'd lived my night like a queen. Or maybe just a girl who wasn't poor and starving.

I hesitated to get up the next morning, wondering if I'd find him still gone. But the aroma of coffee seeped its way under my door, beckoning me to get up.

He had to be there. Unless he had a fancy machine that he could schedule. But it wasn't a regular coffeepot. It was one of those that made it by the cup.

I yanked the covers back and ran to the bathroom, taking time to finger comb my hair into submission. I didn't have a valid reason to have my heart racing, pumping adrenaline through my limbs, urging me to get to him faster. No reason at all.

But this time felt limited and I wanted to enjoy every moment. One day at a time could mean that today was the last day. It could all be pulled out from under me and I'd be dropped off at the trailer like this had all been a dream.

And I wanted to see him. I could be honest about that.

I'd watched him move about the office, taking in his easy movements, shocking for a man his size. His long fingers had flown across the keyboard between running through his short hair. Sometimes he'd even take a moment to lean back in his chair and drag a finger across his full bottom lip.

Each movement had drawn my attention to the strength under his suit. Each movement stoked the flame of attraction burning through me.

I had a crush. How could I not after all he'd done for me? It was normal, I rationalized.

Taking a deep breath, I began my descent downstairs and loved the shot of happiness tingling through my limbs when I saw him sitting at the island with a cup of coffee and the newspaper.

His back muscles strained under his t-shirt and my mouth

watered as I imagined touching him. I needed to get myself together. It was one thing to have a crush and another to fall headfirst into a pool of lust because I'd put the man on a pedestal.

"Good morning," I greeted in my most calm voice.

He didn't look up. "Good morning. Sleep okay?"

"Yes. It's kind of impossible not to in such a comfy bed."

I turned my back on him to look over the coffee machine. My hands hovered over the buttons trying to decide which ones to push, but hesitating because I didn't want to break it. I gasped when a strong arm reached past me and grabbed a mug, placing it under the spout. I stayed still, forcing myself not to step back into his heat as he grabbed a little white cup, put it in a slot in the machine, and pushed a few buttons to bring it to life.

"Thank you," I breathed when he stepped back.

"No problem. You'll probably want to figure out how to use it."

I turned to face him, mirroring his stance of leaning a hip on the counter. "You'll have to show me how you made the cup from yesterday. It was delicious."

"Just two creams and a sugar. Nothing fancy."

"How do you make yours?"

"I just have it black and a stronger brew. Keeps the hairs on my chest," he joked with a smile.

I couldn't help but smile in return. It'd been the first time he'd joked with me and it added fuel to the fire keeping my crush alive.

"Once you have your coffee, I was hoping we could sit and talk. I've been thinking about what to do and I have a plan. Just need to know if you're interested."

"Of course."

"Good. Meet me in the living room when you're ready."

I willed the machine to make my coffee faster and even forewent the cream and sugar just to get to the room faster. I immediately regretted my decision when I sat and took a sip, cringing at how bitter it tasted.

Erik didn't comment, just raised his brow at the black liquid in the cup.

"So, what's up?" I asked.

"Okay." He set his cup down on the coffee table and rested his elbows on his knees, his hands clasped between them. "I'd like you to stay and work for me. During that time you can save up money to find your own place. The ten thousand at the end of the month should help with that." My eyebrows rose, my heart thumping harder with each word from his lips. "If business is still your interest for college, then you can submit for our internship program. We pay for any schooling that you can't cover from scholarships and grants. But you would need to begin applying for scholarships immediately. As well as get your college applications in."

"Are you serious?" I barely breathed the words, scared that he would begin laughing and say just kidding. It all seemed too good to be true.

"As a heart attack. The only catch is that once you complete your degree you have to work for Bergamo and Brandt for two years before applying at any other jobs."

"That doesn't seem like a catch. That sounds like a guaranteed job."

"We like to at least try to keep our investments. Take some time think it o—"

"Yes," I interrupted. I didn't even need half a second to consider this. "Are you kidding me? I'd be a fool not to take an opportunity and I'm not one to look a gift horse in the mouth."

"Good. I'll help you get all the applications you'll need."

"Of course. God, Erik." I looked down, embarrassed by the tears burning my eyes. "Thank you. Thank you so much."

He grabbed his mug and stood, ignoring my emotional

display. Taking a deep breath, I got myself under control and had to tip my head back to meet his eyes.

"You're welcome. Now get dressed and we can run out to get you some clothes. Unfortunately, until we get those clothes, you'll have to wear what you wore yesterday."

Blood flooded my cheeks. "Um, I-I don't have money for new clothes. I can just run back to my home and grab some things."

"I already said no. And I'm buying. I highly doubt you have office wear either."

I didn't, but this felt like a charity case.

"Like you said, Alexandra, don't look a gift horse in the mouth."

9

ERIK

THE FLUORESCENT LIGHTS shined down on her wide eyes. She walked into the store like she'd never seen a Target before. According to Hanna, it was one of the greatest places on earth, but I didn't get it.

"I've never let myself go in these places before because I couldn't afford them." The words were soft like she was saying them to herself. But then she turned her full attention on me with a wry smile. "Leah liked to come here, though. But only because she stole the things she couldn't afford."

"Sounds amazing."

She shrugged, one side of her mouth quirking up ruefully. We stood at the threshold of the sections and I waited for her to lead the way.

"Are you going to go look around?"

"No," I answered dryly. This store wasn't my top pick for my wardrobe. "I'm good on clothes."

"So, you're going to walk with me?" she asked slowly, one brow cocked.

"Is that a problem?"

"No. Not at all. I'll be quick and just grab a few things."

I stayed a few paces behind her watching her. I became lost in watching her smile when her fingers grazed a certain top. She would hold it up to herself and look at herself in the mirror, biting her bottom lip like she didn't want to let too much happiness show. Then she'd shake her head and put it back, instead grabbing a white button up and other simple clothes.

I began plucking the discarded clothes off the rack and holding them to buy later. She ran her hands down a stack of cotton shirts and admired each color, but settled on a white one.

"What's your favorite color?"

She blinked like she was coming out of a trance, having forgotten I was there behind her. "What?"

"What's your favorite color?"

"Umm...green."

I stepped by her side and grabbed a green shirt, adding a blue one for good measure. It would look good with her eyes.

"What are you doing?" She turned, seeing my armful of clothes. "What are all those clothes?"

"The clothes you want."

"I don't need those. I've got the basics here. I just need things for the office." She held up her two pairs of pants and monochromatic selection of tops.

"You'll need casual clothes, too."

"I don't need all that," she argued.

I gave her a hard stare and pinched my lips in disapproval. "Just keep shopping."

Heaving a sigh, she continued but watched me out of the corner of her eye as we made our way through the racks. Each time I'd pick up a discarded item, she'd give me her own disapproving look, but my stare allowed no arguing.

After I picked up seven more items, she stopped touching things and only picked up a few sparse items. We got to the end of the section and crossed the aisle when she stopped and a huge grin spread across her face. She hunched over to look at the movies lined up in a cardboard stand.

"Oh my God, I loved this book." She held up *Gone Girl*.

"Have you ever seen the movie?"

"No. Movies weren't in the budget. I hung out at the library a lot so I've read a ton of the books that were made into movies. But this one was one of my favs. *Girl with the Dragon Tattoo* is my favorite. I heard the movie wasn't as good as the book, but if I could have splurged on seeing one movie, that would have been it."

"I hear most books are better than movies."

"You hear? Do you not read?"

"Not for leisure. It's mostly reports and articles."

"That's boring."

"I actually enjoy it."

She set the movie back down and continued down the aisle. I made sure she wasn't looking before I grabbed the movie and slid it under the pile of clothes. I didn't know why I did it. We were there to buy clothes for the office. There was just something about her smile that made me want to see it again. I'd just hidden my contraband when she turned and backed into the underwear and pajama section, a devious smile tilting her lips.

"Want to pick these out for me too?"

I gave her a hard glare without answering.

She picked up two scraps of underwear, one on each finger and held them like scales. "What do you think? Lacy or silk? Boyshorts or thong?" Apparently, we were going to finish this trip with me glaring at her the whole time. "Or maybe granny panties."

I would much rather imagine her in cotton granny panties than that scrap of teal lace. Not that I should be imagining her in anything.

"You're hilarious."

"I've been told by my coworkers I make the time go by with my awesome sense of humor." She dropped the wispy fabric and grabbed a selection of simple cotton. Thank God.

"Were you the class clown?"

"Not really. But having a sense of humor is better than feeling sorry for yourself."

You can laugh about it or you can cry about it, Erik. Pick your poison, but I'd prefer to laugh.

Sofia's words when she was dumped right before prom hit me. She'd been the most resilient girl I'd ever known. I couldn't help but be reminded of her when I looked at Alexandra. They both had the same stubborn will.

Alexandra looked at a pair of silk pajamas, but put them back and grabbed a pair of basic cotton pants. She'd taken two steps and I made my move to grab it.

I'd just wrapped my hand around the hanger when she jerked around.

"No." She stepped close and did her best glower, her eyes narrowed to slits and her lips pursed.

"If you want them, then just get them."

I went to lift them off the rack when her hand slapped mine. I dropped the hanger, shocked at the slight sting across the back of my hand.

"I *don't* want them. I was just testing you. You failed."

Her words barely registered. "Did you just slap me?"

She stepped back and clutched at her chest with an exaggerated gasp. "You sound like an 1800s grandma shocked because I just showed some ankle."

She waggled her eyebrows and tugged her black pants over her ankle.

It was so unexpected, I laughed. It was rusty and unused, but it choked up out of my chest almost like a bark of sound. She stood upright again and her eyes softened.

"You should smile more," she proclaimed softly.

The same tension from that first night in the kitchen flowed like a bubble around us. My chest warmed and it should have been the warning to take my family up on their suggestion and have Alexandra stay somewhere else.

But that wasn't the way this would work. I shook my head and looked away, breaking the moment.

She hooked her thumb over her shoulder. "I'll just grab some pajamas and we can go."

"Make sure you grab enough," I called to her back.

She twirled around and lowered her brows. "Yes, sir," she answered in a deep voice and a salute.

And as much as I wanted to stop it, I couldn't help but smile.

ALEXANDRA

"WINE ISN'T SO BAD," I said, a little lightheaded from the second glass.

"It's a good pairing with the steak." Erik sat with me on the couch, holding his own glass. "My mom loves exploring new wines and always let us have some with dinner. She said we were exploring our European heritage and everyone in Europe enjoyed a good wine with meals."

"Thanks for letting me have some."

"You're hardly a child."

"Yeah, but I'm not twenty-one either."

"It's just wine. It's not like I'm taking you to a bar and letting you do shots."

We'd gotten home and ordered dinner in. It felt like a

halfway normal experience, just two people eating dinner. I'd been able to wear anything other than someone else's clothes, and we'd talked about what I'd learned at the college of YouTube.

Now we both sat on the couch with our drinks, a business channel playing in the background. He'd been reserved earlier in the morning, but as the day went on, he relaxed in small increments, leading to him slouched back next to me.

I sat criss-cross applesauce and faced him, only a foot separated my knees from brushing against his strong thighs straining against the denim of his pants.

He finished his glass in one big gulp before turning to me. "Ready for bed?"

I mimicked his movement and emptied the red liquid before setting it on the table. "Sure."

"You're going to want to drink a glass of water with some ibuprofen before bed."

"Yes, sir," I said with a deep voice and salute.

He smiled again and it reached across the space, stroking my skin, pulling a smile from me too. Kind of like when he'd laughed in the store. It was so sexy. Deep, a little dark, and a rumble that shook me even from a distance.

When was the last time I'd felt this at ease? Had I ever? And all because of this man. I wished for something I could give in return, something to show how much I appreciated everything. I didn't have anything. Except for me.

He'd been on the site for a reason and maybe it wasn't to buy a virgin, but probably some form of sex. Maybe I could give him some intimacy, show my thanks with my body.

I inched forward and the smile slowly slipped from his face, but he didn't move to pull away. When my knees brushed his thigh, I slicked my tongue across my lips and leaned in. The kiss was soft and tentative. I didn't know what I was doing, as I'd never kissed anyone before. Taking my cues from him not jerking back, I pressed a little harder—explored a little more. I trembled with nerves that I was doing it wrong, trembled with excitement at being so close to a man.

I rose to my knees, resting my hands on his shoulders and wrapped my lips around his bottom one, loving how soft and plush it felt between mine. I nibbled at it, causing a groan to rumble from his chest. The simple kiss I'd planned on giving him went out the window as Erik took control.

His hands gripped my waist, holding me to him. His head tilted and his tongue pressed against the seam of my lips, demanding entrance. I obliged and opened, my tongue meeting him halfway, tasting the red wine he'd been drinking. His grip tightened and I whimpered, trying to rub my legs together around the ache between them. He tugged me and I threw my leg to the other side of his, straddling his lap.

Erik's hands spanned my waist and settled me atop him, a thick ridge greeting my core. I'd only worn leggings and a tank top and I could feel everything. Whimpering again, I held on to his shoulders and gave in to my body's cravings, rocking my hips, gaining friction. Heat blossomed from my core and rose up, making my nipples pebble. My cheeks were on fire as he guided me back and forth making the ache stronger. His hand moved to cup my breast, stroking his thumb across my nipple. When he pinched the sensitive tip, I detonated.

I moaned against his lips and rocked harder and faster as my body shook from the pleasure wreaking its havoc. My movements slowed as the orgasm ebbed and I pulled my lips from his to catch my breath. His hands still held me in place and I floated back to earth. Leaning in, I placed gentle kisses along his jaw, the corner of his lips, whispering words between each one.

"Thank you. You saved me."

He stiffened and pushed me back until I sat on his knees rather than his hips.

"This can't happen," he growled.

I blinked, my mind trying to catch up to his drastic change in mood. "What do you mean?"

His jaw clenched and rather than the heat I'd imagined seeing, his face had grown cold and distant. "Don't romanticize this. Don't romanticize me. I'm not some hero you dreamed about fucking you slowly."

Lightheadedness swamped me as a fire burned through my whole body. "I-I'm not. I just...I just wanted to say thank you."

He paused for a moment and I waited for him to pull me back to him and accept all I had. Instead, his hands gripped me tighter, sitting upright to sneer in my face. I pulled back, seeing the same look I'd seen in the hotel when he'd been trying to scare me. Who was this? Was this the real Erik? Was the man I'd spent the day with an act?

I swallowed the lump in my throat and grabbed onto the small ball of anger at his quick change in mood.

"I'm not someone to be repaid with sex." He sat me aside and stood, turning to look down at me. "Have some respect for your body."

He stormed upstairs, leaving me cold and shell-shocked.

I'd held tight to the swell of anger and at his words, it exploded, consuming me. It burned every other feeling of tenderness and joy into nothing.

If he didn't want my thanks, then my anger was what he'd get.

10

ALEXANDRA

THREE DAYS HAD PASSED since Erik shifted into a giant, silent asshole.

And despite his return to a colder behavior, I didn't feel any less safe around him. Safe enough that I didn't need to sleep in front of my door. I just now felt the need to punch him in the face each time he answered me with a grunt.

On Sunday, I'd stayed in my room. I'd been a petulant child by not responding when he'd knocked on my door saying he was going out. I did it again when he came back saying he had something for me. I didn't want anything from him, unless he was willing to give me the piece of my pride he took from me Saturday night.

We didn't talk Monday morning and he'd had Laura take me back to the apartment at the end of the day. He hadn't spoken directly to me unless it was to give a brusque command at work. And the "internship" I was supposed to be in consisted of the most menial tasks known to man. I didn't see anyone else grabbing everyone's coffees and printing off papers. Laura had been getting up from her seat to do it herself when Erik let her know I could do it.

She at least had the grace to wince each time I had to complete another mundane task.

But I'd swallowed it down and did it because I was still better off here grabbing Erik's lunch than I'd been at the grocery store. So, I'd set aside more of my pride and been as polite as possible to him, even if we didn't actually speak to one another.

"Hey Alex, can you watch the desk while I go on lunch?" Laura asked. She'd begun calling me Alex for short and I kind of liked it. I never knew anyone well enough to give me a nickname, besides Leah.

"Sure."

"It shouldn't be too busy, but call me if you have any issues."

"No worries. I'm not as dumb as it seems when Erik gives me such basic tasks."

She laughed softly. "He's a complicated man."

Maybe five minutes later a tall blonde in a hell of a business suit came strolling in. I gawked at her cream wide leg pants and black blouse, in awe of the authority she strutted with. She was halfway to Erik's office when I picked my jaw off the ground.

"Excuse me, can I help y—"

"No," she answered before I could finish, throwing a hand up like she was waving me away. She didn't even turn to look at me when she spoke.

My admiration for her dropped like a dead weight. Erik was at his desk and had just locked eyes with me when she shut the door. What a bitch.

The minutes ticked by as I stared at Erik's door waiting for Miss Bitch to come back out. Five minutes passed and I came to the conclusion that maybe she had a meeting, even if it wasn't written down on the calendar.

I took the time to pull up some more information on the

University of Cincinnati's business program. Each button I clicked made me a little more breathless. The campus was beautiful, the programs were top notch. I never imagined attending a college like this. I figured at best I'd end up at a community college with an associate's degree.

"It's a good school to attend."

I jumped at Jared's voice, not having heard him come down the hall back from lunch.

"I'm pretty excited about the possibility. I have to get accepted first."

"How'd you do in high school?"

"Good. Mostly As and Bs. But I never got to take my exams because I couldn't afford them. So, we'll see how those go."

"Erik will take care of those fees."

I tried to stop from rolling my eyes, but it didn't work. "Yeah."

It only served to make Jared laugh. "He's not so bad. A little rough around the edges, but mostly good."

I was saved from responding when there was a thud against Erik's door causing both of us to jump. We jerked our heads waiting to find out what the hell was going on when all of a sudden another softer thud hit the door, followed by a moan.

My eyes bulged and heat infused my cheeks.

Thud. Thud. Thud.

The heat in my cheeks turned to a fire burning through my whole body. I wanted to crawl under the desk and plug my ears. The last thing I wanted to do was hear that woman getting screwed against the door.

'I'll uh...I'll just head to my office," Jared muttered, walking away.

Lucky bastard.

The thuds came faster and the groans got louder. I squeezed my eyes shut and pressed my fingers against my ears, praying for it to end. I was only granted my wish five of the longest minutes later when she moaned his name just before a deep groan followed.

I'd heard my sister and Oscar go at it many times, but this was worse.

Even though I'd been pissed at Erik for his cold attitude, I still hadn't been able to stop the small embers of my crush from staying lit. It was such a minor lingering crush, but pain and embarrassment spread and took up every spare inch when I heard him fucking that woman. Blinking, I fought to hold off the fire burning the backs of my eyes.

I was just as stupid as he claimed me to be—just as naive.

A few minutes later, the door opened and I did my best to keep my eyes glued to the screen, not seeing anything.

"When can I see you again?" the woman asked.

"We weren't supposed to see each other this time," came his terse reply.

I glanced up from under my lashes to see her hand on his chest. He stood like a statue, his hands in his pockets and his face stoic.

"You didn't seem to mind." She dragged her nail down his dress shirt and he stepped back.

"Go, Angela."

She stomped her foot—literally stomped her foot—before finally giving in and walking out.

I didn't look up again, but I could feel him there as she went to the elevator and waited. As soon as the doors shut, he sighed like he'd been holding his breath and prepared to fight her off.

I still didn't look up.

But before his office door could close, my mouth had ideas of its own that didn't include ignoring him.

"For someone who's all high and mighty about respecting a woman's body, you sure are a dick to them."

I looked up then and watched him slowly turn back to me, his brows lowered. His green eyes sparkled like emeralds under thunderclouds. He took two long steps away from his door and smirked down at me. "Trust me, I didn't disrespect her body at all. Didn't you hear?"

He'd wanted me to hear. That asshole wanted me to hear him fucking some woman. Why? So I wouldn't *romanticize* him? I stiffened and took a deep breath to push down the anger. He turned to walk away again, but I wasn't done.

"No, you just disrespect women as basic humans."

He turned back, taking another step closer. "Are you jealous?"

He hit a little too close to home. What did that woman have that made him decide to give in to her and not me? Why was her body worth *disrespecting* but mine wasn't? I scoffed. "No."

He walked slowly around the desk until he stood right in front of me. His hands moved from his pockets to the arms of the chair and leaned down, bringing his face too close to mine. I stayed upright, unwilling to pull back and cower.

"Disappointed then?" he asked softly. "Disappointed that I didn't bend you over and fuck you in the disgusting hotel room? Even more disappointed now that you know how good I can make a woman feel?"

"Fuck you," I ground out.

I remained still as he dragged his nose along my cheek, only letting my eyes slide closed a little. They snapped back open when he pushed away to stand upright.

"Maybe it was your ploy all along. Maybe you're not even a virgin at all. This is just your way of guilting some poor man into giving you so much more than a measly ten grand. You sure didn't feel like a virgin when you rubbed yourself all over me as you came."

I didn't know how I kept my body glued to the chair when all

I wanted to do was stand up and shove him. Maybe even smack his face for insulting me.

Instead, I clenched my fists and managed to growl past my clenched jaw. "Screw. You."

With a triumphant smile, he stepped back and headed to his office.

"Call the Precinct and make a reservation for two at seven. Then, please notify Miss Stutz of our plans. Her number is in my contacts. Laura can take you back to the apartment again." He stopped before closing his door and gave one last parting shot. "I'll be home late tonight. I have a woman's body I need to show some respect to. Again."

11

ERIK

MY KEYS DROPPED to the carpet with a muted crash. Resting my hand against the door, I groaned and leaned over, trying to focus my eyes enough to grab the chunk of silver on the dark carpet.

I stood upright but didn't remove my hand from the wall. The world spun and it took two attempts to finally slip the keys in the lock. Before I pushed the door open, I checked my phone for the time. Ten thirty-two. That was late enough. Hell, I'd been done with dinner almost three hours ago. It'd been a petty mistake to meet Angela for dinner.

I'd come out to find Alexandra there, her cheeks stained red and her chin high and mighty in the air. She'd opened her sassy mouth and I'd reacted, shutting her down. Joke was on me when I had to endure almost forty-five minutes with Angela rambling about how happy she was that we had dinner. It gave her the wrong idea and she began talking about a wedding next month and getting a hotel for the both of us. I'd scarfed down the eighty-dollar steak and made excuses to leave.

There was no way I could sleep with her again. I hadn't really wanted to in the first place. She'd strolled in and I'd caught a glimpse of Alexandra's wide, innocent eyes, and I'd wanted to toss Angela out to call Alexandra into the office and pick up where I'd stopped everything Saturday night. Which was why I'd given in to Angela's overt come-ons and even fucked her against the door. I had a point to make and I had to make it savagely.

I was beginning to realize Alexandra didn't take shit. She called me on my rude behavior and I'd snapped. The fact that I'd needed to remember Alexandra's soft cries to come while fucking Angela pissed me off and I'd taken my frustration out on her. I'd taunted her and cornered myself in a situation I hadn't wanted to be in.

Hence why I'd gone to a bar to drink and was just now stumbling into my own apartment as quietly as possible, hoping she'd already locked herself in her room like she'd done every day this week. I held the knob as I eased the door closed, thudding my head against the solid surface when I heard her voice.

"I assumed you wouldn't be coming home."

I peeled my head from the door and shook myself off before turning to face her. She was a nineteen-year-old girl in *my* home. She was also a young, beautiful woman whose legs were currently on full display along with the rest of her skin. She finished filling her glass of water before turning to rest her back against the counter.

I slowed my pace and tried to stop my eyes from trailing over her exposed skin. She wore a pair of running shorts and a t-shirt. No bra. Because why would fate be nice and at least put her in a damn bra?

My hand gripped the island granite for support, trying to appear more sober than I was under Alexandra's assessing stare. "How was she?" she asked, her tone mocking. "Different from earlier? Better? Or does it even matter?"

"None of your business." I grabbed my own glass and reached past her to fill it in the sink.

"God, did you fuck her drunk?" She scrunched her nose like the smell of scotch disgusted her. "That poor woman."

My glass thudded to the counter. Her words easily undoing the loose rein I had on my temper. "Yeah," I taunted. "She was real sad as she screamed my name."

Her lip curled. "You're disgusting."

"Didn't think so Saturday night," I said with an easy shrug.

Her own glass thudded into the sink and she went to storm past me. I should have let her go, escaping another chance I could have touched her. I should have gone to bed knowing I'd won another victory at pushing her away. Instead, I snatched her wrist to hold her back.

She whirled and stared at my hand easily encircling her wrist. "What?"

What? That was a good question. What did I want? I looked around the kitchen like it would give me an answer to keep her there with me. My eyes landed on the far drawer and a light bulb went off. "I need to give you this while you're not holed up in your room."

Letting go, I brushed past her and ignored the way she gasped when my arm touched her chest. I grabbed the white box with an apple on it from the drawer and laid it on the counter.

"I don't need a phone."

I ground my jaw. I hadn't meant to buy her a phone, but I'd been walking past the store on Sunday and maybe felt bad for how rude I'd been and bought one for her. However, she'd shut down my plans and apology by ignoring me when I knocked on her door, inciting my irritation again. Just like she was doing now.

"Yes, you do," I grumbled. "I need to be able to get a hold of you for work."

She barked a laugh. "No thanks. I don't need you to reach me and give any orders more than you do. In fact..." She sucked in a frustrated breath and I prepared for her sassy retort. Instead, her shoulders sagged and her voice got quiet. "Me staying here is a mistake. We obviously can't get along and this is just a waste of time." She didn't wait for a response, just tried to walk past me again.

I grabbed her wrist again and held her back, growling the least logical thing in that moment. "You'll stay if you want your money. I bought you."

"You're not my keeper." Her quiet voice was gone and her eyes burned with fire.

"No, I'm the man saving you from your shitty future. You're being an ungrateful shit about it."

"I didn't ask to be saved," she yelled.

It hammered against my throbbing skull and was like gasoline on a fire. My temper spiked, but I didn't yell back. No, I backed her up into the counter and cornered her, using my size to intimidate her. "No?" I asked. "Did you want me to let some predator come take you? Did you want to be pinned to a bed as he shoved his dick in you and laughed at your tears?" I inched closer and lowered my voice. "Then when you think it's finally over because he'd taken every hole you have, he drugs you. Only for you to wake up on some cot in a trailer so man after man can pay twenty bucks to stick their dick wherever they want."

"Stop," she whispered, her wide eyes glowing like silver in the dim light.

But I wasn't done. I took the final step to press myself against her, barely holding back the groan at feeling her soft body accept my hard edges. She watched my hand move to push her hair back. "Or maybe you changed your mind when you saw me. Maybe you liked what you saw and hoped I'd strip you naked and make love to your tight, virgin pussy."

I leaned down, brushing my nose along her cheek, breathing in the lemon and vanilla scent clinging to her skin, and whispered in her ear. "The truth is, Princess, I won't be any softer. I'll take what you offer and love every cry you let free. The only difference is that I'll make you like it and beg for more."

By the time I'd finished my speech, my cock was hard and my body urged me to rub against her until I came.

"You're an arrogant prick with a hero complex."

She tried to sound hard, but the breathy words ruined it and she couldn't hide the fact that she hadn't pulled away when I stroked her skin. Clenching my hands on the counter, I fought for control. The alcohol and her nearness made me warm and hard. Thankfully, there was still a rational part of my brain that told me to back the fuck up—a part of my brain that told me she wasn't completely wrong.

I listened to the small sliver of reason and stepped back, ending the night before it spiraled too far out of my control.

"Take the phone," I ordered, walking away. I stopped before heading up the stairs. "And you're not leaving. I may be an asshole, but at least you're safe here. So, suck it up and don't make me chase you down."

When I reached my bedroom, I shed my clothes on the way to my bed and collapsed on top of the covers.

"God," I groaned, dragging a hand over my face. I'd fucked up tonight. Over and over again. And to make matters worse, my dick was standing straight up from my body, fully erect from being pressed against Alexandra. She'd been so soft, her curves and her skin. My length jerked when I remembered how good it felt to have her grinding on me, sucking on my tongue. I remembered her whimpers.

The strength that had me walking away in the kitchen broke down behind closed doors. I'd give in tonight, and tomorrow I'd be strong again, putting more distance between us.

I gripped my cock and stroked it softly. My eyes slid closed and I sunk into the memory of her soft whimpers.

12

ALEXANDRA

THE ENDING CREDITS of *Revolutionary Road* scrolled up the screen. Erik had taken to buying movies on Amazon for me to watch. It made being mad at him hard. He was a conundrum of being a dick and having these redeeming qualities.

The way he left me alone most nights in the apartment allowed the annoyance to grow. I clicked off the TV and looked out at the shining lights of the city.

Maybe I should take the five thousand and go. It was a lot of money. I could get an apartment by the bus station. I could make it work.

But barely.

I'd still struggle and I just wanted a little more to life than to constantly struggle. I'd be able to accomplish more with ten thousand. I'd be able to reach all new levels if I had a college degree and guaranteed work.

It won't be like this, I reminded myself.

But the lights of the city called to me and this empty apartment wore on me. I needed fresh air, a little of the freedom I was working toward. Staring down at the phone on the coffee table, I thought about texting Erik to let him know I was going for a walk, but why bother. He was off on one of his many dates and I'd be back before he even knew I was gone. I'd only walk a few blocks and come right back. Maybe grab a bite to eat while I was out. He couldn't be too mad if I was just getting some food.

The decision made, I grabbed my coat and a couple bucks from the box Erik kept money in. I tried not to use it, but he said it was for food and other essentials. At most, there was fifty dollars in there and I could replace anything I took with my first paycheck.

The cold air washed over my face and instantly I felt better. The weights holding me down in the apartment lifted. I walked slowly in no specific direction, just enjoying the sound of cars driving by and not being alone. It only took a block before my mind strayed to Leah. I thought about her more than I wanted. I wondered how she was, wondering if she was safe. The idea of her alone, being abused by Oscar turned my stomach.

I'd planned on leaving everything behind once I had the ten thousand dollars, but I'd been fooling myself. I would never be able to completely cut myself off from my sister.

Things hadn't always been so bad. Life in Ireland had been great actually. Even when we moved in with Mom, we'd still banded together. When we first moved, we'd sat on the floor of our shared room and made a blood pact. Us against the world.

When older boys had asked me on a date, she'd done my makeup and helped me dress. She'd also punched my date in the throat when he'd tried to kiss me after I told him no. Then Mom had gotten really bad, working less, taking more drugs. Then Leah met Oscar and it spiraled from there, the good memories becoming nothing. But there were enough good memories to keep me from completely leaving her.

I stopped at a crosswalk just as a bus stopped to pick people up. Making a rash decision, I checked where it was going and hopped on. My leg bounced harder with each stop we made closer to my destination. When we'd got as close as we'd go, I hopped off. Zipping my jacket up higher, I looked side-to-side. This area of town was familiar but much more dangerous than the swanky downtown area I'd just left. The buildings disappeared and trailers took their place.

The sign for our trailer park came into view, a streetlamp only half illuminating it. Standing in the shadows, I considered turning around and going back. Erik would be pissed if he knew where I was, but I just needed to know she was okay. I took a deep breath and rounded the corner, heading to Leah's trailer. Funny how it'd only been a little while, but the trailer no longer felt like home.

I kept my head down and avoided the few lights that would make my presence known. I didn't really have a plan once I got there. Didn't really think I'd do anything other than look in the window to confirm she was alive and Oscar hadn't gone insane and hurt her.

But when I made the final turn, the trailer was completely dark. I walked softly, avoiding making any extra noise to announce my presence. It wasn't too late, but they could be asleep inside. I looked inside the best I could through the dirty windows, finding everything dark and no one passed out on the couches. Moving to lean back against the trailer, I rolled my lips between my teeth and thought about what to do. The wind blew and I shoved my cold hands into my pockets, one connecting with the large rectangular phone.

I could at least leave my number. Maybe she realized her mistakes and wanted to reach out, but didn't know where to find me. I wouldn't be an accomplice to her ruining her life, but I wanted to be there if she ever needed help. Staying quiet, I pulled out my old key and eased inside. Cringing, I took in the ashtrays, needles, and lighters littering the coffee table.

This is a mistake. My subconscious screamed at me to turn around, that I was being as naive as Erik accused me of being, but I had to try. There was no harm in hoping. Moving quickly, I found a piece of paper and pen and wrote down my number, rushing to the bathroom to shove it in Leah's makeup bag. Oscar would never be in there, but Leah was sure to see it.

I left the drawer open, hoping she'd notice what was off, and got out of there. I clung to the shadows until I made it to the streets, and then I ran. I even passed the first bus stop, heading to the next one, needing to put as much distance between me and that nightmare as I could.

The bus was just pulling up when I reached the stop and I got on. I took the drive to catch my breath, wondering if I just made the biggest mistake yet.

I JUMPED when my new phone vibrated across my desk next to Laura's the next day.

"Still not used to it?" Laura asked, laughing at my reaction.

"Not really."

It'd been three days and I'd barely done anything with it. Jared helped me add music yesterday. He'd stared at me in wonder when I told him I barely knew how to turn it on.

"Leave it to Erik to find someone to work at a tech company that doesn't know how to use an iPhone."

I laughed. "Hey, at least I know how to use a computer."

The phone vibrated again with a reminder that I still hadn't checked the notification. I swiped it open and thought I might crush it in my grip when I read the message.

Mr_E: Grab me a coffee.

No please. No asking. Just a command like it was a foregone conclusion that I'd be a coffee girl. I'd seriously considered dropping the damn thing in the trash or giving it to a homeless person.

But I couldn't ditch it because now I needed it in case Leah called.

I hadn't heard from her yet, but I figured it was only a matter of time. Leah had been the eighteen-year-old to claim me when Mom died, but I'd been the one to really take care of us.

I thought about telling Erik I'd gone back to the trailer, but it was messages like the one he just sent that kept me from sharing anything beyond what I needed to. I deleted the message because it irritated me to see the list of commands, before heading to the lunchroom to grab Master his coffee. I was watching the black liquid drip from the machine when a deep voice interrupted my internal debate of whether to put eye drops in Erik's coffee or not.

"Hey, new girl."

I turned to say hello and stalled, the words frozen on my tongue. Holy hotness. The guy standing on the other side of the table, currently giving me a lazy smile, was hot. Like Abercrombie and Fitch model hot.

"Um, hi." Real smooth, Alexandra.

"I'm Wyatt." He reached his hand across the table and I stepped forward to shake it. Surprisingly, I didn't feel a jolt of excitement when we touched. Not like I did with Erik, which was kind of irritating because this guy should have been turning me into a bonfire. He had the styled, short on the sides-longer on the top, dirty blond hair and eyes like the sky on a sunny day. He'd obviously perfected his slight smile, making his eyes twinkle with ease and a hint of something devious.

Yet, instead of warmth, I only felt appreciation for an extraordinarily attractive guy and a minor thrill that he was aiming a smile at me. What girl didn't like to feel like she could garner the attention of a guy that looked like him?

He raised an eyebrow and I realized I'd been silent too long. Crap.

"I'm Alexandra. But people have been calling me Alex for short."

"Alex."

A spark flickered hearing him try my name out on his tongue, that smirk still firmly in place. Maybe I'd dismissed him too soon.

"So, what do you do here, Wyatt?"

"I've been an intern here for two years. I graduate in the spring and then it's on to an actual salary position."

"Sounds exciting."

"Yes, and no. A little terrifying. If I make a mistake now, I'm just learning. If I make a mistake later, then they tend to look at it differently."

"Can't handle the pressure?"

"Oh, I can handle more than you think," he said, his eyes dropping down and back up my body.

My cheeks warmed and I looked away. Clearing my throat, I diverted the subject away from his meaning. "So, what do you do?"

"I'm mainly in analytics on the floor below. What about you?"

I gestured behind me to the coffee maker. "Right now, I'm the errand girl."

He winced. "They must be a bit harder on you up here on the CEO floor. We barely had to do any errands. But when they did dole them out, we rotated who got stuck with the task."

"We?"

He came around to lean against the table, facing me. His shirt stretched across his muscles when he crossed his arms. He wasn't big, but he definitely wasn't scrawny either.

"Yeah. There are three of us on the floor below. I don't think I've seen an intern be placed on this floor before."

"Huh."

He ignored my eloquent response, thank goodness. "We should grab drinks sometime."

"She's nineteen," Erik growled from the doorway. "She can't drink."

Wyatt stood upright but didn't jump to give his attention to Erik.

"Wow. I had no idea," he said, smiling at me.

Behind him, Erik looked like he was about to explode. "What are you doing on this floor?"

Wyatt turned with an easy smile. "Sorry, Sir. Miss Brandt wanted me to drop this off to you. I was on my way to your office when I happened to see Alex here and thought I'd welcome her to the team."

Erik took the thumb drive Wyatt pulled from his pocket. "You can leave now."

"See you around, Alex."

I smiled and waved at Wyatt before he disappeared around the corner. Erik however, remained glued to the floor with his pissed off scowl still in place.

"You're just so desperate to lose that hymen, aren't you?"

I rolled my eyes and clenched my fists. I should be used to his comments, but they still pissed me off. "Not every girl talking to a guy is trying to have sex with him."

"He sure wanted to fuck you."

"Good for him." Sarcasm bled into my words.

Erik's posture relaxed and he crossed his arms, a small smile playing on his lips. Unlike Wyatt, Erik's arms clearly strained against the material, showcasing spectacular muscles. On cue, my body heated like the traitor it was.

"What?" he began. "Was he not rich enough to pay the ten thousand for your virginity?"

"Stop being an asshole." I turned back to his coffee to hide the blush staining my cheeks. "What are you doing here anyway?" I asked, trying to change the subject.

Hearing steps, I turned to find Ian walking in.

"I came to check on my coffee," Erik answered, undeterred by Ian's presence. "You were taking too long."

I grabbed the mug and set it down with a thud, sliding it across with a condescending smile. "Sorry, *Sir*."

"Hey, happy people," Ian greeted, his eyes volleying between us.

Erik snatched up his mug and harrumphed a response to Ian before leaving.

"Is he always such a dick?" I asked before thinking. Shit. Ian was Erik's friend and the other half of the company that was employing me and I'd just called his partner a dick. I cringed. "Sorry."

I stared wide-eyed as Ian's head fell back and he laughed long and loud. When he got control of himself he pretended to wipe tears away before focusing his intensely gray eyes on me.

"It's totally okay. And yes, he's usually pretty gruff. Hell, that dick went in with Jared and got me a prank Christmas gift. Set me up to take boudoir photos with a blind date."

I should have been surprised by Ian calling his business partner a dick, but ever since working here, I'd gotten to know him, and discovered he's unapologetic about who he is and rarely curbs anything about himself when around others.

"Joke was on them because she was hot as hell." He cocked his head to the side and stared at me. "But Erik seems to have a soft spot for you."

"Great," I deadpanned.

Ian went to the fridge and grabbed one of the prepared salads. "Hey, some of the best sex of my life came from that blind date, even though she drove me bananas. She kept arguing with me about every damn thing." He shook his head like he was baffled someone wouldn't just fall in line with him. "Just wouldn't admit I was right."

"Well, I don't plan on sleeping with Erik."

Ian pointed his fork at me with a smile. "Good. Stick with that. Maybe if you say it enough you might have a chance of it not happening."

I stared slack-jawed as he walked out of the room.

He was wrong.

I would *never* sleep with Erik Brandt.

13

ALEXANDRA

"Miss Russo, welcome to Bergamo and Brandt," Erik greeted the stunning brunette.

My mind went back to the bitchy blonde who had dismissed me as she walked into Erik's office. She'd looked like a badass boss lady when she walked in too, but everything about Miss Russo's demeanor was different and I liked it. She came in and acknowledged Laura and me with a smile before reaching out to shake Erik's hand.

"Hello, Mr. Brandt. And please, call me Carina."

Her hand didn't linger as she batted her eyes at him. Watching her, I realized that *this* was a true badass boss lady. She wore sky-high stilettos like she wasn't walking on needles. Her suit was stylish and sexy, but she wore it like it was for her alone —not to impress anyone. *This* was a businesswoman I wanted to study and take notes on. My heart skipped at the thought of being anything like her. Even imagining the kind of authority she walked in with gave me a high none of the drugs Leah took could reach.

I swallowed down the giggle rising up as I realized I was in lust at first sight with a woman.

"Of course. We can ditch all formalities and you can call me Erik. This here is my assistant, Laura, and a new intern, Alexandra."

"Nice to meet you," Carina said, taking a step forward to shake both our hands.

As soon as she stepped back, I dipped my head to subtly check for any drooling.

"If you would like to follow me, we can get started in my office." Erik held his hand out, gesturing toward his open door.

Just as they were about to cross the threshold, Laura winked at me before speaking. "Don't you think talking about your new office plans would be a good opportunity for Miss Hughes to learn in her internship?"

Erik turned, looking over his shoulder at me with a glare, his jaw tight, like I had put Laura up to it. My pursed lips, trying to hold back a smile, probably didn't help my case.

"I'd be completely fine with that," Carina said.

He was officially cornered into a decision.

In case he was thinking of coming up with an excuse, I decided to lock in the pressure and cocked my brow, challenging him to say no.

"Sure," he ground through his clenched jaw before it relaxed into a devious smirk. "But make sure you grab some waters for us. Unless you'd like a coffee," he offered Carina.

"Water is fine, thank you."

"Waters then, Alexandra."

He turned and shut the door behind him missing my growl of frustration. Laura didn't though. She laughed and kept typing. "Don't let him win. Run to get the waters and be back faster than he expects."

"Thanks, Laura."

I did as suggested and was rewarded when Erik's eyes widened before narrowing at my entrance.

"That was fast."

"What can I say, I'm a good employee."

Carina thanked me for the water and was finishing setting up when I sat on a chair to the left.

"I'm excited to be working on the next project for Bergamo and Brandt. I know you worked with my father when you originally structured your company."

"We're happy to have Wellington and Russo helping out."

Carina smiled my way. "It's good to see you taking on a female intern. I've done some research on your company and it is a male dominated office with only male interns."

Erik gave an easy smile. "I assure you, it's completely unintentional."

"I was kind of an accidental intern," I explained. "But I'd like to think I'm the best kind of accident."

Carina laughed. "We have to take every opportunity we can." She winked and turned back to Erik. "Okay, let's get started, shall we?"

"Yes." Erik sat up and I took that as my cue to remain quiet and absorb as much information as possible. "I'm sorry Mr. Bergamo couldn't be here, but I'll be sure to fill him in."

The meeting moved quickly and I was confused through most of it but took notes so I could look things up later. Sometimes Carina would take a moment to explain a technique or the lingo. Erik didn't acknowledge that I was there, but I didn't care. I became a sponge and sucked up as much information as I could. There was no YouTube video that came close to this kind of learning.

Carina began packing up and had just put her sleek leather bag over her shoulder when she gave me her full attention, but talked to Erik. "I'd love to work with Alex whenever possible. I'm always willing to extend as many opportunities to another female in the business as I can."

I think my jaw hit the floor. Erik's tightened as he gave me an annoyed look. But he didn't fight it. He sighed heavily and gave in. "Of course."

She shook both our hands. "Good. I look forward to our endeavor, Erik."

Just as she left, Jared came out of his office looking a little frantic. "Erik, we need to have a meeting now."

Erik gave a curt nod and told Laura to hold his calls before he and Jared disappeared into Erik's office.

"How'd it go?" Laura asked.

"Amazing." I fell into my seat with a dreamy sigh. "I may have a lady-crush on Carina."

"Couldn't say I blame you. She is a woman to idolize."

"She said she wanted to work with me on the project. I'm not sure I have anything to offer, but I'm willing to learn."

"I bet Erik loved that."

I laughed. "You should have seen the joy on his face."

Laura shook her head but was smiling. "I'm going to head to lunch. You okay watching the front desk?"

"Sure. Shouldn't be too hard since Erik isn't taking calls."

"Okay. I'll be back soon."

I'd been sitting at the desk for only a few minutes when a UPS man came to deliver a package. After signing for the package, I held the box and considered my options. Erik was pretty adamant about getting anything delivered as soon as it arrived and I knew he'd been expecting one from HudTech, the company on the label.

Deciding it would be better to have them stop talking for less than a minute than hold a package that may be more important, I went to knock on the door. I raised my hand but stopped when I noticed it wasn't completely shut.

"You found her on the same site that Alexandra was on?"

"Yes. She was listed as sixteen and a virgin."

"Same username as before?"

"Yes." Jared sounded disgusted.

My heart pounded so hard, I was worried they'd hear it through the door.

"Hire MacCabe to collect her and take her to Haven and they'll take over from there to get her settled."

"Haven isn't complete yet."

"It's done enough. She can be a trial of how everything will run."

What the hell were they talking about? Squeezing my eyes shut, I tried to organize the thoughts rushing through my mind. I tried to focus on the most rational answer but the scarier ones kept breaking through everything. He was on the site again. For a virgin. A young one. Maybe that was why he didn't take me. Maybe I was too old.

No. I shook my head. Erik wouldn't do that. He was an asshole, but none of this was true. I was hearing wrong. There had to be a logical explanation. There was no way Erik was going around buying young wo—

The door jerked open and I gasped, stumbling back in shock at seeing Jared standing there, his hand still on the door. One eyebrow crept up before he shifted his gaze from mine back to Erik, behind him. I tried not to, but I couldn't help but follow his stare to Erik as well. He sat at his desk, jaw clenched and eyes hard.

"I'm so sorry, I wasn't trying to eavesdrop. I didn't hear anything. I wasn't even listening." I kept rambling, spouting out random short sentences that seemed to make it worse and worse while internally I was screaming at myself to shut up. "You have a package."

Jared turned back to me and one side of his mouth twitched. "Well, I'll let you go ahead and handle that."

He brushed past and left me standing in the open doorway, wide-eyed, heart still hammering, and clutching the package that got me into this mess. Erik didn't say anything, just gestured me forward and held his hand out. I took slow steps forward and thought over all I'd heard.

What if he was buying up virgins? What if he wasn't who I thought he was? Was I just going to ignore it? How did I bring it up?

My mouth made the decision for me before I could think through the repercussions. My body even joined in and cocked a hip with my hand on it, like I was Miss Attitude.

"What? You didn't get me, so you're back on the site looking for someone else?"

His hand dropped and his eyes turned almost black. "Don't."

He looked a little murderous, but now that I'd begun, I was committed and wanted answers. "No." I slammed the door behind me and took long strides forward until I stood in front of his desk. "Tell me if you're bringing another girl to the apartment. Maybe you're trying to make a harem."

"Alexandra," he growled my name and his hand curled into a fist on his desk. "You don't know what you're talking about."

"Then tell me," I almost pleaded. I didn't want any of it to be true, but my mind struggled to form another option. "Because right now, I'm a little scared you're keeping girls in different places for yourself."

Erik heaved a breath and leaned back in his seat, his hand coming to rub across his mouth as he looked around the room. I stood there watching him, not moving no matter how long it took. Even if it felt like the seconds ticked by like minutes.

"Erik," I whispered. All the challenge had left me, leaving behind desperation that I was wrong. I slept down the hall from this man. I'd sat astride the man and kissed him. I fought with him and trusted him. I *had* to be wrong.

"I keep an eye on the dark web for girls being sold into sex slavery," he finally said. The words were soft, but rattled through me like he was yelling, shaking me to my core. "I hire a team once I've—or Jared—tracked them down and they extract the girl."

The rush of adrenaline and fear seeped out of me, leaving me weak and empty, and I fell back into the chair in front of his desk. "So, this is something you do."

He turned his head and met my stare. "It's a thing I do."

My mind tried to piece the puzzle together of how he retrieved me and what he told me about retrieving others and question after question piled on top of each other. "Do you always bring them back to your place?"

He huffed a laugh but didn't smile. "No."

"Then why did you with me? Why didn't a team come and get me?"

"You were...different." The words sounded dragged from him. "You were selling yourself. I went because you were alone. Because..." He looked to be fighting with what to say next. "You were just different."

I nodded like I understood, but I wasn't sure I did. "What do you do when you find them?"

"I set them up and get them into rehab if needed. Most are addicted to the drug they'd been fed depending on how long they'd been captured. My goal is to offer them a fresh start. If they have a family, we take them there and work with them to move on."

"What's Haven?"

"Haven is a foundation I began a few years back, but I always had goals to make it more. I wanted to create a place for these girls to go that will provide them everything they need in one place until they're ready to go out in the world again. However, it's not quite set up yet."

I wished he would look at me. Instead, he stared down at his finger drawing figure eights atop his desk. I thought maybe if I could meet his eyes, I'd understand more.

"Why? Why do you do this?"

That got his attention. His hand stopped moving and he looked up from under his lashes. The green of his eyes darkened and pain flooded his expression knocking the wind from me. I'd seen Erik angry. I'd seen him laugh with friends. I'd seen him irritated. I'd seen him turned on. But I'd never seen him in pain. I sat back, collapsing deeper into the chair as fire burned the backs of my eyes. I didn't even know what it was but watching the hurt inside him, I knew it'd be bad.

"My sisters were kidnapped when they were seventeen and on vacation in Florida." My hand flew to my mouth, covering the gasp. "I hadn't been able to go because of work."

"Erik..." Part of me wanted to stop him. I knew it'd be bad, but I hadn't been ready for how bad.

"It took me four months and seven days to find them." The words came out like they were ripped from his body. He looked back down at his hand that was curling into a fist. "When I finally got to them, Sofia hadn't made it."

Tears slipped down my cheeks and my fingers trembled against my lips. "Erik. I'm so sorry. So, so sorry." Sorry I pried. Sorry for his loss. Sorry for his pain. Sorry for it all. Hatred settled heavy on my chest. Why did I bring it up? Why did I push?

"Hanna took years to recover. Sofia was her twin and she'd watched her die."

Erik cleared his throat and sat up straighter. I mirrored his actions and swiped at my tears. If he could pull himself together right now, then I could respect him enough to do the same. My pain wasn't his responsibility. He had enough of his own.

"Alexandra." I looked up to find his eyes blank, a wall blocking any hurt that had escaped. "It goes without saying that this doesn't come up. Ever."

"Of course."

"And what I do doesn't come up either. It's not common knowledge and I made a splash when I first started rescuing women and coming after the people who ran the operations. I made enemies. It's one of the main reasons I hire people to complete the rescue rather than going myself."

"Of course," I said again. What else could I say? I was done asking questions. I wasn't sure I could handle any more answers. His fingers had resumed their figure eights and after I'd given my compliance he looked back down at the movement. He appeared to be closed off, but I watched the way he swallowed again and again. I watched the way his other hand clenched and unclenched. I could only imagine what he was mentally reliving.

I'd heard what he said, and what he didn't. The way he talked about not being on vacation with them, the way he talked about taking so long to find them—he blamed himself. Maybe he did all of this as a penance for what he believed were his mistakes. As much as he pissed me off, I hated to watch another human being hurt. Especially one who had chosen me as someone to help.

Scooting forward in my chair, I reached my hand across the desk until I was able to place it over his. His hand stopped and he briefly flashed his eyes to mine. I didn't say anything, just rested my hand on his for comfort for as long as he'd take it. Air rushed from my lungs when he adjusted, turning his palm up to hold mine.

We sat there for maybe a minute, but a huge shift occurred. He accepted my comfort and a silent truce fell between us. After a while, he eased his hand back and I did the same.

"Don't ever talk about it," he said again. "Don't ever tell anyone."

"Yes, sir." I gave him my compliance. No sarcastic remarks and petty battle.

"Good." He sat upright at his desk and moved his mouse to bring the computer back to life. "Now, go get me a coffee."

I almost bristled at his brusque order, mad that I'd apparently been the only one to feel a middle ground. But then he glanced my way and one side of his mouth ticked up.

I relaxed, realizing Mr. E had a darker sense of humor.

14

ERIK

"I know I'm not supposed to talk about what you do while we're out, but can I ask you questions while we're home?"

I looked over my shoulder to Alexandra sitting on the other side of the island. She leaned forward with her elbows resting on the marble counter, causing her t-shirt to gape and expose damn near all her cleavage.

Ignoring the way my chest ached at hearing her call my apartment her home, I forced myself to turn back to the sink. I'd never shared this place with anyone and I didn't plan on keeping her here for long. But if I had a gun to my head, I could admit that I guessed it wasn't so bad having her around.

"You can. I may not answer though."

She laughed softly. "Fair enough."

It'd been a week since I'd confessed about what I did on the side—since I'd told her about my sisters. An unspoken truce had formed. I was still conservative with my time around her, but I stopped punishing her for my own attraction. I didn't stop making her get my coffee, but I did give her more meaningful tasks. I even made it a point to CC her on emails regarding Carina's project. Mainly because if I didn't, Carina did.

To feel better about spending more cordial time around Alexandra, I still overtly dated. I came home more nights last week than I had before, but other evenings I had Laura take her home and left at the same time as them, meeting my date outside with an over the top kiss.

Distance was the key to having Alexandra around but not giving in to the way I craved her. Showing her how I hopped from woman-to-woman forced her to keep her distance. It forced her to not stare at me as she wove fairytales about how I rescued her or other women. God knows I hadn't been strong enough to stay away. Every time she'd worked herself closer to me, I'd given in. I'd caved and touched her, told her in one way or another what I really wanted to do to her.

Distance was the key, even if it was just me forcing her to keep hers because I was a weak, horny, son of a bitch.

"Did you get the girl?"

I thought about not answering, but it would only be stubborn and we were past that. There was comfort with her knowing. Everyone close to me—all five people—knew what I did. Her knowing took the stress away of her finding out. And somehow admitting what had happened with my sister hadn't hurt as much as it usually did when I said it out loud. It had hurt even less when she'd slipped her soft palm over mine, sharing her strength and comfort with one small touch.

"Yes," I answered simply.

"How was she?"

"She was okay...not great." We hadn't gotten to her soon enough. It'd been two days after she was sold before we found her.

"Is she at Haven?"

"No. She had a family that had been looking for her. A good one."

"That's good."

"Yes. Not many have that to fall back on."

"Don't I know it," she mumbled as she looked down into her wineglass.

Her shoulders slumped and she made circles with her glass, swirling the dark liquid around and up the sides. Part of me wanted to wrap my arms around her, offer her some of the comfort she'd given me.

I shook off the notion before my feet could start moving. *Distance.* If I went to her and she let me, I'd cave.

"Are you done?" I asked, gesturing to the half-eaten slice of pizza in front of her.

She stared at it before smiling. "Just a couple more bites. Who knew I'd like mushrooms on pizza? Any other time I've had them, they were so gross."

"It's the cheese and sausage that make them even better. Whole new flavor blend. I'm still sad you wouldn't let me add pineapple."

"Fruit isn't supposed to be cooked."

"What about pies?"

"I've never had one. At least not a fruit pie. Chocolate pie is to die for."

I didn't know why it still surprised me to discover all the things she'd never tried, but I'd taken our time together to help her experience new things. It made me appreciate them all the more watching her enjoy them.

"I'll have my mom make one. She makes the best apple pies."

"I'm willing to try. Hell, I doubted your mushroom on pizza and look at me now."

She lifted the slice to her mouth and bit down, her eyes

sliding closed as she hummed in pleasure. Alexandra was always so happy when she ate and I liked watching her enjoy the things she hadn't been able to before. We'd probably had pizza about five times in the last two weeks because she said she loved it so much but could never have afforded anything past the occasional Dollar Store cheap stuff.

I never turned her down when she asked for pizza, even if it meant I had to work a little harder at the gym.

She'd been so thin when I first met her and after a couple weeks, she'd put on some weight. Her cheeks were less hollow, her skin had more color to it. Her breasts fuller. Her ass and thighs thicker. More weight was doing her good, even if it did have my gaze lingering longer than necessary.

She took one last bite and pushed the plate away. "I can't eat anymore. Take it."

I laughed and grabbed the box.

"Hey, you want to watch a movie? I'm so behind on everything since we didn't have a television."

Warning bells rang in my head. *Don't be dumb. Go to bed and keep your distance. For the love of God, walk away.*

She stared at me with crystalline eyes, wide and hopeful.

"Sure."

You're so fucked.

But her smile shut down the negative voice. She was so damn positive and everything made her giddy. No one who had been through what she'd been through should be that happy, but she was. It was admirable and it would get her far. She would have gotten far even without me, but I liked that I could make her success easier.

By the time I had the kitchen cleaned up and everything thrown away, she had *Blockers* ready to go. She flipped the blanket back and patted the couch next to her, all innocence.

There was no seduction shining behind her eyes, no ulterior motive. It lured me into a false sense of security like maybe all my pushing had her thoughts of heroism gone and she no longer was attracted to me.

That lie got me through the whole movie. It helped me keep my hands to myself as she laughed so hard she was wiping tears from her eyes. The lie made me feel safe enough to voice my own curiosity.

"Can I ask you a question?"

Her head tipped back on the couch and turned to look at me with one brow arched. "You can. I may not answer though," she repeated my same words back to me.

"How are you nineteen and still a virgin?"

"It's not like I'm forty," she scoffed.

"I know, but it's uncommon in this day and age."

"I don't know. There wasn't anyone really great around where I was. No one that I felt safe enough with to even consider feeling attraction." She shrugged before shifting to face me. "Plus my sister didn't make it seem all that appealing."

"You ever have a boyfriend?"

"Nope."

"Kissed?" The question slipped out, lower and more intimate than I'd planned.

A slow smile curled her lips. "Well, yeah. I kissed you."

"Was I your only kiss?" I asked, shocked.

Her eyes dropped a bit before looking back up, a blush staining her cheeks. "Among other first experiences."

Her soft moans as her hips moved faster over my lap flashed in my mind, instantly bringing my dick to life.

"Actually," she began, "I don't think you get credit for my first orgasm. I kind of did that myself against you and I could have accomplished the same thing against a pillow. So maybe you're not that great."

No inner voice giving me warnings about giving her space and to keep this neutral could stop my male pride from rearing its head. I narrowed my eyes and shifted to face her, leaning an arm on the back of the couch to crowd her. "Not that great?" I growled.

The smile she'd been trying to hold back broke free even as the slight blush became a rosy red that spread down her neck. "Nah. I'm still waiting for someone to give me my first real orgasm."

A roaring sound filled my ears, like a wave washing away all common sense. In its place was me beating my chest demanding she acknowledge that she came against my crotch because I made her. I leaned in closer. "*I* gave you your first orgasm."

She shrugged casually, but I saw the pulse thudding against her neck. I watched the way her tongue slicked out to coat her lips. "Sorry to crush your spirits, but I did all the work. You just sat there. Kind of like a pillow would."

"I was."

"Weren't."

"Was."

"Weren't."

"Was," I growled, reaching the end of my patience.

She giggled. "Were—"

My lips crashed down on hers, stopping the childish argument. A small part of me knew how fucking stupid this all was. I'd pushed her away, made decisions, gone on dates I didn't want to, all to make sure she stayed away. And here we were, kissing because I had to make a point that I was some caveman.

I was an idiot.

But I didn't care much when her soft lips were under mine. I didn't care how much I was screwing all my hard work up when she pressed her breasts against my chest and moaned. I didn't care as her tongue tentatively snuck out to touch my lips.

I opened and the rich plum flavor of her wine exploded in my mouth. I brushed my tongue against hers and explored every inch, tasted every part of her. I buried my hand in her hair and controlled her, moving her where I wanted to gain better access.

Her hands gripped my shoulders as I pressed her back to the couch where she spread her legs to fit me between them. Thinking of nothing other than making her come, my hand slipped past her breast and down her body. I lifted just enough to work my hand under the thin pajama pants she wore.

"Has anyone touched you here?" I asked, my fingers lightly skimming over her damp panties.

"No," she confessed breathlessly.

I watched her eyes as I pulled the material aside and exposed her. I fought to keep from leaning back on my haunches and pulling her pants down to look at her pussy. Instead, I felt my way, groaning when my fingers encountered smooth wet skin.

"You shave." She lifted one shoulder and looked away, but I gripped her chin and made her look at me. "Don't be embarrassed. It's sexy. It makes me want to touch it all."

To prove my point I flattened my hand and cupped her, rubbing the smooth skin. Her gasp went straight down my spine to my balls like an electric shock.

"I did it for the hotel and just kept up with it since."

"I like it," I growled against her neck.

Using my middle finger, I dipped between the lips of her pussy and dragged it up until I brushed her hard bud, circling the moisture around and around. She arched her back and whimpered. Moving back to her entrance, I collected more moisture before slowly easing a finger inside. Oh my fuck, she was tight. She would squeeze my cock like a vise.

I pushed in and out, bringing my thumb to her clit. Her eyes widened before squeezing shut. When her mouth fell open on a moan, I latched on, eating every sound of pleasure from her lips.

Again and again, I penetrated her with just one finger, occasionally swirling around her nub until her juices were running down my hand.

"Listen," I demanded. I pushed in hard and moved my finger, wet sounds reaching our ears.

She moved her hands to cover her face, but I pulled them back.

"Don't hide. I love that you're so wet I can hear you. I want to hear it all, so make sure you scream when I finally let you come."

Her chest heaved, drawing my eyes to her breasts rising up against her cami. "Has anyone seen these?" I asked, still slowly moving my finger in and out. She shook her head and that caveman feeling came roaring back, demanding I be the first. Just one more thing I could be the first on. Just one more. "Show me."

With shaking hands she gripped the top of her shirt and tugged down, until two beautiful mounds spilled free, her light pink nipples pulling tight into hard buds. I wanted to lean down and suck them into my mouth, but I settled with just watching.

"Beautiful," I groaned. "I want to taste them, bite them, mark them as mine. But I'll save that first for someone else."

She opened her mouth to argue and I stopped her by pressing my lips to hers, really working my fingers over her. Her whimpers grew to moans. Her core squeezed tight and a rush of wetness flooded her smooth pussy.

"Erik. Yes."

Goose bumps prickled across my skin at hearing her groan my name. I almost came in my pants when I imagined how tight she'd squeeze my cock.

When her core finally stopped spasming, I eased my finger from her and brought it to my lips, sucking as much of her off as I could. She was sweet and tangy and delicious. I shouldn't have done it because it made her all the more tempting. Tasting her from my hand made me crave to taste her directly from the source.

"Mmm," I moaned. "You taste good. And I'm tempted to pull your pants down and shove my tongue up inside you to get every drop, but I'll leave that first kiss to someone else."

Her eyes softened. "What if I don't want anyone else?"

My body stiffened and the voice I'd been pushing aside finally broke free and shouted *I fucking told you so.* I let a blank wall drop over my eyes and rose to my knees, taking a minute to shift her top to cover her breasts. "Don't Alexandra. I told you not to romanticize this."

Her eyes bounced between mine and the corners of her lips dipped down. "You just had your hand in my pants. Just licked my orgasm off your fingers. I-I... I don't understand."

Of course she didn't. Because she was naive and no matter how much I showed her otherwise, she was too positive to imagine I was anything other than a man who would save her and not hurt her.

I backed up to the other side of the couch and shut down any emotion, projecting a cool aloofness I didn't feel. "I had to prove a point. Just because I made you come and touched you doesn't mean we're anything. I make a lot of women come. They at least have the decency to return the favor."

Her eyes dropped to the way my cock tented my pants before popping back up to look at me. "Is that...is that what you want? For me to suck you off?"

"I wouldn't hate it." I rolled my eyes. "But God knows you'd probably take my cum down your throat as a proposal."

Her jaw clenched and she scrambled to get up from her prone position. "Fuck you, Erik."

Standing, I gave her a hard glare. "No matter what world you're in, Alexandra. Men are still just men."

I ignored the glassy sheen slipping over her eyes and stormed off for my room. The movie had been a mistake. It all had been a mistake and all I was left with was us back to square one and another cold shower.

15

ALEXANDRA

"Great job Alex on the marketing mock-up you sent me," Carina said when she exited Erik's office. "I may have stolen a bit of the layout to create another one I'm working on."

Erik's eyes slid to mine over Carina's shoulder. Despite how cold he'd been to me all week, something like pride sparked behind his eyes at Carina's praise.

"You know, if you don't love working with Erik here, I have a spot open for you."

I damn-near melted out of my chair. Every time I was around Carina, I studied her—in a completely non-stalkerish way. Self-confidence poured off her, and she walked with power and assurance. She was everything I wanted to be as a businesswoman.

I was so focused on keeping myself in my seat that I almost missed Erik's brows furrowing as he glared at Carina's back. They softened when she winked at him over her shoulder.

"You can poach your own company, but leave mine alone. Besides Alexandra is perfectly happy where she's at."

I cocked a brow but didn't comment at his over the top smile he gave me.

"Let me walk you out."

Erik disappeared down to the elevators and was back in a few minutes. I hoped he'd come back with some of the humor he'd shown a moment ago. It would make the upcoming weekend in the apartment a little less awkward. We'd backtracked on our truce in the past week. He was back to barking orders at me. The only silver lining was that the orders were actual work.

"Alexandra, get me a coffee."

Well, most of the time it was actual work.

I should have been more mad than I was. Mad at how he'd treated me Saturday night. But I still felt his finger inside me— stretching me. I still tasted his lips and tongue on mine. I still heard his voice demanding me to show him my breasts. I still had butterflies fluttering in my chest whenever I locked eyes with him and it was hard to push the want down.

I got that he was trying to prove the night on the couch was nothing. I got that he was proving to me that he was a womanizer and I shouldn't expect more from him. Even hinting to the fact that I'd like more had been an obvious mistake. I'd been lost in the moment of the orgasm, my lips moving before my mind could think it through. I'd been ready to give him everything.

Then he'd pulled back. Hard.

Even with how the night ended and how embarrassed I'd felt at his rejection, it hadn't stopped me from fantasizing. I'd never fantasized about a man before. I'd never felt safe enough to consider being close to someone. And that was what it boiled down to: I felt safe around Erik. I felt safe enough to close my eyes and imagine being intimate with him.

He'd pulled back Saturday night, but he'd also pulled back other times only to get close again. I wasn't dumb enough to push the issue, but my daydreams had me holding out hope that maybe we'd find ourselves in another position where some of my fantasies could come true. Maybe I'd get to feel him against me again.

I lightly knocked on the cracked door to alert my presence. Erik waved his hand for me to come in without looking away from Jared who sat in front of his desk talking. When I got halfway to his desk, Erik's eyes slid my way as if he couldn't help himself. They started at my legs and as I moved closer they slid up until they rested on my breasts. When I finally reached his desk, I expected a quick dismissal, but he was too busy staring at my chest to tell me to go. So, as Jared continued to talk about reports, I stood there, letting him look his fill, slowly burning from the inside out under his gaze. Thank goodness for the padded bra otherwise he'd see the way my nipples pebbled underneath.

"Erik," Jared called his name. "You with me?"

Erik's eyes snapped to mine. The usually grassy green eyes burned like melting emeralds. One side of my mouth ticked up, letting him know I noticed his heated gaze. His brows dropped and his lips pinched in frustration at being caught. A wall fell over his eyes and any heat became a blank slate of nothing.

"Yeah," he said to Jared without looking away. "Alexandra, you may leave now." I set the coffee down slowly, not letting my smile drop. Before I could close his door behind me, he called out, "I'm leaving early today. I'll have Laura take you home."

I nodded and headed back out to my desk, feeling the warmth of his gaze for the rest of the afternoon.

He left fifteen minutes before us, only talking to Laura as he walked out. I wondered if I'd see him tonight or if he would try to avoid me all weekend. Only time would tell, but my stomach fluttered at the possibilities. I told myself I was only being optimistic that I'd get to feel that kind of pleasure again with someone I trusted. I took Erik's words to heart and didn't romanticize him. I didn't picture a future with him. He didn't seem like the relationship type. But I couldn't help but hope to enjoy my time I was with him.

"Ready to go?" Laura asked.

"Yup." I shut down the computer and grabbed my things.

The elevator had just opened when she snapped her fingers. "Shoot. I forgot the file on Erik's desk. Go ahead and head on down and I'll meet you by the car."

I stepped out of the elevator and any warmth I'd had lingering from earlier vanished as a bucket of freezing water crashed over me. Across the lobby against one of the pillars off to the side was Erik. And his date for the evening.

He had her pinned to the wall, their lips locked. One of his hands was buried in her hair and the other was smoothing along the curve of her ass.

As much as I talked myself up about not romanticizing him, about how I knew he wouldn't want a relationship and I only wanted pleasure while it lasted, my heart still seized in my chest. Rocks still sank to the pit of my stomach.

I felt like a voyeur watching a private moment. The lobby was completely empty and most of the lights were out. I went to step back into the elevator and pretend I hadn't witnessed anything when the doors slid closed and I was stuck. I stepped softly not wanting him to witness me catching him when all of a sudden his lips separated from hers and he looked right at me.

His eyes trapped me in place. His lips tipped up on one side, giving me the same cocky look I had given him earlier today. With his smirk firmly in place and his eyes locked on mine, he slid his hand lower until it eased under her skirt and shifted up. The woman gasped and Erik didn't look away from me as his arm flexed and made big movements so there was no doubt what he was doing. Her moans came faster and harder, the sound hammering like a chisel against my chest. I wasn't going to stand there a second longer to listen to her come.

Not caring if I made noise alerting my presence, I stomped off to the front door needing to get out of there. I would have to walk the long way to the garage, but I didn't care. I held my chin high even when I left the building. I didn't let any emotion show until I rounded the corner and was out of view.

I was wrong. I was just as naive as he accused me of being. I was just as stupid to not listen to his words and brush them off when he still gave me heated stares, when he gave me an inkling of approval. I swallowed back the tears, the full weight of my immaturity crashing over me. I'd always felt older than my nineteen years because I'd experienced more than most. But as I leaned against the stone of the building, there was no questioning the fact that I was just another dumb girl with silly dreams.

Erik had tried to prove a point Saturday night and I'd brushed it off and accepted it with a shrug, not really believing him. But he sure proved his point now. Just because I was in his world now, didn't mean a man still wasn't just a man. It was about time I accepted it and stopped hoping that maybe some of my fantasies would come true.

I met Laura by the car and remained silent during the drive home. The apartment door had just closed when my phone vibrated with a message.

Unknown: It's Leah.
Unknown: Hope you're good.

I stared at the phone with hesitance like it was a bomb waiting to go off. I'd told her to contact me with an emergency and I waited to hear what it was, but no other messages came through. My mind raced with the possibilities, but after the emotional roller-coaster I'd been on today, seeing Leah's name on my phone eased some of the pressure in my chest. Maybe my sister was messaging me just when I needed her. Maybe me not being there to take care of things had forced her to grow up a bit and she was reaching out.

Me: Hey. Yeah. How are you? Where did you get a phone?
Unknown: Oscar got me one.

The pressure was back when she mentioned his name. If Oscar was still around, Leah wasn't getting any better. I rolled my eyes at my own naivety. Looked like today was a day for realism—optimism be damned.

Leah: Are you with that guy that came storming in our place?
Me: Why?
Leah: He gave me that money. I figured if you were still there, maybe you could get me more.

Tears burned the backs of my eyes. When would I learn to stop hoping for the best?

Me: No.
Leah: Liar. Where are you?
Me: Safe.
Leah: With money. I'm sure he's paying you well for your *services*

I let her assume what she wanted. The sister I had hoped to be on the other end of the message was long gone. This Leah was mean and angry. She wasn't the supportive friend I'd had before Mom died.

When I didn't respond, she turned to guilt.

Leah: Are you going to let me suffer?
Me: You can take care of yourself.
Leah: I'm trying. Please.
Me: Leave Oscar.
Leah: Why? He loves me and I need him.
Me: Then I can't help you.

I didn't wait for a response. I tossed the vibrating phone on the counter and headed to my room. All I wanted to do was wash the day away and fall in bed.

———

I JERKED awake when my door flew open, crashing against the wall. Clutching the comforter to my chest, I scurried back against the headboard and took in the large figure in the door. My heart thundered and my lungs struggled to take in air.

I squeezed my eyes shut, fighting off thoughts of the worst. I always locked my door and the one time I didn't a man comes storming in. The bad dream faded when my bedroom light was flicked on and a scowling Erik stood illuminated in the door. He took two long strides to the bed and I held the blanket tighter like a shield.

"What the fuck is this?" he growled, holding up my phone.

"What the fuck are you doing?" I screeched, adrenaline still pounding through me. I was only in my underwear and a cami with no bra. If he wanted to talk to me, he could at least have the decency to let me get dressed. "Get out."

He ripped my shield from my hands and I curled my legs up, using my hands to cover as much of myself as possible, even though he wasn't looking anywhere but my face.

"What. The. Fuck. Is. This?" Each word was snarled from his clenched jaw.

Between the panic still coursing through my veins and being jarred from a deep sleep, I struggled to think. I took in the black rectangle and answered with sarcasm. "It's a phone, asshole."

He tossed the phone, hitting the pillow next to me, not saying anything. I brought the screen to life and saw some of the messages from my sister.

Leah: We can work together.
Leah: Meet me and help me.
Leah: It's just a little money.
Leah: Stop being so selfish. He won't miss it.

"When the hell did you give her your number?"

"I...I did—"

"Don't lie to me," he shouted, taking the last two steps to bring him by my side. He crowded over me, placing his hands on each side of my head, trapping me against the headboard. "When?"

The pressure on my chest came back the more he intimidated me. It reminded me of the night in the hotel, but this was different, his anger seemed more dangerous. Closing my eyes, I took a deep breath, trying to calm my racing heart. "I just dropped it off. I didn't even see her."

"Are you kidding me? When did you leave? When did you have time?"

The more I became acclimated to being awake, the more my panic shifted to anger. How dare he use his size to corner me in bed in the middle of the night? It was pissing me off and I relied on the rage rather than cowering.

"One of the many nights you think you lock me in while you

go fuck your way through women," I sneered. The image of him fingering that woman came roaring back.

"Why? Why did you do it?" His tone was marginally softer, but the heat of his anger still barreled down on me.

"She's my sister."

"She's a waste."

"Shut up," I shouted.

"She will use you," he shouted back. "She will ruin you and you're too fucking stupid to see it."

"Stop calling me that," I yelled, shoving him back. He barely moved, but the whole day was piling up and I was on the brink of explosion.

Him calling me stupid hit harder than it had before because I felt stupid. I knew the decisions I made were mistakes and they were done without thinking about the reality of a situation. I'd given Leah the number in hopes she'd get better and come to me. I'd held out hope for Erik because I'd wanted to believe in the best situation, not the real one.

"Then stop acting like it." He stood up and stepped back. My vision blurred and I dropped my eyes to the carpet at his feet. "Delete the messages and the number and never answer her again. Cut your ties as long as you're here. You might be fine wasting your time, but I'm not. I won't help you if you keep choosing to fuck it up and work against me."

"She's my sister," I defended again, wanting it to mean more than it did.

"Open your eyes, Alexandra. She's a cancer and she's using you."

When I didn't continue to fight, he flipped the lights off and closed the door like he'd never even been there.

I scrolled through the messages. There were more than what I'd read as Erik stood over me. Over an hour, Leah had sent probably fifteen messages, each one getting meaner than the last.

Maybe Erik was right. Maybe I needed to be more realistic and make my decisions based on the things around me, not what I wanted to happen.

My wants didn't matter.

They never had.

16

ERIK

ANOTHER WEEK and I was no more comfortable with Alexandra than I'd been since that first kiss.

Only this week, a new emotion had been added to the mix. Guilt.

I hated emotions.

And I'd felt more in the past month since she'd been here than I had in the past five years. Desire, frustration, confusion, want. All of them had mixed in a chaotic cocktail I was losing control of. Guilt was the most recent.

I didn't usually question my actions, I made them with confidence. But I questioned the way I'd hurt Alexandra intentionally. I'd wanted her to catch me with another woman, and not just walking away on a date. I wanted her to see me intimate with another woman because words hadn't been working. Add in how angry I'd been at my inability to fully distance her from me, and I was a bomb waiting to explode.

I hated that I still smiled with pride when she did something correct. I hated that I couldn't stop staring at her and getting lost in thinking about all the things I wanted to do to her. I hated that she caught me staring. After the way I'd treated her Saturday night, she should have rolled her eyes and told me to fuck off when she caught me staring. Instead, she smiled with a flush staining her cheeks.

So, I'd lashed out, acting like a dick. And despite my immediate guilt over my actions, I continued to be a dick, not knowing how to stop myself.

I'd ignored the way she'd cowered last night, telling myself it had been for the best. Maybe if she was scared, she would finally protect herself from all the dangers around her. She needed to learn that turning a blind eye to them would get her hurt.

Just like Sofia had been naive about the dangers around her and gotten hurt.

"So, you have a crush on the intern."

I jerked my gaze away from Alexandra leaving my office to a smiling Carina.

"What? No," I denied a little too adamantly. Carina stopped packing her briefcase to deliver a dubious stare.

"Okay."

"Don't patronize me," I growled. Carina and I had formed a friendship of sorts. Our meetings were no longer about just the marketing plans, but also business in general. I respected her. I liked that I could talk to her without feeling like she was trying to get somewhere with me. Talking to her almost felt like talking to Ian. She was straightforward and didn't hold any punches. Hence why she was currently calling me out on my staring at Alexandra's ass.

"I'm not," she said, holding up her hands. "I'm just pointing out the obvious."

I scoffed instead of trying to answer.

"Fraternizing at the office can be hard. You have to make sure it's worth the effort."

"Aren't you engaged to your business partner?" I remembered

hearing it at a meeting somewhere. The Wellington and Russo company would officially be a family company, rather than just partners.

"And now he's engaged to his boyfriend."

My eyebrows rose slowly as I took that all in and refrained from commenting.

"Yeah." She laughed, pulling the bag over her shoulder. "Well, I have to go. If it makes you feel better, she seems to have a crush on you. Even though she also seems to be trying to light you on fire every time she looks at you. So, maybe you've already fraternized."

"Let me walk you out," I grumbled, ignoring her knowing smile.

When I walked past Laura's desk to head back into my office, she let me know she was leaving for the day.

"Can you take Alexandra home? I've still got work to do and won't be leaving until late."

"Of course."

I closed my door behind me without looking Alexandra's way, even though I could feel her gaze doing exactly as Carina claimed: trying to burn me to the ground with her look alone.

The sky faded from the orange of sunset to night and my eyes blurred from staring at the computer screen for so long. I was shutting it all down when a soft knock came before the door slowly opened.

"Hey." Hanna leaned through the cracked door, her long hair falling over her shoulder.

"Hey. What are you doing here so late?"

"I could ask you the same thing." She pointed an accusing finger at me and narrowed her eyes like her small frame would intimidate me. We all looked so much alike with our dark hair and green eyes. Hanna had gone through a phase when she was a teenager and hated looking like Sofia, so she dyed her hair, cut it, used self-tanner to darken her pale skin. Anything to differentiate herself. Her short pink hair had been how I'd known she was alive and not Sofia when I'd finally found them.

Now she wore her hair long and naturally dark, just like Sofia had.

"I always work late."

"Yeah, yeah." She sighed and fell into the chair in front of my desk and I moved to sit in the chair next to her. "So what are you working on?"

I hesitated telling her about cases but decided to confess. Hanna hated when I held back, accusing me of coddling her. "I was just looking over a report from MacCabe from last week."

Even though she insisted on being strong enough to handle information about others, she still had a moment of honest reaction. Her eyes dropped to her lap and she swallowed. Her hands curled around the leather arms of the seat, but then she forced herself to relax, her shoulders dropping back with her slow exhale. "You do good work, Erik." Her eyes lifted and she gave a hard stare. "But don't run yourself into the ground paying for sins you didn't commit."

My jaw clenched and I cocked my head to the side, not openly pretending I didn't know what she was talking about, but not confessing either.

"I know you blame yourself for not being there. You think if you were, you could have stopped us from being taken. But you're being ridiculous thinking your presence on vacation would have changed anything. You know Sofia and I would have ditched you no matter how hard you'd try to keep an eye on us."

We rarely talked about what had happened. We'd each done therapy with Hanna to help with her recovery, but we still never talked about it. I wanted to shut it down now, but she had brought it up and I wouldn't deny her the right to discuss what she needed.

Looking down, I swallowed. "I miss her," I confessed.

"Me too. Every day."

The tears I heard in her voice had me scooting forward to the edge of the seat and reaching for her hands. Gripping them tight, I waited for her to look up. Her eyes, glazed over with tears, shined like emeralds. I ran my fingers under the thick cuff of her bracelets, feeling the thick ridges that circled each wrist. The scars from rope a constant reminder that she'd fought through it and had never given up.

"I'm proud of you. I don't say it enough. I'm proud of how strong you are."

Her hands held mine tight. "I'm strong for her. She was the positive one. She was the one that talked about getting out. When I wanted to—" She stopped, swallowing what she was about to say. "She painted a better picture. I live for the both of us. It's the least we can do."

I pulled her in for a hug and let her stay in my arms as long as she wanted.

She sniffled a few times before pulling back. "This is more depressing than I was hoping to get tonight," she said with a laugh. "Let's go grab some dinner."

"Sure. My treat."

"Damn right."

We decided to hit the pub just down the block since she was demanding a cheeseburger to replenish after all that emotional crap. Apparently, we were more alike than just our looks.

We walked in the door and waited to be seated. The place looked like an Irish pub with dark wood and hunter green leather seats. On the far end of the restaurant were a dance floor and stage.

We'd just ordered our drinks when Hanna spoke. "Looks like our interns had the same idea as us."

My eyes followed hers to the round table close to the bar and on the edge of the dance floor. Two male interns had their elbows leaned over on the table with beers in hand as they watched the dancing. My eyes tracked where they were looking and landed on a couple standing close, swaying to a slow song.

An ocean of white noise roared in my ears blotting out all other sounds in the bar. I took in the long legs bared by the very familiar black dress I'd seen Alexandra in earlier. Her hair stretched down her back almost brushing the bottom Carina had caught me staring at earlier. She stared up into the eyes of none other than Wyatt, the boy who'd been flirting with her a few weeks ago in the breakroom.

Fire burned through my veins as I watched his hands skirt above her ass, his fingers dipping down to crest the full curve. She didn't pull back, instead remained plastered to his front, smiling up at him.

"She's very pretty," Hanna said.

Forcing myself to look down at the scarred wood of the table, I took deep breaths trying to cool myself off before raising my eyes. I ground my jaw when I took in Hanna's smirking mouth. "I wouldn't know," I ground out.

"I don't know how you don't when your eyes can't stop glaring at her. Does it bother you she's dancing with Wyatt?"

"Shut up," I growled.

Her head fell back and she laughed. "Man, Ian was right."

I was saved from having to respond when our drinks were delivered. But she was right, I couldn't force myself to stop looking over. Finally, the streak of slow songs ended and the two detangled, heading back to their seats.

Just as Alexandra was going to sit, Wyatt gestured to the bar and grabbed her hand. In the back of my mind, I knew Hanna was talking, but I didn't think she expected me to listen. She'd been nice enough to not say anything more, but she kept smiling at me every time I turned back from watching Alexandra.

Wyatt ordered a drink and then leaned against the bar, facing Alexandra. They were too close, closer than they needed to be. It was eight in the evening on Thursday. The bar was hardly crowded. But she didn't pull back. No, she stood perfectly still as Wyatt leaned in and brushed her hair back behind her ear. She stayed perfectly still as he leaned in and tipped her chin up so he could brush his lips against hers.

A base of anger thundered through me. She didn't pull back. She didn't even stand there prone. She turned her head and lifted on her toes, pressing her lips to his. When her mouth opened, bringing her tongue into play, I snapped and was out of my seat before I even realized what I was doing.

Hanna's laughter rang behind me. "I'll see you tomorrow," she called out.

I wove between people, my eyes not leaving the couple making out like some kind of porno against the bar. I walked right up and into her personal space just as she was pulling back from sucking face with the boy band model.

"Let's go," I managed to get out between clenched teeth.

She jerked and looked up at me with wide eyes. "Erik. What are you—"

"I said, let's go."

"What?" Her eyes narrowed, the word snapping like a warning. A warning I ignored.

"Don't make a scene, Alexandra."

She stood tall and didn't cower against the bar like my height should have made her do. No, she took a step toward me and glared for all she was worth. Wyatt was smart enough to not interfere in the battle of wills currently happening.

When his drink was slid across the bar, he finally spoke up. "Hey, I'm gonna head back to the table," he said cautiously.

Alexandra gave me one last hard glare before a devious smile slowly stretched her lips.

She turned to face Wyatt and stepped into him, pressing her hand to his chest. My fingers curled into fists against the bar to keep from ripping her hand away.

"Thank you, Wyatt, for the dance."

He smiled, confident about himself now that she was pressed to him. "Sure. We'll have to do it again sometime."

Alexandra cast a side glance my way before winding a hand up into his hair and pulling him down for a deep kiss, moaning for effect.

Barely holding back a growl, I snaked my hand around her elbow and walked away. She stumbled but didn't fight me until we pushed through the doors. Once we were on the street, she jerked out of my grip and stormed off in the wrong direction.

"You're such a dick," she yelled over her shoulder.

"I said no fucking the interns. And the car is over here."

She didn't answer, just kept walking.

"Alexandra, I will toss you over my shoulder if I have to."

That got her to stop. People around us were staring but I didn't care. Fire raged through me and I needed a strong drink and to lock her in a closed off room away from everyone, including me.

She whirled around and stomped over but didn't look up. She didn't look at me the whole drive home. I was completely fine with that.

When we got home, she escaped to her room without a word and slammed the door.

I poured myself a full glass of scotch and fell back on the couch. Maybe if I drank enough I'd be able to shut down my brain from thinking of all the reasons I behaved like a caveman tonight.

You're jealous.

The words whispered through my mind, but I didn't want to

believe them. I downed the contents and left the glass behind, instead grabbing the bottle to take to my room.

The guilt that had been hounding me all week vanished, anger taking its place. She wanted to get back at me for rubbing that woman in her face. She wanted to be defiant and go to a bar without telling me and making out with some boy toy.

Too bad for her, because I played the game better than anyone and she would learn that if she lashed out, I would lash out harder.

17

ALEXANDRA

"How was dinner with the boys last night?" Laura asked.

Despite the way the night ended, I smiled. "It was good. I had a lot of fun."

"I'm glad you ran into them in the lobby."

We'd been on our way to the garage when Wyatt had called my name. I'd turned to find him and two other Abercrombie and Fitch models with him. He'd invited me to head out with them and the thought of going back to the apartment alone had me agreeing before he'd even finished asking.

He'd been so polite and handsome and kind. When we'd been standing at the bar and he'd leaned over to kiss me, my stomach had flipped and I'd held still for him. I wasn't sure what I'd feel when his lips touched mine, but my mind had immediately conjured the only other man I've kissed. I compared Wyatt's soft tentative pressure to the way Erik had held me in place and consumed me. I compared the way small flutters tickled in my stomach to the way Erik's kiss had caused me to feel lost in a storm. I'd even put more effort into the kiss hoping I'd feel more.

As if my mind had conjured the man himself, he'd growled in my ear. I'd been shocked at first which quickly shifted to embarrassment. My blood had heated to a boil and everything in me raged at the man who plagued me. I'd seen the jealousy in his eyes and it had only served to piss me off more. He didn't want to have me, but no one else could have me either.

I'd remembered catching him with his hand up that woman's skirt and I'd decided to give him a taste of his own medicine. He'd reacted about as well as I'd expected when I'd attacked Wyatt, but it hadn't brought me any joy in my revenge.

"They're good boys," Laura said, bringing me back to the present.

Erik walked past, a scowl firmly in place, obviously having come in at the perfect time.

"Yeah, I may go out with them again. Wyatt is pretty cute."

He glared and I refused to look away. His jaw ticked and I forced a smile just to poke the bear.

"Laura, can you make copies of the Emerson files, please?"

"I was just about to head to lunch, but if it can't wait, I can do it now."

Erik returned my smile with one of his own. "That's okay. I'll have Alexandra do it."

"Are you sure? I can wait on lunch."

"That's okay. Thank you, Laura."

Erik went back into his office and Laura gave me a concerned look. "If it's too much, just wait for me and I'll help you."

"I'm sure I'll be fine making a few copies."

Another concerned look and then she grabbed her purse and left.

Erik strolled out with a box filled with papers and dropped it with a thud on the desk. "I need five sets of copies."

My jaw dropped and I stared at the chunk of white papers spilling out. "Are you kidding me?"

"Afraid not," he answered, his tone bored.

"That's going to take me forever."

"Better get started then."

He waited until I looked up before giving me a wink and heading back into his office, whistling. Before he closed the door, he poked his head out. "And bring me a coffee when you're done."

The door closed before I could growl what an asshole he was.

Taking a deep breath, I calmed myself before grabbing the box and heading to the copier room.

It went quicker than I'd thought once I found my rhythm. After about forty minutes, I was back at the desk with coffee and files in hand.

The door was cracked and I didn't hear anyone talking in Erik's office so I pushed the door open, looking down to make sure the coffee didn't spill as I slid the door back closed. I'd taken one step into the office when I looked up and froze, staring wide-eyed at the scene on the couch.

The coffee almost slid out of my numb fingers.

Erik sat with his legs spread wide, his head tossed back and his eyes closed. A woman knelt in front of him, her red hair swaying as she bobbed up and down over his crotch.

Holy. Fucking. Shit.

Every muscle in my body stiffened and chaos reigned inside me. A voice screamed to run—to get the fuck out of there before anyone noticed I'd come in. I needed to look away. Why couldn't I look away? This was worse than him pleasuring a woman, this was so much more intimate.

A muffled moan came from the woman and it snapped me out of my trance. I went to take a step back when all of sudden Erik's head lifted and his eyes opened, landing right on me. His hand buried into the woman's hair and he fucking winked at me. *Winked.*

He was doing it on purpose. He'd planned for me to walk in on him getting a blow job and I wanted to storm over there and punch him in his stupid face. Pressure beat down on my chest and my cheeks lit on fire. He was an asshole and in that moment, I hated him.

I went to step back to leave the room when his mouth parted and a groan ripped from his chest. His hips thrust up and he bit down on his lip, his eyes sliding closed for a moment as he came.

Finally, I was able to look away and turned to leave.

"Stay." My body froze again—as if his words alone commanded me—and looked over my shoulder.

The woman shifted to see me and giggled. "Are we having a threesome, Erik?"

My lip curled in disgust. "I'm leaving."

"No, Chloe was just leaving."

"What?" The woman sat back unblocking Erik's crotch where his softening dick was laying stark against the black of his slacks. My eyes widened and my thighs squeezed involuntarily. I'd never seen a penis before. At least not one outside of pictures. I hated that the sight had a heat burning from my core. I hated that I stared at all.

Erik breathed a deep laugh before tucking himself back in his pants, a knowing smile on his arrogant face.

"Yes. I'm sorry, but work calls," he told the woman—*Chloe*. "Thank you for our lunch break."

She blinked like she was trying to process the fact that she'd just sucked him off and now he was so coldly dismissing her.

"Can we finish this later?" she asked, dragging her hand up his thigh.

His smile was fake. "I will try."

I scoffed, loud enough for them both to hear.

"Problem, Alexandra?" Erik asked, victory pouring off him.

His smug smile begged for me to take him down a peg. This

was one too many times for me to not lose my temper. "He won't call, Chloe. He finds being a dick to me and flaunting his sexual activities as funny. You were a means to an end." His smile slipped. "I know what you're doing Erik. Acting out because I kissed someone else?" I tsked. "So childish. Now who's naïve?"

"Obviously I need to talk to my intern," he growled at me over Chloe's head. "Pay her no mind, Chloe. I assure you, I enjoyed our lunch." She turned to look up at Erik, completely ignoring me in the room. He brushed her hair back but met my eyes. "*Very* much."

It seemed to appease her because she lifted to her toes, pressed a lingering kiss to his cheek and left. I tried to follow—needing to get the fuck out of that room before I exploded—but he stopped me.

"I'm not finished with you yet, Alexandra. I need my files and coffee."

I glowered at him as I stormed over to his desk. He stood and made a show of adjusting his crotch before buckling his pants.

"You're disgusting." I slammed the box down, feeling mild satisfaction at the thud. I was more pleased that I spilled a little coffee on his hand when I shoved it at him.

"And you're accompanying me to an event tomorrow."

"Hah," I barked a laugh. "No."

"It wasn't a question. You're coming."

"It doesn't have to be a question for me to tell you, hell no."

"Too bad. Everyone at the company is attending, including you," he said with arrogance like my rejection was futile and nothing but a pesky fly. "I'll give you money before you leave tonight and you can go buy a dress."

"No," I said again, this time stomping my foot.

"Yes. End of argument. Don't bother wasting your time."

"I'm not going with you because you're a dick. So, buy whatever dress you want, but I'm not wearing it."

He ignored my rebuttal, bringing the coffee to his lips and cringed after drinking. "It's cold."

"Well, next time don't have your dick down some woman's throat and you can have it while it's hot."

I spun on my heel and stomped out before he could say anything else. Unfortunately, he followed. Laura rounded the corner as I fell into my chair, my arms crossing over my chest like a pouting child.

"Laura, just the woman I wanted to see," Erik greeted jovially. "Can you take Alexandra to find a dress after work for the banquet tomorrow?"

She cringed at his request. "I'm sorry, I can't. I would but I have dinner plans tonight."

Erik's brow furrowed as he scanned the office like another willing candidate would appear out of nowhere to take me shopping. Maybe he'd just give up and I wouldn't have to go. A smile was already making an appearance when he wiped it away.

"Fine," he grumbled, turning to me. "I'm taking you. Be ready by five. Don't make me wait."

My jaw dropped and I was ready to tell him to shove it, but he turned and slammed his office door before I could say anything.

"Yes, sir," I grumbled.

"Should be fun," Laura said, holding back a laugh.

Yeah. That was exactly the word I was going to use to describe anything with Erik. *Fun.*

At least I could enjoy myself. I'd make sure it was the most tedious night and he regretted ever forcing dress shopping on me.

18

ERIK

Me: Hey, are you free?

Me: I decided it'd be a good thing if Alexandra attended the event tomorrow and she needs a dress. Can you take her?

I FIGURED a text message would be able to hide my desperation as the minutes ticked closer to five. I didn't want to take her shopping. I didn't want to spend the afternoon with her. It negated the distance I kept trying to push between us.

Of course, having her come tomorrow at all might have been a bad idea. But her not going would look weird, when everyone else in the company was attending. I'd been so swamped with preparations, I hadn't even thought about her coming until Laura mentioned it.

> **Hanna:** Ahahahahaha! Absolutely not. Even if I wanted to, which I do, I can't. I have a dinner meeting with a client.
>
> **Hanna:** Take her to the boutique in Covington. I may

swing by after dinner just to watch you squirm as you help her pick out a dress.

Me: I hate you.

Hanna: I'm messaging Ian now. He could probably use a good laugh.

Me: It's the middle of the night in London.

Hanna: He'll think it's worth it.

Hanna: Have fun.

I wanted to stomp down to her office and demand she take Alexandra and remind her that I was her boss. Then she'd probably tell Mom and I'd have to explain why I was bossing around my baby sister. Apparently actually being her boss and being an adult weren't good enough explanations to get your mom to leave you alone.

"Are you ready to go, sir? It's five-o-clock sharp."

Squeezing my phone, I closed my eyes and took a deep breath before turning to face her.

"Yes, I just need to shut down my computer."

"Cool. I'll wait by the elevators."

Cool? Sometimes she spoke and I was reminded of how young she was. She had faced so much that had forced her to grow up, but moments happened that made her nineteen years apparent. In those moments, I felt like the biggest pervert for all the things I'd done to her. For all the things I still wanted to do to her.

I shook it off and met her at the elevators. We didn't speak the entire drive. I kept my jaw clenched shut, worried about what might slip out if I relaxed. Instead, I suffered through the silent drive, inhaling her sweet lemony scent.

It wasn't until I crossed the bridge that she spoke. "Where are we going?"

"A place my sister recommended in Covington."

"Is this where you take all the girls shopping?" she asked, her tone dry.

"Contrary to popular belief, I'm not jumping at the chance to take girls shopping."

"Well, I hope you're ready for this because I'm gonna take my time and be picky about my first formal dress. It may take hours. Aren't you happy you forced me to do this?"

I groaned at her jovial tone. "You're enjoying this."

"You deserve this."

I went back to clamping my jaw shut because she was right, after what I did today, I did deserve any punishment she dished out. I once again hadn't meant for it to go so far. I'd only meant to invite Chloe to lunch and make Alexandra see her. Then Alexandra had walked in, frozen, staring at me and I'd come. Her blue eyes burned me from across the room and had my balls pulling up tight as jets of my cum spilled, and I completely forgot the actual woman sucking me off.

The drive went surprisingly fast for Friday traffic, but as soon as we parked, I climbed out of the car and took my first deep breath that wasn't saturated with the young woman next to me. We were greeted by two women who asked Alexandra all kinds of questions about her preferences. She'd stuttered and turned wide eyes to me.

"She needs a gown for a black-tie event tomorrow."

"Of course," one of the women said. "I'm Tina and this is Audrey. If you'll follow us to the second floor we can get you started."

"Oh, um..." Alexandra's head whipped between me and the woman dragging her toward the back hallway. "Can he come with me? I'll need his help."

"Of course, we have a sitting area." She didn't bother to turn back around. Just waved her hand for me to follow.

"Can we get you some water? Maybe some champagne?" Audrey asked.

"Water for both of us will be great." When she walked away, I mumbled, "Straight liquor would be better."

"Actually, I'd love a glass of champagne." Alexandra turned, smirking, enjoying my discomfort. "It's going to be a long night."

However, she wasn't smirking much when Tina cornered her again.

"Do you know your sizes?"

"Um." Her eyes kept flicking to mine. "Sizes?"

"No problem, dear. Just follow me and I'll get you all figured out." Tina tugged Alexandra to the dressing room, causing her to stumble. "You'll need to strip so I can get an accurate measurement."

Audrey appeared with my water just as Alexandra disappeared behind a curtain. Before it closed she looked over with wide, pleading eyes. I raised my glass in a salute and took a sip, not bothering to hide the smile at her discomfort.

Maybe two minutes in, a yelp came from behind the curtain, followed by a grumbled, "They're just boobs. Everyone has them. No need to be modest."

I made sure I laughed loud enough for Alexandra to hear me on the other side.

After a few more yelps and awkward laughs, the curtain was whipped back and out came Tina. "We'll gather some dresses to get started."

A traumatized Alexandra stood against the mirror with a cream silk robe clutched tight around her chest. Her eyes locked on my smile and narrowed to slits.

"They stripped me," she whispered, stomping over.

"Sounds like you had a fabulous time."

"You knew this would happen."

"I didn't, but I can't say I'm disappointed."

She lifted a finger and opened her lips to start rioting at me when both women came back, their arms filled with every color of fabric imaginable.

"These should get us started."

"Jesus. We'll be here forever," I moaned, falling back in the stiff cushioned chair.

She smiled victoriously until Tina tried to head into the room with her. "Let's get you stripped again and I'll help you in an—"

"No," Alexandra shouted, her hands up to hold off Tina. She softened her tone when she realized how harsh she sounded. "I've got it. Thank you so much. I will definitely call for help. Really appreciate it."

"Are you sure?" I asked, adding fuel to the fire.

Her head jerked my way, her eyes angry slits that tried to laser through me. "I'm sure," she ground out.

"Well, call me if you need me," Tina said, walking away, Audrey on her heels.

"So, what's the event for?" Alexandra asked from the other side of the curtain.

"It's the annual fundraiser for Haven."

There was a long pause before a soft, "Oh."

"It's very important to me, so I'd appreciate if you took it seriously."

Her head popped from behind the curtain. "Just because I want you to suffer for being a giant asshole, doesn't mean I would do anything to ruin your event. Especially in front of people."

"Really? Like you didn't make a scene in front of Chloe?"

"You're lucky I didn't make a bigger scene," she challenged before disappearing behind the curtain.

I supposed I was lucky, but right then, I didn't feel very lucky.

The next fifteen minutes passed in a blur of rustling fabric behind the curtain and Alexandra coming out in one stunning dress after the next. I thought the first one was a winner with its high neck and long sleeves. She'd rolled her eyes and flung the curtain closed.

She didn't show me the second one and Audrey had just come to check on us when Alexandra came out with the third one on, her back pressed to the curtain.

"Oh, that's beautiful," Audrey gasped.

Alexandra cringed. "I like it, but I can't tell how it will look with the right bra."

"Oh, that's no problem at all. Let me grab you some undergarments," Audrey said, disappearing back through the door.

"Let me see," I demanded.

"No."

"Turn, Alexandra. Now."

She rolled her eyes but complied. The back of the dress was like a racerback, but the sides were cut deep, exposing the sheer, black band and straps of her bra.

"I can see the dilemma. Why not just go without a bra."

"Umm, because I have D-cup boobs."

I dropped my gaze, not thinking. "I noticed."

"Well, this dress has no support and I need something to hold me up."

"Here you go." Audrey came back with two sets of lingerie proudly dangling from her fingers.

I almost choked on my tongue at the scrap of underwear that she carried. It was black and lace and not a whole lot of anything.

"I figured you'd only need the bra, but they come in a set."

"Thank you," Alexandra said. "I'll try these on."

And then we went back to dress after dress, only now I imagined them all with a tiny lace thong underneath.

"I really like this one," she announced before coming out from the dressing room.

"Let me see."

She slid the curtain open slowly and my cock went from one to sixty in less than five seconds. Holy shit. "No."

"What?"

"I said, no," I growled.

The emerald silk hung off her curves perfectly. The slit bared her pale leg with each step she took. It cinched at the waist and separated into a vee that didn't even try to cling to her breasts. They swayed with each movement, almost making me beg that she'd make a wrong move and they'd fall out for me to ogle.

"Why don't you just ask every man to stare at your tits?"

She popped a hand on her hip, the material swaying one way and the soft curves in another. "Like you are right now."

"Exactly. And I don't even want you."

"You're a dick."

"Pick a different dress."

"You know what?" She stomped two steps away from me. "If you have such a strong opinion, then you come help me find a dress."

"No."

"Then I want this one."

We were in a standoff. She stood over me, her eyebrow raised in challenge. A rumble grew in my chest, but I managed to swallow it down. "Fine," I caved.

"Good. Follow me."

She flicked through dresses and I stood behind her giving my opinion on each. After a while, I held about seven more dresses and my arm was starting to get tired. These damn things were heavy.

"So, how did you start your own business?" she asked, still flicking from one dress to the next.

"I hit a bit of luck my senior year of college and sold an app which got me a good amount of money, but it was Ian's idea that we start our own company. He came from money, so it was easier for him. We started small in our shared apartment, selling a few more apps and programs. A few years later we were able to get actual offices."

She nodded and held out one dress. It was pink and the color was all wrong. I shook my head and she put it back with a shrug.

"What do your parents do?"

"They're both high school teachers."

"That's cool."

"Not when they teach at your school."

She laughed and it eased some tension I'd been trying to hold on to. "I bet it really killed your game with the ladies."

"Hardly. What about that one?" I reached past her and flipped back to one she just passed.

She pulled it out and looked the burgundy fabric up and down. "Sure. Come on, I think that's enough."

"Thank, God."

She disappeared behind the curtain and I opened my phone to respond to some emails. A soft thud pulled my eyes up and my heart stopped. A small crack remained between the edge of the changing room and the curtain. I barely held back my moan at the beautiful curves that were reflected in the mirror.

Alexandra was bent over, stepping into a dress, her skin pale and soft against her plain black cotton panties. She stood upright and wiggled the dress over her hips, her full breasts swaying in a barely there lace bra that hinted at her pale nipples beneath. I must have made some sound because she gasped and I looked up to find her eyes locked on mine through the reflection. Color the same as the dress tinted her cheeks, but she didn't rush. She took her time to slide her arms in the sleeves and eased the material up over her luscious chest, not once looking away.

I thought about apologizing, but I wasn't really sorry. The curtain hadn't been closed and I wasn't sorry I devoured the picture of beauty on the other side.

She turned and slid the curtain open. "I need you to button me." Her voice was husky and deep, letting me know she was just as affected as I was.

There was no hiding my erection, but I still tried to be subtle about adjusting myself. Her eyes dropped and more color stained her cheeks before she turned her back to me. Almost all of it was exposed and I made fists to keep from stroking it just to find out if it felt as soft as it looked. I worked the little buttons all the way up to just below her shoulder blades, the heat of her skin burning me each time my knuckles brushed against her.

"You look beautiful," I strangled out, my eyes meeting hers in the mirror.

A gasp pulled our attention to the doorway. "Oh, that's the one," Tina exclaimed. "So beautiful. Let me grab a pair of shoes."

"Oh, no, that's —" Alexandra tried to object, but Tina was already gone.

She came back a moment later and pushed Alexandra onto a chair, kneeling at her feet, getting ready to put the shoes on. Alexandra's hands were clenched tight around the arms of the chair and her shoulders rose, preparing to be assaulted by Tina again.

"I've got it." I stepped up beside her and gently extracted the shoes from Tina, giving Alexandra a break.

Her shoulders relaxed and her hands loosened their death grip as I fell to my knees. I slid the gold strappy shoes gently on her feet and fastened them around her ankles, before holding out my hand to help her stand. After a moment of hesitation, she slipped her fingers in mine.

"Just perfect," Tina proclaimed. "Please tell me this is the one."

Alexandra's eyes met mine again in the mirror. "Yeah, this is the one. Good job, Erik."

Tina went to step forward, but I held up my hand. "I'll make sure she's taken care of."

"Of course. I'll meet you downstairs."

"Thank you," Alexandra whispered.

I stripped her of her shoes and helped her to stand again, turning her back to me so I could work on the buttons. Giving in to the weakness of my desires, I stroked my finger down her spine once the buttons were all done. She shivered as I approached the dip in her back, just ending above her ripe bottom. A bubble surrounded us. No one else remained in that part of the store and with her back to me, I felt I could give her a little.

"I'm sorry about earlier."

She stiffened. "I understand."

She didn't understand, but it was what it was and I had to live with my actions from here on out.

I also had to live with the image of her swaying breasts and full ass on display. It went in the same vault as the feel of her pussy squeezing my fingers, as the feel of her sitting atop me, grinding on my cock, and her breasts heaving as she panted and moaned her pleasure.

A vault I only opened at night when I was weak and already had my hand fisting my dick.

"Let's grab some dinner on the way home," I suggested when she went to undress.

"Okay."

"Is there anywhere you're wanting to try?"

She poked her head out, her nose scrunched up. "Would you kill me if I asked for pizza again?"

Shaking my head, I laughed. "Only if you try it with pineapple this time."

She made fake gagging noises but conceded. "Fine, but let's get a sausage and mushroom for when I'm right and it tastes horrible."

I called in an order while she finished changing. After a dress, shoes, underwear, and jewelry were all purchased and Alexandra's eyes almost bulged out of their sockets at the price, we were on our way.

"I don't know about this, Erik," Alexandra said once we were back at the apartment, both of us standing on either side of the island.

She looked at the pineapple, onion, and ham pizza with skepticism. "Drama queen."

Eyeing the slice, she slowly brought it to her mouth, took a deep breath, and then bit. Her eyes slid closed and I took the moment to take in her soft features. I became lost in her full lips moving, almost moaned when her tongue slicked out to catch any sauce.

"It's..." She swallowed. "It's not bad."

My arms flew up in victory. "Yes."

Her laughter rang like the perfect melody, filling the apartment. "Don't get too cocky. I'll eat this piece, but then I'm back to sausage and mushroom."

Rolling my eyes, I dug into my own pizza, enjoying the comfortable silence.

"How did I not know about the charity event tomorrow?" Alexandra asked after she finished her water.

"Hanna and I do most of the work for the function, and the last month is usually the final touches. You wouldn't see anything come across Laura's desk."

"I guess that makes sense. How long have you had the charity?"

"I've had the charity for five years, but this is the third year for the fundraiser event. It took me a while to have everything together enough for the gala. When I first started, I had almost everything invested in our new company."

"That sounds exciting."

"It was definitely a busy year." I drained the rest of my beer, setting it on the counter between my hands. I spun the glass in circles, the scraping sound loud in the quiet kitchen. "Getting our company ready to move into the offices was why I didn't go on vacation with my family that summer."

She looked up to meet my eyes. Hers were wide and filled with questions, but she stayed silent, letting me talk if I wanted. I didn't usually want to talk about it. I'd gone to family therapy with Hanna, but otherwise, I didn't speak about it. But something about tonight had me wanting to talk to her. Explain to her what I'd lost—why I pushed her away so hard. Once you lose someone you love more than yourself—when you feel that pain—you do everything you can to not feel it again, including not letting anyone close.

"We'd had the family vacation planned for months but Ian and I had opportunities too good to pass up. Mom was pissed, but I figured she'd get over it because I'd be there for the others. Hanna always tells me it wouldn't have mattered if I was there or not, but I had to believe I could have kept them from going out that night or gone with them."

"No seventeen-year-old girl wants to go out with their older brother, Erik."

I breathed a laugh. "Hanna says Sofia would have found a way to get past me. Which is true. She was the sneaky one, always attacking each adventure like it held nothing but fun."

"Where'd they go?" she whispered.

"Sofia somehow got them in at an eighteen and older club. They knew the rules about going out. They knew how to protect themselves, but they were taken anyway." Her soft hand covered mine where it was fisted on the counter. "A woman lured them to the back and a van was waiting. My parents called me the next morning and I flew down. I was too late. The cops looked into it, but said missing girls were common from that area." I swallowed hard past the anger building in my throat. "I became obsessed," I growled. "I researched every single thing I could. I asked about old cases, how they hunted the traffickers, anything I could get my hands on. I'd always been fluent with the computer but had only dabbled on the dark web just to prove I could. But once I found it was a way to track sales, I buried myself in it. It took me two months to narrow down who'd most likely taken them. I spent two months after that tracking them, always missing the group, sometimes by days."

I stopped to take a deep breath, trying to calm my racing heartbeat, focusing on her cool hand soothing mine. "Four months," I choked out. "It took me four months to find them in some hovel in Utah. Over the months, I'd worked with a security company, knowing I couldn't do it alone. They helped me raid the place." My eyes burned, remembering walking in the dank, dark, concrete building. It was filled with office dividers, a string and curtain partitioning off the rooms. "I stormed through the rooms, knowing they had to be there and that no matter what they'd been through it wouldn't matter because I'd bring them home."

Alexandra sniffed and I looked up from under my lashes to find silvery tracks down her cheeks. Hating my weakness, but unable to stop it, matching tears fell from my eyes and I stared down at the counter. I cleared my throat and wiped the wetness away, getting myself under control.

"When I finally found them, I was too late."

"ERIK...?" Hanna stared up at me with glassy eyes, none of the life shining in them. She laid stretched out next to another girl on the double bed, her pink hair flat against the filthy pillow. I ran to her side, hovering my hands over her, not knowing where to touch, but

desperate to assure myself she was real. She was so thin, wearing only a stained dress shirt.

"Hanna .... Hanna," I said her name over and over. It was her. I'd found her.

"Erik. Oh God. Erik," she cried. Instead of launching herself into my arms, she curled to her side next to the still form I could only hope was Sofia, but the dark hair covered her face. "It's too late. It's too late," Hanna muttered.

"No. Hanna. I'm here. It's not too late." I gently brushed her hair back from her forehead, but she jerked away, clutching Sofia's too pale arm. "Sofia. Wake up. I'm here." I gently brushed Sofia's hair back, coming face to face with blank open eyes. "No."

I stumbled back into the divider, rattling the hollow walls, Hanna's sobs shaking through me like an earthquake. No. No, no, no.

"It should have been me. It should have been me," Hanna repeated.

I covered my mouth with a trembling hand, holding back the bile burning up my throat. Hanna's frail body shook and I forced myself to get it together. She'd been through God knows what for four months and it was over. She didn't need the storm of emotions trying to drown me. She needed her brother like she'd needed me on vacation. Swallowing it all down, I stood on shaking legs and went back to the bed, being the rock.

"Hanna, it's time to go home."

"No," she shrieked. "I don't want to go home without her. I don't want to do this anymore. I can't without her."

"Hanna," I choked out. "I'm taking you both home. You're both coming home."

"SHE'D DIED the night before and no one had taken the time to move her. I'd been so close." I slammed my fist down. "Twenty-four hours and I could have made it."

Alexandra's chair scraped against the hardwood and she moved around the island, not hesitating to wrap her arms around me. I shouldn't let her, I should push her back. But for the first time in years, I talked about my worst nightmare and I just needed the comfort.

I wrapped my arms around her and let her warmth and strength fuel my own. "I promised from that moment I would do anything to help any way I could. I figured I'd use the skills I'd acquired over the months and put them to use. Once I saved the first few women, I needed to help them get back on their feet. And Haven was born."

She held me a moment longer, stroking her hands up my back. When my body stopped vibrating with memories she pulled back, leaving her arms at my waist. "You're an amazing man, Erik Brandt."

"Hardly," I murmured.

Her eyes, still shining with the remnants of her tears, lightened and one side of her mouth quirked up. "I mean, you're kind of an asshole, but a good one."

Her words lightened the mood and helped pull us out of the past. I stared down at the girl in my arms and something cracked.

"I should get to bed," she said, stepping out of my arms. "It's a big day tomorrow and I'm excited to be a part of it."

"Thanks for coming."

"I hardly had a choice." She winked to let me know she was joking. "I'm glad I am though."

"Me too. Get some sleep and I'll see you tomorrow."

"Goodnight, Erik."

"Goodnight, Alexandra."

19

ALEXANDRA

THE DAY MOVED IN A BLUR. I'd woken up to Erik banging on my door. He'd greeted me with a coffee, a breakfast sandwich, and an order to haul ass because I had appointments to make. I'd thrown on some clothes and was whisked away to a salon. I guess I was lucky since he at least stopped the car for me rather than ordering me to tuck and roll.

I'd been plucked and tugged and polished everywhere. Who needed their legs waxed when the dress was floor length? I'd backed up and almost grabbed a brush to fight off the woman who suggested a Brazilian wax. Erik had probably put her up to it.

Asshole.

Except maybe he wasn't such an asshole. Last night had been fun. We'd been more at ease on the way home. I should have been livid after walking in on him getting his dick sucked, and it still pinched my chest each time the image flashed behind my eyes. But then I remembered that I had accepted who he was, closed off any hopes of more and the pinch eased. At least I pretended it did.

When I looked like a whole new woman, I messaged Erik and

he'd told me a car was waiting for me outside to take me home and he'd meet me back home at six-thirty to pick me up.

But six-thirty had come and gone twenty minutes ago and I was pacing, my mind running a million miles a minute.

He decided to leave me at home. He was embarrassed by me. He didn't want to be seen with me. He had taken another woman. This was all just another scheme to show me how little he cared. It was another scheme to hurt me.

It didn't matter how irrational the thoughts were, they were there, and they hurt me. They poked holes in my denial about being realistic about him, exposing how much I cared.

Just as tears burned my eyes and I feared my makeup would be ruined, there was a knock at the door. I froze, unsure who it could be since Erik wouldn't knock on his own door. Stepping softly, I looked through the peephole to find a blond-haired man I didn't know.

"Who is it?" I asked because, of course, they would let me know if they were a serial killer on the other side.

"Miss Hughes. I'm William, your driver for the night. Mr. Brandt was held up and sent me to get you myself."

I cracked the door and when he didn't come barging in, I opened it all the way. "Let me just grab my purse."

I grabbed the little gold bag and followed William to the elevator. Somehow I managed to keep my jaw from hitting the ground when he led me out to a Rolls-freaking-Royce. I didn't know anything about cars, but I knew a Rolls Royce was an over-the-top impressive name. The car even smelled like luxury, like they rubbed freshly printed one-hundred dollar bills over everything.

The only thing that penetrated my complete fascination with the vehicle was my anxiety. Each mile we rolled closer to the event, I became more and more nervous. All of a sudden the reasons I thought Erik had left me behind came rushing back.

What if I embarrassed him? I'd never done anything like this before. I'd never dressed up and mingled with rich people. In that car, I felt young and naive about the world.

And as if she knew when my guard was down, Leah messaged me.

Leah: I miss you.
Me: I miss you too.

It was an easy response and it wasn't a lie. It just wasn't what she thought. I missed my sister from five years before, not the one messaging me now.

Leah: Please help me out. I just need a little cash.
Me: Leave Oscar.
Leah: Why are you like this? Why are you trying to take away the one good thing in my life? You're being a controlling bitch.

Closing my eyes, I swallowed the pain and took a deep, cleansing breath, and powered the phone down. We stopped in front of the Cincinnati Music Hall and William came around to open my door. Stepping out, my sister's words fell away and I refocused my attention on the large, red brick building. I followed behind the people walking in pairs and groups up the steps and through the glass doors.

William had informed me that Erik would meet me in the far left corner of the room and was expecting me. I strolled into the large foyer and walked slowly as to not bump into anyone. I couldn't stop looking around at the old architecture. The tall cream pillars supporting the second-floor balcony. The lights shining down on the deep red and cream checkered floor. All around sat tables with items to bid on, tables for people to chat around as waiters moved silently offering drinks and hors d'oeuvres.

I wove my way between the crowd until I saw Erik's dark hair and broad shoulders. My steps slowed and I took him in. I'd seen him in many suits, but a tux was a whole new ballgame. He looked debonair and delicious.

I thought of the first time I'd met him and how he'd taken up too much room. He took up too much room here, too. Even ten feet away, I could feel his presence as though he stood right next to me.

"Mr. Brandt." I spoke his name quietly as not to interrupt the other man talking. I hadn't known what to call him and decided to err on the side of formal.

"Alexandra." My name fell on a breath from his lips as he took me in from head to toe and back again. His gaze stroked every inch of my body like a possessive touch and I could only imagine that my cheeks matched the burgundy of my dress. I hoped the amount of makeup I wore covered most of the blush. "You look stunning."

Someone cleared their throat and snapped Erik out of his stupor.

"Alexandra, you look gorgeous." Carina stepped across their circle and gave me a hug, easing my anxiety.

"Thank you." I stepped back and took in her cream, empire waist dress. "You don't look too bad yourself."

She smiled and shrugged, completely confident in her own looks. She was awesome.

"Let me introduce you to the other half of our company. This is Jake Wellington."

One of the men stepped forward and smiled. He had the softest blue eyes and I struggled to not get lost in them. "It's nice to meet you. And this is my fiancé, Jackson," Jake said, gesturing to another tall, broad specimen with eyes begging me to keep staring.

"Alexandra," Erik growled my name and pulled my attention back to him. His narrowed eyes and pursed lips let me know he didn't appreciate my ogling. Well, too bad. A girl could stare.

"Alexandra is an intern and helping me with the Bergamo and Brandt project," Carina explained. "She came up with the marketing layout I showed you," she said to Jake.

His eyebrows rose. "Very impressive. Erik is a lucky man to have you at his company."

Heat rushed to my cheeks at his praise. "Thank you."

"If things don't work out there, make sure you give us a call," Jake said.

"Don't bother, I already tried. Erik is possessive of this one," Carina joked, smiling at Erik.

"I know a good investment when I see one." Erik rested his hand on my upper back, moving me closer to his side. "Carina, it was great to see you and Mr. Wellington. We appreciate your donation and I'm sorry you all missed my partner, Mr. Bergamo. Enjoy the night and I hope you win a very expensive prize."

"Nice to meet all of you," I managed before Erik dragged me away.

"Alex, wow," a familiar voice called.

I turned to find three boys all dressed in tuxes. "Wyatt. Hey."

I disentangled my hand from Erik's and greeted Wyatt with a hug. "You look amazing."

"Thank you."

"Mr. Brandt, thanks for letting us be a part of the event. As always, each year is better than the last," Wyatt greeted.

Erik didn't respond, only nodded. He probably couldn't speak past his clenched jaw.

"Can I get you a drink?" Wyatt offered. "Then we can maybe have another dance?"

"She can't," Erik finally spoke—or growled was more like it. "I'm introducing her to our clients. I suggest you boys do the same and use this as a business function. I'm sure Hanna is around somewhere. Just please remember you're representing our company tonight."

"Yes, sir," they all responded, standing a little taller.

Erik's hand moved to my back again and guided me away.

"That was rude," I mumbled.

"This is a charity gala hosted by our company, not some rave they can get drunk at and grind on you."

I couldn't help but laugh. "That's a bit over the top."

He looked down his nose at me and shrugged. "Either way, it will be good for you to come around with me and learn how to interact with clients."

I held my arm out. "Lead the way."

Erik spent most of the night moving around the room and I stuck by his side, entranced by all the beauty and excitement. He was in his element talking with everyone, pushing them all toward the auction prizes, animatedly discussing the plans for Haven. It had me softening even more after last night.

I couldn't deny how safe I felt with him. Not that it made any sense. Looking from the outside in at the relationship we'd formed, he'd been rude and cruel to me. But I couldn't deny the way I felt. I knew what fear felt like and never once had I questioned my safety in Erik's presence. I never worried he'd seriously hurt me. It may have sounded crazy, but I was able to breathe easier around him.

I just no longer held out any hope that he would come around to wanting more from me. So, for the time being, I relished the relaxed ease I had with him. I enjoyed feeling sexy each time he looked at me. I enjoyed the rush of tingles down my spine when his fingers grazed the skin on my back to direct me a certain way. I'd never had this safety to embrace my sexuality and as the night progressed, I wanted more.

After a while, we moved to a ballroom upstairs where speeches were made and dinner was served. Erik stood and gave the keynote speech that had tears burning the backs of my eyes. Knowing the story behind how Haven started, made the simple words he spoke about helping women and the community ring through me with so much more feeling.

Then everyone applauded as Hanna announced the auction winners before the party moved back downstairs where everyone danced under dim lighting to a jazz band playing off to the side.

"How about that dance?" a deep voice said behind me.

I already knew who I'd find when I turned and wasn't disappointed to meet blue eyes and an easy smile. Wyatt walked up with his hands in his pockets and I couldn't help but smile. He was handsome and there was no denying it. He might not inspire the same heat that Erik did, but I could still appreciate his good looks.

Tonight had been a unique experience and made me weightless and free from the day to day stresses—comfortable. Why not enjoy a little more attention? Why not embrace the seduction?

"Sure."

I was getting ready to place my hand in his when another snagged it away.

"Sorry, Wyatt. Maybe the next one," Erik said over his shoulder as he pulled me away.

"Really?" I growled at Erik's back.

"I told you not to screw the interns."

"How is that your business?"

I almost bumped into him when he stopped and whirled on me, his brows furrowed over angry eyes. "Because you're my business. Now, are we going to dance?"

"No."

"Erik?" a soft voice called from behind him.

He turned. "Chloe, hey."

I saw her fiery red hair over his shoulder and didn't even bother to not roll my eyes.

"I was wondering if you'd like to dance."

Erik turned to me, a challenge glinting in his green eyes. "I'd love—"

Then I was the one dragging him away. "He can't. Maybe the next one."

Before I made it too far, she grabbed his hand and stepped up close to press her lips to his ear, but spoke loud enough for me to hear. "I miss feeling you inside me."

I looked away from the intimate moment and went to let go of Erik's hand, but he held tight.

"I'm sorry, Chloe. Maybe another time."

He stepped out of her grip, allowing me to lead him to the dance floor. Once we were lost among the swaying couples, he took control, moving me where he wanted me. He lifted my hands to circle his neck before gripping my hips, pulling me close. My heart raced, making me feel lightheaded as we moved in the crowd.

"I thought you didn't want to dance?" he asked, his chest puffed up in victory.

"Shut up." I looked up through my lashes at his laughing eyes and couldn't help but smile. "I saved you. She would have eaten you up and had plans of babies before the first song was over."

He grimaced. "You're not wrong."

People moved all around us, clinging to each other like lovers, and I tried to focus on the soft blend of the saxophone and piano. The music was soft and begged for couples to curl close to each other. For a moment, I gave in to the comfort and let the heat of Erik's hands on my waist burn through me. The fire snaked around my hips and dug in deep to my stomach before dropping between my thighs. I stumbled, losing the rhythm when I took a moment to rub my legs together to ease the ache growing there.

"Okay?" Erik asked, a smile in his voice.

"Perfectly fine."

The song ended and he stepped back, his green eyes darkening. "We should go." His voice sounded just as rough as mine had. Was he feeling the tension between us like I was?

He held the door open and led me to the car. There were seats across from me, but when he followed me in, he chose the one right beside me. Soft jazz filled the small space like we hadn't left the gala at all. We were now just in our own bubble without the hum of the crowd around us.

Chloe's words kept rolling through my head. They bothered me, but they mostly had me curious. Each mile that passed, the curiosity about sex built and built until it slipped from my lips.

"What does it feel like?"

He shifted from looking out the window to locking his eyes on mine. "What?"

"Sex."

One eyebrow slowly rose. "What?'

I barely held back my irritated sigh. "She said she misses feeling you inside her. I can't help but wonder what it feels like to get naked with someone." His pupils dilated almost swallowing the deep green. "What does it feel like to be bare against someone and let them inside you?"

Erik swallowed, his hand forming a fist and relaxing against the cream leather, but he didn't look away from me. "You've let me inside your body."

Just hearing him say it had me squirming in my seat. "That was different. I was dressed."

"It can be fast and with clothes on."

I rolled my eyes. "I know that, but what's it like when it's not? Please," I added softly. The longer he went without answering, the more I needed to know. It thrummed through me and had me holding my breath.

His chest rose and fell on a deep breath. "It's warm," he finally said before clearing his throat. It did nothing to ease the deep gravel as he answered. "Wet. It can be hard and fast or slow and sensual, making you feel every inch inside you. Every part of you is touching, your skin hot and sweating. Then you get to the finish and it's like electricity shooting down your spine, all your nerves centering on the center of your body as you come. It's like a high—a pleasure you can almost black out from."

The rough tone stroked my skin, the friction warming every inch of me. "I want to know," I breathed, almost pleading. "I want to feel that high."

His jaw clenched, but I couldn't miss the long bulge in his slacks. "I'm not going to fuck you."

I didn't expect him too, but I was intoxicated by his words. It was like I stood on the precipice of a bungee jump and I could already imagine how it would feel to have the wind rushing past me and the drop of my stomach, but I wasn't quite there. I needed to feel it.

My body urged me to push him. Not because I thought there would be more, but because I was terrified I'd never feel this safe again. One thing I learned throughout my life, was to take what you could get because nothing was guaranteed tomorrow.

"Is there no other way to feel that? The bare heat you described? To be naked with someone? Is there another way for you to show me?" His eyes flicked between mine and I kept pushing, rushing to reassure him this time was different. "I know there won't be more. You've made that more than clear. But I trust you and I know how rare that is. I don't want to miss an opportunity. Show me."

"You trust me?" He seemed truly baffled by my confession.

"Yes."

His eyes flicked between mine. "Why?" he whispered.

Wasn't that the question of the night. "Because I do." He huffed a laugh, lacking humor. "Erik," I said, getting his attention back on me. "Why wouldn't I trust you? Okay, yes, you've been an ass, but it makes you no less of a great man. You'd never hurt me. You'd never take advantage of me. And I knew that if I ever really needed you, you'd be there. I've never doubted that."

"I'm not the man you think I am."

"Maybe you're not the man you think you are." My words stole his arguments. "Please, Erik. I trust you."

He swallowed again, his head dropping back against the seat, his eyes closed. "Okay."

My heart soared and thudded like a freight train at full speed, only to come to a screeching halt when his words penetrated my bubble of excitement, letting nerves creep in.

"Give me your panties."

I froze but then remembered how much I wanted this.

The rustling of my dress overpowered the sound of the music playing softly. Erik stripped out of his jacket before working the buttons open on his shirt, watching me work my panties off under my dress. Each inch of skin he bared had my heart racing faster. I'd watched his muscles move under his clothes, but I'd never seen him without a shirt. He was built like a Greek god. His muscles hard and rigid, his abs rippling as he tugged the edges out of his pants to expose the deep v on each side of his hips.

He held his hand out once his chest was bared and I placed my panties in his palm with shaky fingers. The scrap of black lace he'd bought me dangled on a single finger for his inspection.

"Now come pull my dick out of my pants," he ordered, stuffing the fabric into his pocket.

I swallowed my nerves and leaned over, working his buckle open with shaky fingers. He didn't move to help me as I fumbled. By the time I'd eased the zipper down, his length was pressing against the cotton of his boxer briefs and I was squirming in my seat. His hips lifted in an invitation to tug everything down to expose him completely. I remembered his softened cock I'd glimpsed in the office, but nothing prepared me for the soft skin that grazed my hand when he sprung free of the confines. Nothing prepared me for the heat. Penises had never been anything I was interested in. I'd only viewed it as a tool to hurt me with.

But Erik's cock was beautiful. Long, thick, and straight with a head I couldn't help but brush my thumb across. He groaned and I pulled back because that wasn't what he'd asked me to do and I wasn't taking more than he was offering. That was the mistake I'd made last time.

"Straddle me. We're going to do what we did before on the couch. Except this time will be with the wet, naked heat you want. It's the best I can do."

My thighs were slick with my arousal and it embarrassed me to imagine letting him know how wet I was.

"Have you changed your mind?"

"No. I-I'm just kind of wet everywhere."

A growl rumbled in his chest. "Good. Let me feel it."

I threw my leg over his lap, pulling my skirt out of the way and closing my eyes as I settled over him. My body shook with nerves, but I didn't let it hold me back from settling and pressing my wet heat fully against him.

"Oh, fuck," he groaned.

His hands disappeared under my dress, moving up my thighs to my core. My thighs clenched and I choked on my breath, the light graze up and down my slit building the ache—the anticipation—to exploding. Both of his thumbs found the lips of my pussy, pulling them apart just enough to settle his cock between my slit. I gripped his shoulders and squeezed my eyes shut, trying to control how fast my breaths were escaping. I didn't want to show how scared I was by being this close to him, how terrified I was that he would stop and I'd never feel this again.

His thumbs slid up and down the edge of my folds, playing in the moisture.

"So fucking wet. Perfect."

He thrust his hips and I gasped as the smooth skin of his dick slid over my clit.

"Open your eyes, Alexandra. Look at me."

I obeyed and became lost in the forest green that watched me through half-opened lids. He pushed my hips down so I was settled perfectly atop his cock as he thrust again and again.

"Ride me, Alexandra."

The command slid through me, controlling my muscles. I moved my hips slowly at first, biting my lip to hold back the whimpers. His cock was thick and touched every part of me. I slid all the way to the tip, feeling him at my entrance, before sliding back down. We moved in tandem and each time the soft head would graze my opening, I almost wished he'd push in and take me. I swallowed my plea on each stroke.

His hands came out from under my skirt and moved to my back. They fumbled with the buttons before he growled, "Fuck it," and ripped the material. He tugged it off my shoulders, trapping my arms at my sides before yanking the thin lace bra to the side, baring my breasts.

He wasted no time falling forward and latching on to my nipple. The wet suction shot straight from my breast to my core like a live wire burning down, closer to explosion. He sucked and nipped before kissing up my neck, pressing his chest to mine as he bit at my ear.

"Do you feel it? Do you feel my heat? Do you feel my heart thundering against you like a wild animal desperate to get closer? Fuck you feel so good."

"Yes," I whispered. "More."

He pulled back and flipped my dress up exposing where his length slid between my folds. Feeling him moving was one thing, but to watch the head of his cock slide underneath me and reappear coated in my juices was another.

"Each time I feel the head of my cock at your entrance, I want to shove up and take that tight pussy for my own. I want to watch your tits bounce as you move up and down on my cock. I want to look down and see the blood of your innocence coating me and know it's mine. I want to take everything."

"Oh, God." The pleasure burned my cheeks and slipped down my chest.

"But I won't. Tonight, I'm going to watch the lips of your pussy coat me in your cum and jack me off. I'm going to fuck your slit until you rub every ounce of my cum from my body."

I moved faster, harder. I was so close. Every nerve began and ended at my core and I was desperate to explode—to feel it all. There was no room for shame. There was no room for fear of what came next. All I had was need.

"Look at you. Look at us." I looked down to where he stared. "Look at your pussy lips on each side of my cock, too small to do more than stroke the top. Your little clit poking out, desperate for each brush of my cock."

His words, the hard thrust of his length dragging across my clit, it was too much.

I exploded.

Tears burned my eyes, the pleasure too much. Cries ripped from my chest as my whole body exploded. The driver could probably hear me, but I didn't care. Nothing mattered but the pleasure consuming me.

"Fuck, what I wouldn't give to feel that tight cunt squeezing me right now."

"Erik. Oh, God."

He leaned back and gripped my hips hard, staring down at us

and moved me hard and fast. A moment later, his own groans filled the car as we both watched his cum shoot across his stomach. I never knew watching a man come could be so sexy. The way the first few ropes shot high on his abs and the last bit leaked and slipped from the small slit. I wanted to make him do it again and again.

Once he stopped sliding between me, he relaxed his grip marginally and took a deep breath.

Fascinated by the white fluid dripping between the ridges of his abs, I dipped my finger, collecting some and bringing it to my mouth. The salty tang exploded on my taste buds and didn't taste like I thought it would. I'd heard Leah talking about cum before, but Erik's had a salty, rich flavor. I slid my finger from between my lips and looked up to meet his eyes.

He'd watched me and his breaths that he'd been trying to get under control, picked back up again.

"Sorry. I was curious."

He breathed a laugh. "Don't be. I'm finding it hard to control myself knowing you want my cum in your mouth."

He dipped his own fingers through the white liquid and brought it to my lips. I moaned and sucked them in my mouth, making sure to get every drop he offered me.

"Satisfied?"

"Definitely yes."

"Mr. Brandt," a voice came over the speaker. "We're here."

The embarrassment that hadn't mattered before hit me now. The man up front probably knew what we'd done. I tugged my dress back up my shoulders but had to hold it in place because he'd torn through the buttons in the back.

Easing off Erik's lap, I moved to my seat and rearranged my skirt. Erik used my panties to clean up the rest of his cum and tucked himself back in his pants. He gave me his jacket to cover my ruined dress.

Before he opened the door, he turned to face me, his large hands framing my face. "Now you know how it feels," he whispered across my lips before giving me the softest, most gentle kiss.

He pulled back and opened the door, holding his hand out to help me exit.

I stared for just a moment, unsure of what happened next. I tried to stay in the moment—tried to be realistic about what happened when we went upstairs, but my mind was a mess of pleasure and nerves and hopes. We'd never ended a moment we gave in on such good terms. It usually ended in an argument. Not with him kissing me gently and offering his hand to help me stand.

Giving in to whatever happened, I slid my palm against his and stepped out. He gave a soft smile and closed the door behind us.

"Erik?" We both froze at the female voice behind us. "Erik, please talk to me. I miss you and I just wanted to talk."

The words were slurred and when Erik stepped back, the red-headed woman stumbled to reach him. He let go of my hand and caught her before she fell on the pavement.

"Chloe, what are you doing here?" His voice was cold, but she missed the obvious, continuing to cling to him.

"I miss you. I miss fucking you."

Again, I looked away at her intimate confession.

"You're drunk."

"Not really. You can take me upstairs and do whatever you want."

"I'm going to take you home."

She perked up and gave him a lazy smile, her eyes half shut in what she probably was hoping was seduction, but really just looked like she was about to pass out.

Me, on the other hand? My heart shriveled in on itself. "I'll just head up," I muttered, trying to move past without looking at him.

"Alexandra," he called, halting my progress. "I'll be back."

I nodded without turning to meet his eyes and kept going, but then his hand was on my bicep, forcing me to face him. I willed the tears to subside as I raised my eyes, hoping they were as cold as I felt inside.

"I'm not going to fuck her. I just want to make sure she gets home safe."

His eyes pleaded with me. I'd never seen Erik look so earnest before, making the decision to believe him easy.

I stroked his cheek and gave him a reassuring smile.

"Get some sleep and we'll talk in the morning."

I nodded, my chest managing to relax enough to breathe again.

20

ALEXANDRA

I TRIED TO STAY AWAKE, but when two in the morning rolled past, I gave up and let myself fall asleep.

He wasn't there in the morning when I woke up either. I'd quickly brushed my teeth and finger combed my hair to casually stroll down the stairs to find an empty apartment. Maybe he'd never come home. Maybe Chloe had convinced him to stay with another stupid blow job.

I plopped down on the bar stool at the island and let my head fall into my hands, groaning my frustration.

"I'm so stupid."

No matter how much I shut down thinking and hoping, nothing was stopping my body. My body had a mind of its own when my heart flipped in my chest at the thought of seeing him in the morning. My body was a traitor as my face stretched into a smile, remembering what he'd given me last night. My mind was screaming at my body to get itself together and stop being a desperate idiot, but the way my stomach fluttered at his name, it was a losing battle.

Sitting in the kitchen, my body just hurt and my mind was sitting there muttering, "I told you so."

Lifting my head, my spirits perked up when I saw a glass beside the sink that hadn't been there last night. He'd come home. Hope was short lived because it was eight in the morning and he was already gone. On a Sunday. I had to wonder why he didn't want to be here.

Maybe he regretted it but had the decency to not be a dick about it like he usually was after we'd been intimate. Maybe I should at least thank him for that reprieve.

Taking a deep breath, I did the best I could to shake it off to keep myself busy through the day. I sat at the dining room table and pulled out the laptop Erik let me use and began applying for scholarships. It took longer than I thought because a lot required me to write a paper about why I thought I deserved the money. I could have summarized it in one sentence. "Because I'm poor as fuck but work as hard as anyone else." I decided to use more eloquent wording than "poor as fuck" when I had to.

The words began to blur in front of me and I decided that was enough for one day. It was somewhere between lunch and dinner and my stomach growled, reminding me I hadn't eaten anything after breakfast.

I still hadn't heard from Erik. To be fair, I hadn't messaged him either. I was too scared of his reaction when I was forced to face it. So, instead, I pushed on through the day and decided to make spaghetti for dinner. Maybe he was on his way home and we'd be able to sit down and enjoy a meal together.

I ended up sitting at the dining room table again—alone—twirling noodles endlessly around my fork, staring out at the twinkling lights of Cincinnati. I almost jumped out of my skin when my phone vibrated across the table.

I fumbled the phone as I turned it over to see who was calling. *Leah.* I hesitated, weighing the pros and cons of a phone call.

So far she'd stuck to text messages, but the fact that she called had me anxious something was wrong. Before it could go to voicemail, I swiped to answer.

"Hello?"

"Alex?"

I sat up, everything in me on high alert at the tears in her voice. "Leah, what's wrong? Are you okay?"

"It's...It's Oscar. I left him and he was mad and he scared me. I left, but he just messaged me letting me know he tracked my phone and he's coming to me. I'm so scared Alex."

I stumbled in my rush to get out of the chair, catching myself on the back of the couch. Every neuron was firing through my body causing my limbs to tremble like I'd had too much caffeine as I ran up the stairs to put on a pair of leggings and shoes.

"Where are you? Are you hurt?"

"Not much. I'm at the Budget Inn on Eighth. Can you come get me?"

I froze, looking around the room, trying to come up with a plan. "I don't have a car. Shit."

"What about an Uber? You have money for an Uber right?"

"Yeah. I'll do that. I'm on my way, Leah. Hang in there and don't answer the door until you hear me on the other side."

"Thank you, Alex. Thank you."

I hung up and opened the Uber app, thanking the heavens that one was only three minutes away. I skipped the elevator and rushed down the stairs, just bursting through the door when the car pulled up.

The ride was less than ten minutes but each one passed like a lifetime.

Leah: Room 10
Me: On my way. I love you.

I cringed when I imagined what Erik would say, but he had to understand. Leah was in trouble. He helped girls all the time and Leah needed help.

Making a decision, I quickly dialed his number. He did stuff like this all the time, maybe he could help. Maybe he had plans in place. But with each ring that went unanswered, I knew I was on my own.

"Can you wait here?" I asked the driver when we pulled up.

"I've got another job waiting for me to accept."

"Please. We'll be right out. I promise."

He screwed up his mouth but gave in. "Five minutes. If it takes longer than that, I'm out of here."

"Okay. Be right back. Thank you."

Shoving my hands in my jacket, I hunkered down just in case Oscar was waiting to pop out somewhere. Maybe he wouldn't recognize me. I walked up to room ten and knocked on the chipped green door. "Leah. It's me."

The door cracked open and Leah's face appeared. "Thank God. I didn't think you'd show."

She reached through and gripped my hand, yanking me inside and slamming the door.

And there stood Oscar, leaning against the wall with a smarmy smile on his gaunt face.

I stomped over, ready to punch him in his junk. "You son of a bitch. You leave her alone."

He shoved me back and I spread my arms wide so he couldn't get to Leah.

"Oh, Alex. I'm so glad you're here." He reached his hand out. "Come here, Leah."

My jaw almost hit the floor when she moved out from behind me and went right into his arms. He tucked her close against his body and dug into his pocket, producing a pill that he placed on her waiting tongue. "You did good, baby."

She swallowed and smiled up at him like she had a million times, not at all scared or trying to get away.

"What the fuck is going on?"

I inched my way to the door. This was wrong. Nothing was adding up and everything in me screamed to get the fuck out of the room.

"Ah, ah, ah, Alex." Oscar took a wide step, blocking the door. "We needed you here to fulfill the deal."

"What deal?" I hated the way my voice shook. I needed to portray a strength I didn't feel.

He reached into his back pocket. "Your sister found this in your room one day. Ten-thousand dollars for a night with a virgin."

My stomach dropped and the world spun, but I couldn't pass out. I had to focus.

"I'm not willing to spend ten-k to fuck a virgin," a deep voice came from the bathroom before a tall guy walked out. He looked normal enough with dark jeans and a plain t-shirt covering a lean, muscular body. But his eyes were hollow and dark and leering at me like I was an animal about to be eaten. "But one thousand seemed like a good deal."

"Leah?" I breathed her name. It escaped like a plea, wanting her to tell me this was all a horrible joke.

"Yeah. Leah showed me and we decided you most likely hadn't fucked that guy yet from what you'd told Leah about him. But Bill said it didn't matter, he'd pay either way. I would just owe him about two-fifty back if you don't bleed when he fucks you."

Taking a few steps back, I shook my head. This couldn't be real. This couldn't be happening. I almost collapsed, everything was shaking so hard, but I had to get out of here. I had to run. Eying Oscar, I figured I could slam past him and knock him off balance enough to get to the door. He had my sister's swaying body in his arms, he wouldn't be able to move as fast. I pushed off, ready to flee, but only made it a couple steps before two strong bands wrapped around my body, lifting me off my feet. I kicked out, trying to hit anything or anyone, only swiping at air before my body was slammed on the bed.

Adrenaline coursed through my veins and I moved every inch of myself, lashing out to fight. But Bill's heavy weight sat on my thighs as he gripped my wrists in one hand, using the other to maneuver a zip tie around them and through the old wooden frame of the bed.

"No," I screamed. "No. No." Maybe someone would hear me. Someone could stop this.

Bill laughed. "Scream all you want. Where do you think you are? Do you think people here give a shit what happens in these rooms? As long as they get paid for the night."

I dug my heels in the bed, trying to lift him off, but he sat on my thighs and I couldn't gain an inch against the slick bedspread.

"You know, Oscar. We have the room all night. I have some friends who'd pay to fuck her. She won't be a virgin when I'm done with her, but they're not picky."

"I think we could get at least ten in tonight. Maybe more."

I flexed every muscle and screamed as hard as I could. This couldn't happen. Tears streamed down my temples into my hair as the picture Erik had painted for me in the same hotel all those weeks ago was coming true.

My screaming stopped when his palm struck my cheek, a stinging fire engulfing my skin. I took a deep breath, trying to focus and get through the pain, to stop the ringing in my ear. I'd never been hit before.

"Not that I don't want to hear you scream, but that's a bit excessive. Don't make me duct tape your mouth shut."

My chest shook with the sobs I was trying to hold back, but I stopped screaming. I didn't want to have my mouth covered. It would prevent any chance of anyone hearing me. I stopped for now, but if the opportunity struck, I needed to be able to speak.

"Please. Please don't do this. Please." I wasn't above begging. I would do anything to get out of this situation. There was no pride here. There was only survival.

"You beg so pretty." His finger dragged down my cheek softly, an illusion completely opposite of what was to come. "Maybe we can keep you here for a while. Let people come and go as they please. My own little whore."

Oscar laughed. "Maybe I'll get to shove something up your tight asshole other than the prude stick you have."

I shook my head, looking over at him lazily sprawled in the chair, Leah in his lap.

"Leah, please. Please. You can't let this happen."

Her glassy eyes met mine, mostly vacant except for a small flare of anger. "You should have helped me when you had the chance. But no, you're a selfish bitch. So, I'm helping myself."

"Shh, baby," Oscar palmed her head and pressed it into his neck. "Don't worry about her. Just enjoy the high." He pulled another pill from his pocket and fed it to her.

"Leah," I cried, but she didn't look up. Betrayal washed over me. "Leah," I screamed her name, forcing her to acknowledge what she was doing, but she ignored it like I didn't exist in whatever world she slipped in to.

Bill leaned over me, reaching for the radio to turn the knob to blare the music. I jerked, trying to head butt him, but it didn't work. My hands were secured and the plastic tore into my skin when I moved too far. It didn't stop me from pulling. The wood was old, maybe it would crack. Maybe a miracle would happen.

He flicked a knife open and the world closed in on me.

"We won't be needing this." He put the tip of the knife at the top of my shirt and cut just enough for him to tear it all the way to the bottom. I froze as the cold metal then slid against my breast bone, under the center of my bra to cut that away too.

I watched him toss the blade on the nightstand and I swore I'd break free and cut off his dick with it. I'd destroy him. I squeezed my eyes shut so tight bright spots appeared behind them as he peeled back the cups of my bra.

"Look at these tits. God*damn*."

Heat washed over my body and I tried to picture Erik's face as two foreign hands cupped my flesh, his thumbs rolling over my nipples. I pulled back, trying to make myself one with the bed, but it didn't help. Nothing helped. There was no vision to pull me away from the moment.

"I'm gonna fuck these tits too," he stated, pinching and rolling my nipples painfully hard. "I'm gonna come all over you. I've got first dibs on it all."

"Except her ass," Oscar spoke up. "That's mine."

"Yeah, yeah."

Bill moved, shifting the bed so he could bow over me to suck a nipple into his mouth. I jerked side to side to avoid it, bile churning in my stomach. His palms held me still as his teeth latched on.

"No," I cried. I tried to scream again, but my throat was sore and any sobs I'd been trying to hold back were breaking through.

He scooted back and I tensed my muscles, prepared to kick if he moved off them. Instead, he tugged my pants down my hips, past my thighs and stopping at my knees.

"No. No. Please." My words were like desperate bullets as he bared my body. I just needed one to hit a soft spot. I just needed one to penetrate this psycho in front of me to reach him to let me go. I had to try. "Please. Stop. Please. Please. Just let me go. Please."

"Let's see if she's still a virgin," Bill said, smiling at Oscar.

He moved his hands between my legs and I fought, thrusting

up and down and any way I could move to dislodge his fingers, but nothing worked. His finger slid through my slit and pushed up inside me. I cringed and cried out at the burn just his one finger caused. He pushed in and out a few times and my world fell in on itself. I'd never be the same after this. My chest ached and crumbled.

"Fuck, she's so tight." He pulled his finger out and moved them to his belt buckle. "Dry as a fucking desert though. Not that I'm worried. I'll make it in. You just may bleed more."

Bile threatened to come up at his gleeful tone. His pants parted and he reached in to tug his penis out, stroking it a few times. I stared at the ceiling, anywhere but at him. I counted the textured stars, starting at one end of the room and moving to the other. I pictured Erik's face. I pictured working at his office. I pictured anything other than what was happening.

The tears wouldn't stop coming as my lips kept whispering "please" over and over. If Erik ever found me, he'd tell me he was right. I'd admit defeat. I'd grovel and tell him I was sorry for not being smarter. I'd do anything to get out of this.

"Can't wait to see all that virgin blood on my cock." He leaned over with his hands braced on either side of my head, shifting his face into my line of sight. "Then I'll wipe it off on those pretty tears before I make you suck me clean."

"Please don't do this," I whispered. "Please."

He laughed and sat back up, adjusting himself so he could grab my legs and push them up and back, folding me in half. My pants were still locked around my knees and his hand had a bruising grip on my ankles. His other hand palmed my vagina and stroked down before smacking my ass. The bed moved as he inched his way closer. I jerked my hips making it hard for him and didn't hold back on my screams.

"No." My throat burned, but I didn't stop. "Help me. Help me. Please. Help me."

He grunted, trying to hold me still and get himself lined up.

I let loose a primal scream, but nothing helped. Nothing was stopping him. No one was coming to my rescue.

"Ple-e-e-ease." The word was choppy over my crying, broken up by my shaking chest. "Please, don't."

Something brushed against my entrance and I screamed again.

But it was drowned out by the door crashing open.

Erik's tall broad form filled the door, his face a mask of rage as he took in the scene. His body tense and muscles tight, right before he exploded into action.

21

ERIK

My whole world stood still as all eyes turned to me. I took it in. Oscar and Leah on the chair. Alexandra tied to the bed, every inch of her bared with her folded in half. Some blond asshole on his knees gripping his cock, poised at her entrance.

"Who the fuck are you?" the asshole holding down Alexandra asked.

I met her eyes and I was almost brought to my knees. Hers were red and blotchy from crying and shined with fear and relief. Red slipped over my vision, my pulse thudding in my ears. Everything in me snapped and I took off with a roar, my sight solely focused on taking down the blond.

He thankfully let go of her legs right before I made impact and took him to the floor on the other side of the bed. His lips were moving, but I heard nothing, a dull roar of white noise drowning it all out as I pinned him under me and started punching him.

His fist clipped my jaw when another body collided against my back. Oscar jerked me back and I shook him off before turning to uppercut him, knocking him back on the floor. Then the other one was back, laying punches at my kidneys. I swung my arm wide, backhanding him. He stumbled and I took my chance, grabbing his neck and pinning him to the wall, lifting him until his toes barely scraped the floor.

"Do you know who I am?" I yelled, spit flying from my mouth, hitting him in his bloody cheek.

He shook his head, tears leaking from his eyes, his face red as his fingers scraped at my hands.

"I find sick fucks like you and ruin your whole world. Your whole operation." I pulled him away from the wall an inch just to slam him back in again. "But you? I'd rather not waste my time. I'll just fucking end you here."

"P-ple-please," he stuttered.

I leaned in and whispered. "Did you stop when she said please?" More tears leaked down his face. "Did you?" I thundered inches from his face.

Tires screeched outside before a car door slammed and then Jared stood at the door.

"E..." Jared saw the animal inside me and spoke softly. "You can't kill him. Come on. Cops are coming and you know you can't be here."

Hearing his voice penetrated the fog of rage that had swallowed me whole once I opened the door. Someone whimpered behind me and I looked to find Leah bent over Oscar, crying. And on the bed was Alexandra, her eyes pinched shut tight, her body doing its best to curl in on itself.

"I can't leave without her."

"Then we'll file a report later."

Jared rushed to her side and cut her free, helping her right her clothes. He didn't touch her, because we'd been in this position before. We didn't initiate touch with someone who had been assaulted. If they needed comfort, they came to you. Alexandra jerked away from Jared as soon as she was free, still curling into herself.

I slammed the blond against the wall again. Jared stood, preparing to take me down if necessary. "Mr. E," he barked my codename. "We need to go."

He was right. I'd done many things not approved by the law in my ventures to rescue women. And getting this kind of publicity would limit what I could do in the future. We needed to leave.

The asshole against the wall gasped when I let his feet touch the floor and eased my grip. He fell forward but I got in one last punch before turning to kick Oscar. Then I shed my jacket and held it open to wrap Alexandra in. She didn't shy from my touch, she stepped over Oscar, burrowing in my jacket and pushing against me.

My head swam with relief, feeling her come to me and I needed to be closer. I lifted her in my arms, sighing when she buried her head in my neck and carried her out of this shit-hole nightmare.

I was opening the door for her when two black SUVs pulled up and five men piled out dressed in black, guns ready.

"MacCabe,' I greeted.

"Mr. E." The tall man nodded his head before moving past us and into the room.

I breathed a sigh of relief knowing Oscar and everyone else would pay one way or another for what they'd done.

After gently putting Alexandra in the car, I went to my side and started the trip home.

"Alexandra," I started after only a few minutes. She'd barely made a sound since we pulled out of the lot and I was worried about her stoicism.

"She called me," she said defensively. "She called me crying. She said she was leaving Oscar and he threatened her. She said he was coming for her and asked me to get her. I believed her and I wanted to help her." Tears filled her voice as her tone turned self-deprecating. "I know. I was stupid and naive to believe her."

"No. You're not."

She jerked her head in my direction at my denial of what she'd heard me call her over and over again.

"Do you want to go to the police station and file a report? If you don't, that's fine. We're taking care of this one way or another, but I don't want to make that decision for you."

She sighed, sinking even further into the leather seat. "I just want to go home."

"Okay. Then that's where we'll go."

I parked the car in the garage and was about to get out when her voice stopped me.

"He didn't rape me. You got there before it happened."

"I'm sorry I wasn't there sooner."

If I could have physically hurt myself for not being there for her I would. But no, I was avoiding the fact that I couldn't push Alexandra away again. I'd woken up that morning and immediately wanted to go to her and slide between her sheets. But I'd needed to think—to process what had happened last night. So, I'd bolted, going to the gym, the office, back to the gym—anywhere to not be alone in the apartment with her.

Then I'd gotten the call from Jared about the post selling Alex and my whole world collapsed around me. I'd listened to him tell me about when and where, all while my lungs worked overtime to compensate for the way my blood thundered through me. Terror of losing her had swamped me, almost making me collapse.

"Fuck. Jared. Why?" I almost pleaded with him. "Why would she do this?"

"I don't think it was her. I tracked it to the same library, but it

was last night when she was at the gala. She couldn't have posted it herself. You want me to get MacCabe on this?"

"No. There's no time to wait. I'm checking the apartment first and if she's not there, I'm headed that way."

None of it would have happened if I'd just been there.

We sat there until the dome light went off. She kept staring at her fidgeting fingers and biting her lip. I wanted to reach out and tug it free from her teeth but after everything tonight, I was letting her come to me.

I followed her lead as she got out. I remained quiet when her sniffles began in the elevator. But holding myself apart from her became impossible when the apartment door closed and she fell to her knees on the hardwood in the foyer and gut-wrenching sobs tore from her. One hand supported her against the floor as her back shook. The other was doing its best to hold in the cries as though trying to physically shove them back down where she wanted them.

I eased to my knees in front of her and moved slowly, giving her the chance to pull away before I placed a hand on her back. She didn't stop me. She lifted enough to move her hand to my thigh where she clung to me, her nails digging into my skin through my sweatpants, before moving to ease herself into my arms.

"He touched me," she confessed through her hiccupping tears. "I want to feel clean, Erik. I need to feel clean."

I slipped my hands under her knees and pulled her to my chest, cradling her as I made my way to my bathroom. Her sobs slowed back to sniffles when I set her down on the bathroom tile.

I started the shower and shed my shirt, socks, and shoes, leaving my pants on. Once the water warmed, I tugged her into the walk-in shower, clothes and all. They were quickly saturated and hung from her body but I let her wash away her pain the way she needed to. I held her for as long as she wanted me to until she stepped back and unzipped my hoodie she still wore.

"Do you want me to leave?"

Her hand shot out to grab mine. "No. Please don't leave. I just...I just need it off me. I need it all off me and gone."

"We'll burn it later."

That got a small laugh from her and it was the most beautiful sound I'd ever heard. In the face of her worst nightmare, she found a place to laugh, no matter how small. I kept my eyes high above her head as the clothes came off, falling to the tile floor with a slap. She was vulnerable and taking in her naked skin right then was the last thing I'd do.

She stepped into me, her warm skin against mine. "Please hold me."

"Of course." I ran my hands up, clinging to her when her tears began again.

"I'm so sorry, Alexandra. You are so brave and strong. You will be okay. I promise." I kept whispering words against her hair, over and over hoping one of them would sink in and ease the pain. I had no idea what I was doing. I'd rescued hundreds of women, but I'd never been the one to console them—to make it better. Even Hanna had had therapists and my parents to help her through the emotions. I worried that I would mess up with Alexandra, but nothing would stop me from offering her everything I had.

I held her tighter, needing to remind myself she was safe in my arms. I'd spent years pushing everyone away, not wanting to feel the pain of loss like I had with Sofia and there I was living my worst nightmare. I'd held myself back from Alexandra for so long, and I'd still almost lost her. And no matter how much I pushed her away, I would have been devastated if the night had ended any differently than her standing in my arms.

"Thank you," she whispered. "Thank you for saving me."

"I'm sorry I wasn't there sooner. I'm sorry I wasn't here this morning."

"You're here now."

Unable to stop myself, I pressed a kiss to the crown of her head. "Tell me what to do. Tell me what you need."

Her warm breath puffed against my skin. "I guess I could probably use some soap."

I reached for the bar of soap on the shelf and handed it to her. I expected her to ask me to leave at any moment, now that she was done crying. But resilient, brave, Alexandra did no such thing. She stepped back, soaped up a washcloth, and began washing her body. Every once in a while she'd give me a side glance from under her lashes, but it was as if I wasn't even there.

"Are you going to wash off? You have a little blood on your cheek."

"I can do it when you're done and settled."

She stepped into me and tipped her head back to meet my eyes. Fuck she was beautiful. Even when I didn't look directly at her, even when it was only shadows and blurs from my periphery. She was beautiful.

"I don't want to be alone." Her small hands brushed my sides and tugged softly at my pants. "You can take your pants off and shower with me, Erik. I know you won't hurt me."

"Are you sure?"

She nodded and passed me the soap. I ran the soap efficiently over my body, quickly since she was almost done, and we finished at the same time.

"Are you ready to get out?"

"Yeah."

I turned off the water and reached for a towel off the heated rack and wrapped it around her shoulders. Another towel went around my waist before I grabbed another and gently dried her hair. She held the thick white cotton around her and let me take care of her, wiping away the day one drop of water at a time.

I'd just finished running the towel over my own hair when she stepped back into me. I dropped the fabric and wrapped her in my arms. She didn't cry or even sniffle. She pressed her warm cheek to my chest and breathed me in, finding comfort in my arms.

Holding her, I felt like a giant. Like I could carry the world on my shoulders and I'd happily do it if she could feel safe again. I felt like more of a man than ever before in my life. All because this young woman had been traumatized and was still able to find solace in my arms.

"Do you want to lay down?"

"Will you stay with me?"

"Of course."

I directed her out to my bedroom and she wrapped the towel under her arms and around herself before curling up on the bed. Moving slowly, I lay beside her and let her curl around me however she needed.

I didn't know how long we laid there, but after only a few minutes, she fell asleep. Her soft, even puffs of air against my chest lulled me into my own sleep.

Sometime in the middle of the night, she jerked awake with a cry. I rested my hand on her arm, letting her know I was there, but not trying to trap her against me.

"Shh, Alexandra. I'm right here."

When she curled into my side, I wrapped my arms around her body, holding her close. "Erik?"

"I'm right here. You're home. You're safe." I murmured the words into her hair, over and over until her breaths slowed.

My muscles tensed when her warm lips pressed to my chest. I hadn't been sure at first, but she repeated the process, moving across to the other side before working her way up my neck.

"Alexandra," I moaned. Fuck, I didn't want to take advantage of her and no matter how much I told my cock it was wrong, I couldn't stop it. She felt it and didn't hesitate. She continued to kiss and press her hips against me.

"Touch me, Erik. Wipe it away. Replace it with yours."

"Alexandra," I tried again, but she knew she had me. She could hear the desire coloring my voice.

"Please." Another kiss to my neck, except she opened her lips and slicked her tongue across my skin. "I *choose* this. I *want* this." A puff of air hit my neck with a small laugh. "I've wanted this for so long. You make me feel safe. You take the women you rescue to Haven, but you're *my* haven." She pulled back and looked up at me, letting me see the earnest need blazing from her eyes. "Take me there."

I could give her something. I could give her pleasure.

Keeping my eyes on hers, I moved to my knees between her legs. Her lips rolled between her teeth and I waited for her to pull back in regret. Instead, she parted the towel and exposed every inch of her beautiful skin.

God her breasts were beautiful. Full and just as pale as the rest of her. I lowered to press a single kiss to her mound to let her know what I planned to do, needing to give her every opportunity to stop if she wanted. She whimpered and her legs tensed before relaxing, falling further apart.

"Is this okay?" I growled like a barely restrained animal.

"Please," she whimpered.

I slipped my thumb between her folds and rubbed her clit, loving the way her hips jerked forward and she gasped. Holding her open, I leaned in and licked her from her opening all the way to her clit.

"Oh, God," she moaned, her hand moving to burrow in my hair.

"That's it, baby. Use me."

I gripped a thigh and pushed it up, exposing more. I wanted it all. My lips trailed from her knee, down her thigh before I dove back in, tasting her. I pushed my tongue as deep inside her as I could before pulling back out to play at her bundle of nerves.

She tugged at my hair and moved me how she wanted, her hips thrusting up to ride my face. I hummed when I sucked the bud into my mouth. I flicked my tongue hard and fast listening to what turned her on.

It only took a couple of minutes before she was gasping and crying out, her pussy fluttering around my tongue as I thumbed her clit.

"Erik. Oh, God. Yes. God. Yes. Please." She rambled words, lost in her haze of pleasure.

I softened the pressure and eased back, bringing her down from her high slowly. She finally stopped panting and opened her eyes.

Looking down at me, she stroked my face, a flood of tenderness pouring off a woman who should be hiding under her covers.

"I want more," she stated. "I said I wouldn't ask for more. But, Erik, I want it."

It had been a joke to try and hold off. This woman was strong and beautiful and I'd do anything to keep her whole.

"Anything," I breathed. She looked so innocent staring down at me, her eyes wide and pleading. Her lips rolled between her teeth and I acted. I shifted up the bed, holding myself above her and kissing her lips free until I was the one nibbling at the soft flesh.

If she said she wanted all of me, then I would give her every bit. I couldn't pretend to hold back and give her bits and pieces like I'd done since meeting her.

She deserved more than that. She deserved everything and I was going to do my damnedest to give it to her.

22

ALEXANDRA

I was naked in a naked man's arms who had just put his mouth on me. It had been amazing and more intimate than anything I could have imagined. A giggle almost bubbled up just thinking about it.

Realistically I knew I should be pulling away from every touch after what happened tonight. I should be cowering in a corner after watching him become an animal. He almost killed a man and in the moment—still tied to the bed—I'd wanted him to do it.

Now, as Erik's big body hovered over mine, I was in control. I was choosing to be skin to skin with this man, to have his lips feasting on mine. I chose this sexuality and wouldn't let anyone take it from me.

His tongue tangled with mine and I could taste myself on his lips. It should have been weird, but instead, all I felt was heat building from my core, an inferno consuming me.

"You taste so fucking good," he whispered against my skin, working his way down my neck.

His hand found my thigh and pulled it up on his hip. I used

my foot to work the towel off his hips, needing him as naked as I was. He tossed the towel away before situating his length at my opening and thrusting up and down my slit like we'd done last night.

"Is this okay?"

"Yes," I moaned. "More."

"God, Alexandra, you're going to kill me."

He didn't seem to mind because as soon as the words left his mouth, his lips latched on to my nipple and sucked. I cried out and arched my back, offering myself to him.

My hands gripped his arms before roaming down his back so I could grip his ass in my palms. His muscles flexed when he thrust against me again and I dug my fingers in. Erik came off my breast with a pop and lifted up enough for me to see his chest. I took the opportunity to let my hands explore each groove and bump.

"You are so hot."

He laughed which made the muscles move more and I could have gotten lost in staring at them. My eyes drifted lower to where his cock was pressing against me, the head standing proud from between my legs. I tentatively reached my hand down and let my fingers dip into the slit, collecting the pearl drop before sliding down the length and back up. His body was a statue above me as he let me explore.

"I want to taste you," I whispered, a little worried it was the wrong thing to say. Especially when he groaned and dropped his head between his shoulders.

"This may really kill me," he muttered before rolling to the bed next to me. He supported himself with an elbow and used his other hand to stroke himself slowly. "Are you sure?"

I cocked an eyebrow but was unable to look away from his hand. "Are you?"

He breathed a laugh. "Am I sure that I want you to suck on

my cock? Yeah, I'm pretty sure I'm going to love it. I'm just praying I last through it."

I shifted off the bed to my knees between his legs. Pushing his hand away, I replaced it with my own and held it tall before bringing my mouth to the tip. My tongue dipped inside the slit and I pressed my lips to the top.

"I've never done this before," I confessed, even though it was no secret.

"It may make me a caveman, but I can't tell you how much it pleases me to be the first dick you suck on. It does something to me to know I'll be the first one inside that pretty mouth of yours."

I held him still and slid down his length as much as I could before sucking hard and pulling back. "Is that okay?"

"Hell yes. More, Alexandra."

I smiled at his pained tone before returning to his cock and repeating the process. I used my hand to stroke where my mouth couldn't reach and stopped every once in a while to roll my tongue around the head. He tasted salty and I became fascinated with how hard his length was and how soft the head felt when I pressed my lips to it. He groaned the most when I rolled my tongue along the back, so I did that more.

"Oh, God. Stop. Please."

Scared I'd done something wrong, I pulled back. Maybe I'd read his sounds wrong and they were actually pain instead of pleasure.

"Alexandra, I'm going to come in your mouth if you keep going. And I'd really like to be inside you when I do that."

"Oh."

He stroked my cheek and smiled. "Yeah, oh. You're really fucking good at sucking on my cock. Now come here."

He helped me stand and pulled me on the bed so my head rested on the pillows. We still hadn't pulled back the covers and I laid there completely exposed. He reached in the drawer to pull out a small bottle and a condom but froze when he turned back to the bed.

"You are so fucking gorgeous."

My skin flushed hot at his praise and I fought to not squirm and cover myself. The way his pupils dilated almost swallowing all the green made it easy. He climbed between my legs and sat back on his heels, taking time to roll the condom over himself. That move shouldn't be as erotic as it was, but it held me entranced.

His hands moved up my thighs, easing them apart, but not forceful. When he reached my core, he slid his thumb up and down my slit, rolling around my clit. "Are you sure?"

"Yes." I jerked from his touch, still sensitive from the orgasm he'd given me.

"You probably won't come."

"It's okay." When he wouldn't look at me, I said his name to get his attention. He needed to know how much I wanted this. "Erik. I've already felt so much pleasure with you. The fact that I get to choose you is more than enough pleasure for this."

He nodded, his whole body tight like a man on the edge of losing control. He reached past me for the bottle and flipped the cap. "I want to make this as good as I can. The lube will help."

He squirted some on the head of his covered cock and stroked himself. Then he put some on his fingers before tossing it aside and moving his hand between my legs. One finger slid in easily and I thrust up to meet him. He moved in and out and my hips had a mind of their own as I shifted restlessly on the mattress.

"Erik," I whimpered.

He added another finger, moving his thumb to roll across my clit, stretching me. He only fingered me for a few seconds before adjusting himself over me, lining his cock at my entrance. I could feel the brush of him against my opening and only for a moment, my body stiffened remembering how close I'd come to being raped, but I quickly shoved it aside, staring up into his eyes, getting lost in his safety.

"Tell me to stop at any point. Tell me if it gets to be too much."

I only nodded, finding it hard to breathe. My limbs shook with adrenaline and excitement. I clung to his shoulders and held my breath when he began pushing in slowly. Each time he'd get a little further and I began to ache with wanting. I knew it would hurt, but I just wanted to feel him inside me. I needed it.

A pinch of pain had me wincing and he pulled back, but only to push back in until I winced again.

He moved a hand to my cheek. "Open your eyes."

I did as he demanded and with our eyes locked, he pushed in all the way. It burned and my body went rigid, but he stayed still for me to adjust. When my muscles began to relax he pulled back just a bit before pushing back in. My muscles stayed tight as he moved slowly inside me. Despite the burn, my heart was ready to explode. It thundered in my chest with each small movement. Erik was inside me. Tears burned the backs of my eyes and he froze.

"Am I hurting you? Do you want me to stop?"

I shook my head on the pillow as a few tears leaked out down my temples. "No. Please. I'm just...You were right. It's so much pleasure."

"Relax your muscles, baby." His hand moved to my thigh and massaged, slowly easing the tension. "Tell me if anything feels wrong."

"This is perfect, Erik."

He bowed his head and attacked my lips, nipping and sucking at them, as he pushed in all the way. I cried out, but he swallowed the sound.

"More," I groaned against his lips. The burn shifted to a fire that grew until it consumed my whole body and I wanted more. I wanted him to take his pleasure, I wanted to watch him come inside me.

He picked up the pace and while it still hurt, it wasn't as sharp. It became more of a dull throb. Any time I tensed, he would rub at my legs and slow down until I relaxed again. Sweat beaded along his brow and his muscles bunched under my searching hands. I gripped his shoulder and dug my nails in, holding him to me as his hips thrust faster.

He'd go from kissing me like he was starving to licking at any piece of my skin he could reach. I was unable to stop my hips from rising to meet his when he sucked on my nipples. I could have done this forever. The pleasure didn't peak like it had when he ate me out, but it was there, a thrum under the surface that had me eager for more. He began to lose his rhythm. He stared down at me and he pushed in harder each time until finally he dropped his forehead to mine and groaned, holding himself inside me as he came.

He pressed soft kisses to my lips between his gasping breaths before he slowly slipped out and fell to my side.

"Holy fuck, you're tight."

I laughed. It started small and then grew until my whole body was shaking and he was laughing too. He rolled over to wrap his arms around me and kiss me.

"Let me clean up."

He stood and went to the bathroom while I shamelessly ogled his backside. I heard the water running before he came back out. I repeated the ogling process to his frontside, cocking my head to the side as I analyzed his softened cock.

"It's really crushing my ego with you staring at my dick with that narrow-eyed look."

"Sorry," I laughed. "I've never seen a fully soft penis before."

He shook his head and smiled, climbing back up on the bed between my legs. "Let me clean you up."

I tensed again when he dragged the washcloth down my thighs and across my pussy. I watched as he wiped away the blood and pressed the warm cloth to my opening.

"I'm sorry you didn't come. It may be the first time I haven't been able to get someone off."

I shrugged. "I hear it's normal."

"It won't always be." He tossed the towel aside and moved to lay flat on the bed, his head in perfect line with my pussy. "Let me kiss it better. I want you to come."

He didn't move to touch me until I nodded my head. I wasn't going to turn down more pleasure from him.

He licked me softly, sucking each of my folds in his mouth. Easing his tongue into my slit, he dragged up until he was circling my bud. He pulled back with a smirk and moved to kiss up my thighs back to my center where he repeated the process.

My hips thrust up when he brought me close to the edge only to pull back. "Erik," I cried. "Please."

"I think I love hearing you beg."

But he gave in and sucked on my clit, flicking his tongue hard and fast. My hand gripped the comforter and I moved my hips, flexing my ass, digging my heels into the mattress as everything in me pulled tight and snapped. I shot off and didn't hold back my moans. I cried his name over and over as I fell apart only to come back to him softly kissing every inch of my pussy. He lifted himself and kissed up my stomach, past my heaving breasts until he reached my lips and had me tasting myself again.

"Will you sleep with me tonight?"

Tears burned the backs of my eyes and I nodded, managing to hold them back. Tonight had been a whirlwind of emotions and curling up next to him was more than I could have ever asked for.

He shifted the blankets back and neither of us bothered dressing. He asked me if it was okay before he wrapped me in his arms and pulled my back to his front.

"Thank you, Alexandra, for your gift," he whispered behind me.

A smile stretched my lips. "Thank you for accepting it."

He hummed and pressed a lingering kiss to the base of my neck. "Sleep. We'll talk in the morning."

My mind whirled with the possibilities of what he could say when the sun rose and shined a light on what we'd done. I was sure I wouldn't be able to sleep, but in the warmth and safety of Erik's arms, I passed out in an instant.

23

ERIK

For the first time in my life, I woke up with a woman in my arms. Thirty-one years and I'd never stayed the night. My initial thought had been that I had been missing out because Alexandra felt damn good in my arms, but then I figured no one would have felt as good as she did.

She shifted in my arms and I waited for her to open her eyes, but instead, she rolled to her back and threw her arm above her head. The move dislodged the blanket and the way she stretched exposed one beautiful breast. I wanted to lean over and suck on the pale pink nipple. I wanted to drag my finger around the bud before rolling her nipple between my thumb and forefinger. I wanted her to wake up aroused so she would want me again.

I managed to hold back—barely.

Last night had been a nightmare followed by one of the best experiences of my life. She'd been so tight, so responsive, so beautiful. She'd been everything I thought she would be, which was why I held back. She deserved more than the man who was thirty-one and never stayed the night with a woman. She deserved more than a workaholic. She deserved more than a man who purposefully provoked criminals.

I was careful but had a reputation from years of working, and in the beginning, I'd been less than cautious. I'd been loud and angry and wanted everyone to know I was coming for them.

But screaming in people's faces tended to get you punched in your own. And I'd been a hell of a lot more than punched when I boisterously went after too much. They'd set me up. I went in and almost died. I probably would have if Jared hadn't been around ready to call the cops.

After that, I didn't go out anymore. I hired MacCabe and funded the rescue and recovery.

But it didn't make me completely safe from people finding out.

I stared down at her. Her almost black hair stark against the white sheets, her face soft and serene, even after the trauma she faced. She was a light that still managed to shine through whatever darkness she faced. She was smart and tenacious.

And I was done pushing her away. I wouldn't repeat yesterday, leaving to hide—leaving her to fend for herself when I should have been there.

It all felt inevitable like I'd be fighting a lost cause if I tried to get out of bed and act like last night had meant nothing. It would only serve to hurt us both. At least, with her by my side, I could keep her safe—protect her from any more harm.

I eased my arm out from under her and went to the restroom. When I came out she was sitting up, the sheet clutched to her breasts. Her shoulders were slouched as she stared at the bed, looking defeated.

"Alexandra? Are you okay?"

Her head jerked up and she took me in, her eyes dropping to my cock. I hadn't bothered to put pants on and the more she stared the harder I got.

"I thought you left," she answered, still watching.

"No, not leaving. Just had to answer nature's call." She breathed a soft laugh and finally raised her gaze to mine. "Come on. I'll make us some breakfast."

"Won't we be late for work?"

"I called the boss, he said it was fine," I said with a wink, eating up her every smile.

I walked to my closet and tossed a robe on the bed before pulling on a pair of sweatpants. I loved watching her slip the robe over her shoulders while still trying to clutch the sheet to her chest. She stumbled out of bed a bit when she tried to get out without exposing anything. I wanted to call her out on it, tell her how gorgeous she was and how I planned on seeing every single inch soon, but her cheeks were already stained red from her fall.

I decided I'd let her have this moment and just show her later what I thought of her body. She turned on the news when we went downstairs and I made us each a cup of coffee. When she sat at the island, I slid it over and she murmured her thanks.

Her shoulders were pulled up to her ears and she kept clutching her robe closed. My chest pinched watching her. Did she regret last night? Was she scared of me? Were the events from before catching up? I wanted to walk to the other side and pull her in my arms, but the way she almost curled in on herself, I was too scared *she'd* be the one to push me away.

So, like a coward, I turned my back on her and began making scrambled eggs.

We were sitting at the dining room table, almost finished eating when I couldn't take it anymore.

"Alexandra, are you okay?"

She kept her eyes on her empty plate. "Yeah."

"If you need to talk about anything, you can. If you need me to—" The words choked in my throat, fighting to not come out. "If you need me to give you space, I can."

"No," she denied quickly.

"Are you regretting last night? It doesn't have to change anything if you don't want it to."

"No." She shook her head and tucked a strand of hair behind her ear before looking at me with a smile. "Last night was more than anything I could hope for. I guess I'm just nervous. I'm sorry. I've never done this before."

God, I was an asshole. I forgot how few experiences she had. I scooted my chair out from under the table. "Come here," I ordered, patting my thigh.

She moved slowly, but eventually perched on my leg, looking at me from the corner of her eye. Touching her chin, I brought her lips to mine and gently kissed them, just breathing her in. When she didn't pull back, but sunk more into me, I moved my hand to the neck of her robe and tugged it aside to bare her shoulder. I kissed my way down her neck and across her shoulder until I reached her arm.

"Is this okay?"

"Yeah," she breathed. "How about I just tell you if it's not. If I don't say anything, then we can assume it's more than okay."

"Okay." I smiled and pressed my lips to her soft skin again. She gasped when I gently licked back to her neck and kissed up to her ear. "Don't scare me like that again," I growled before pulling back to meet her eyes. I needed her to hear me—to take in my words. "I'm...protective of you. Somewhere along the way, your name calling latched on and I'd miss it if it was gone."

Her gray eyes sparked before she laughed. Then she leaned down and kissed me. My chest expanded at her initiative. It was more than a kiss, it was an acceptance. It was the most relaxed and like herself I'd seen her all morning and it eased the ache I'd had since I'd walked out of the bathroom.

Her gaze turned serious when she pulled back—nervous. "Not to sound like a naive teenager, but what are we doing."

I shook my head. "I keep forgetting how young you are. People will think I'm an old pervert."

She framed my face with her hands. "I don't care what other people think." And then she did it again, she leaned down and kissed me, this time with bites and sucks, pulling groans from my chest.

"We are doing what feels right," I explained when she pulled back to let me breathe. "Having you in my lap feels right." My hand parted the robe and stroked her inner thigh. "Touching you feels right. Not pushing you away feels right. I'm done fighting you. I want to enjoy you for as long as you will let me."

She sunk her teeth into her bottom lip, but it didn't stop her eyes from creasing and her cheeks from pulling up.

"Will I be the only one you enjoy?"

"Only you."

"Then I only want to enjoy you too."

"You better," I growled. I moved my hand higher, pushing my way between her thighs until I could feel her heat against my finger. I pressed between her folds and lightly dragged my finger up and down. I groaned when she squirmed on my lap, brushing against my cock. "Now, how about I introduce you to shower sex before work? I'd have you sit your pretty pussy on my cock right here, but I don't have a condom."

"Okay," she answered breathlessly, her head rolling back on her neck when I pressed harder against her clit. "I like that plan."

"Tell me, Alexandra, how many times do you think I'll have to fill you up with my cock before you finally come all over it?"

"I don't know." She moaned as I pulled my hand out from between her thighs. I slipped them under her legs and stood, quickly making my way up the stairs to said shower.

"Let's go find out."

24

ALEXANDRA

My sister had sold me for sex.

I'd almost been raped as she sat there on her boyfriend's lap, high as a kite, angry at me for not giving her money.

Erik had rescued me.

Erik had taken my virginity. *I gave it to him.*

Erik.

Just thinking his name helped pull me back out of the daze I kept finding myself in. We'd come into work a little before lunch and I'd struggled ever since to focus my attention on the emails in front of me. Laura kept giving me curious side-eyes but was nice enough to not ask.

So, the day progressed. I would respond to emails and stop, remembering how my sister had sold me for sex. I would remember Erik crashing in and almost killing Bill. I would remember wanting him to. Then I would remember asking Erik to make it better.

Part of me had been scared he'd turn me away again, but I'd needed to take control of my body. I *needed* it, and he gave it to me. It had been more amazing than I thought. I remember Leah sneaking into our bedroom at night and telling me how gross it had been, but had turned to me with a smile, telling me it'd get better.

"It was painful and sloppy. Ugh. And fast. But I guess fast was good because of the whole painful thing. But soon it will be better. And then I'll own my body and all the boys who want it. They won't be able to help but give me what I want if they want a piece of this."

"Did you at least like him?" I asked.

She shrugged, staring up at our shared ceiling. "Nah. Makes it better. My expectations weren't high and I didn't really care. So, it makes the sucky experience meaningless. Always let your first few times be with some dumbass you don't care about. Makes it easier to brush it off."

My sister had been wrong. I cared about Erik and he had made it a beautiful experience. And even though I hadn't come from sex, he always got me off.

"Well, that's the first smile I've seen all day." Laura brought me out of my memories.

"Yeah, it had been a long weekend. I think it's just hitting me."

"Well, whatever makes you smile like that, don't give it up."

"I don't plan on it."

I looked over at the clock and decided getting up may help distract me from getting lost in my thoughts again.

"I'm going to grab Erik his coffee."

I thankfully didn't run into anyone while I grabbed two cups. I figured I could use a caffeine boost too, and maybe he'd want to drink with me. I didn't know the protocol for how we interacted at work. He'd said he wanted to enjoy me as long as I let him, but what did that mean? What did *enjoy* entail?

I knocked softly on his door.

"Come in."

I eased the door open and froze when my eyes landed on Jared. Flashes of Sunday assaulted me.

Being tied to the bed, my pants around my knees, my breasts bared. Jared had been over me, seeing me like that as he cut me free and helped me cover myself again.

"Hey, Alex. How are you?" His tone was polite and neutral, like any other day at work.

"Good." I forced a smile that didn't reach my eyes. "Just bringing Erik his afternoon coffee."

"Thank you, Alexandra." Everyone but Erik had begun calling me Alex. I liked that Erik was the only one who called me Alexandra. "I'll catch up with you later, Jared."

Jared collected his things and nodded as he walked past, closing the door behind him. I appreciated that he didn't treat me any different. I wanted to move on from the whole thing. I knew Erik was going to take care of it in some way, and that was enough for me. I didn't want to be coddled and constantly reminded. Because if I let myself sink into the nightmare, I didn't know if I'd make it out. So, I pushed past it, knowing I would fall back every once in a while, but I wouldn't live there. I wouldn't let that night and the memories ruin me.

"Come here," Erik ordered. I placed his coffee on his desk and went to sit back in one of the guest chairs. "No, no." He stopped my movements and tapped his thigh like he had that morning. "Over here."

I bit back my smile and moved around his desk until I could perch myself on his lap. His hand rested possessively on the curve of my butt.

"You didn't have to bring me coffee, but thank you."

"I know you always have one around this time. I figured I'd go ahead and get it without you having to come out and yell at me about it."

"I can see I've trained you well."

I rolled my eyes at him and took a sip of the hot liquid.

"Did you see the email from Carina?" he asked, conducting business as though his hand wasn't caressing up and down my thigh.

"I did."

"Any questions?"

"A few, but I emailed her back personally."

"Good. You can always come to me for help, too."

"Thank you, Erik."

He set his coffee aside and leaned up to press kisses along my neck. "Who knows, maybe marketing is the path you take. I know your internship requires two years here, but there are marketing roles we can have you focus on."

I smiled and tipped my head to the side, liking the picture he was painting of my future. I wanted to respond, but everything became hazy with the wet heat of his tongue slipping along my collarbone.

"How do we do this?" I asked.

He paused his assault and lifted his gaze to mine. "Let's keep it between us. Not because I don't want people to know, but I want to avoid rude gossip. I'm also not big on PDA in the office."

"Says the man who has me on his lap and is assaulting my neck."

"All is fair behind closed doors."

Leaning forward, I pressed my lips to his and shivered as his hand moved from my thigh up to my breast, his thumb stroking my nipple. I was ready to straddle his lap and really dive in when there was a knock at the door.

"Erik," Jared called through the door. "Remember our meeting is in twenty."

Erik sighed and his head fell forward to rest on my shoulder. "Yeah, be there in ten."

"Does Jared know?"

He huffed a laugh. "I think he's always known."

"Umm..." I didn't know what that meant.

"He and Ian gave me shit from the first moment they saw the way I looked at you."

Heat burned my cheeks. "Oh. Do they think..."

"No. They don't think that's the only reason you're here."

I breathed a sigh of relief. "Okay. That's good."

"I have no doubt you'll prove your worth, Alexandra."

"Thank you." I leaned in as he stroked his thumb across my cheek. "Is the meeting with Jared about your other activities?"

He smiled. "No, this meeting is just a boring analysis of a new program."

"Can I ask a question? I don't want to keep you."

"I can make a little more time for a pretty girl on my lap."

I pressed a quick peck to his lips, basking in his praise. "You mentioned before that you made enemies when you first started. What did you mean?"

His eyes dropped and his chest rose with a deep breath, pressing against my arm.

"You don't have to tell me. I was just curious and I worry about you."

"There's no need to worry." He brushed hair back from my face. "I don't go on extractions anymore."

"But you did."

He swallowed. "I did."

"Why don't you anymore?"

He held my stare and the longer he went without saying anything, the more nervous I got.

"Tell me," I whispered.

"I was loud my first year, calling myself Robin Hood, and like I said, I made enemies. One time, about a year into it, one of my enemies caught up with me. I went into his trap and let's just say, I almost didn't come out."

"Erik," I gasped, my hand covering my mouth.

"A few of his guys remained behind to rough me up. I probably would have died if Jared hadn't found me. He was looking into the same sale."

Tears burned my eyes. "Did they catch him?"

He winced. "No."

"Erik, oh my God. And you still do this? He could come after you."

"Baby, relax." He pulled me close and kissed my forehead. "I don't go under the same name anymore. I buried Robin Hood after that and I don't go out anymore. A security firm handles it all. We just track the sales. Besides, for all they know, they think I'm dead."

I took in his words, they eased the pressure his confession had caused in my chest. Then I thought about how he'd shown up at the hotel the first night. "But you came for me."

His eyes softened, warming to a deep green. "Of course I did."

"Erik." I wiped my eyes. "Promise me you won't put yourself in danger again. Please."

"Don't worry, Alexandra. I already promised my mom. And your case was different. I wouldn't have gone otherwise."

"And when you came for me again when my sister tried to sell me?"

His tone turned hard. "Don't ask me to not come save you. I can't ever promise that." He narrowed his eyes. "But of course, we won't have that issue if you don't go off on your own either."

I lifted my pinky. "Pinky promise."

His soft laugh soothed me and his finger slipped in mine. "Pinky promise."

His lips latched to mine and I barely managed to pull back after a moment. "I should get going. I've already made you late enough for your meeting."

"Let me take you on a date tonight," he suggested.

"Oh, um... I've never been on a date."

"Another first," he growled. "You're feeding my inner caveman."

"Oh, then I will stop," I laughed, standing. "We wouldn't want that to get any bigger."

He smacked my ass as I walked away. "I'll plan something for seven."

Perfect. That would give me plenty of time to run to a store after work and get an outfit for my first date. I did nothing but smile the rest of the day. Any stray parts of my nightmare trying to take up residence in my head were shoved aside for thoughts of what I'd wear tonight or where we'd go or how the night would end.

"Holy shit," Erik breathed, watching me walk down the stairs.

His heated gaze made me feel like I wore a designer gown rather than a black and gold geo dress I picked up at Target. I dragged my hand against the wall as I walked down in a pair of new heels. I wasn't used to the staircase with no handrail yet and adding four inches to my height had me extra cautious.

"You like?" I asked when I stood in front of him.

"Hell, yes. I'm tempted to say fuck dinner and keep you here." His eyes scanned up my body before meeting my gaze. "You look stunning."

"Thank you," I muttered past my smile, tugging one side of my hair over my shoulder. "Who knew you'd be such a gentleman."

"I sure as hell didn't," he said, laughing before pulling me close, aligning our hips up so I had no doubt how much he appreciated the dress. "But I'm enjoying the hell out of it with you.

Something about you urges me to try harder—to be a better man."

My stomach flipped over itself. He wanted to be a better man for me. The words had tears burning the backs of my eyes. "I think you're an amazing man."

He pressed a hard kiss to my lips but quickly pulled back. "Okay. We have reservations and if I stand here with you in that dress a moment longer, I'm going to forget dinner and take you here."

He interlocked his fingers with mine and didn't let go the entire drive. This Erik was different than the one I'd been with the past month. Or not so much a new man, because I'd always noticed how caring he could be, he'd just had his guard up too high to relax and let himself be at ease. I tried to keep my expectations low knowing there was a chance he could push me away again, but staring at the man smiling at me over a candlelit dinner, nothing was able to slow the way my heart thudded in my chest. Nothing was holding back the happiness that filled me to the brim and had me almost bursting.

"How long did you live in Ireland?"

"Ten years. My parents were never married and separated when I was born. Mom was young and didn't fight our dad when he said he was leaving with us. So, he took us to Ireland and we lived there for ten years."

"How did he die?"

"A heart attack."

"I'm sorry, Alexandra."

"It was a long time ago."

"But you still have bits of your accent."

I smiled, pulling myself out of the slump talking about my father seemed to send me in. "A little. And not much. Leah and I would practice our American accents all the time because the kids at school would make fun of us."

"I like it when it comes out."

"It's mostly faded, but you can hear it more when I'm tired or mad."

"Or a little tipsy," he said with a wink. "That must be why I've heard it so much. You've been all three around me. More mad than any others."

"You bring out the best in me," I joked.

"Did you like it there?"

"I loved it there," I answered quickly, my tone wistful. "Maybe I painted a prettier picture because I was young. Not that it took much to be better than when we moved with our mom, but I remember being happy. I remember our dad being happy. We lived close to the ocean. It was cold as hell, but the water was beautiful and peaceful. We'd go to play there as often as we could. Leah was always there by my side, never getting in trouble."

"So she wasn't always crazy?"

I laughed. "No. But our mom wasn't around much, and when she was it tended to be better when she wasn't." He frowned and I hated putting a damper on the dinner with my mess of a life. "It wasn't always bad. Leah stayed by my side. Defended me and taught me how to be strong against all the catty girls. It wasn't until our mom died that things started spiraling."

"I can't imagine."

I waved away the topic. "Enough about me. Tell me about your family. I can only imagine the woman who raised you and twin girls."

He laughed and I couldn't help but smile with him. The topic of his mom was a good one. "She's a hell of a woman. A mean one."

"Are you sure you didn't deserve it?"

His brows furrowed and he nodded. "Oh, I totally deserved it. My father would shake his head at my antics, but my mom would still gasp and have an hour-long talk with me about how I should behave." He laughed again as if remembering a specific memory. "Especially since she was a teacher in my high school. A boy had to be creative to not get caught by his mom with the girls. But then I'd get caught and be in more trouble because it was usually for something over the top."

I groaned. "I don't even want to know."

"It was just typical boy stuff."

"Typical boy stuff is gross." I cringed.

He winked. "We'll see if you're saying the same thing tonight."

"Did your sisters have trouble in school with your mom?" I almost wished I could have swallowed the words back, not wanting to make him sad with talk of his sisters, but he surprised me by smiling.

"Oh, no. They had trouble in school because of me. I'd make sure to visit Mom for lunch as much as possible and scare off any boys."

I groaned. "No. Those poor girls."

"Hanna wasn't much of a problem, but Sofia liked to push her limits. I swear she didn't even like boys, she just flirted in front of me to see if she could make me explode." His smile dimmed and he dropped his eyes to his empty plate. "She was always so strong-willed."

I reached my hand across the table to rest atop his. He flipped his palm up and squeezed.

"Thank you," he whispered.

"For what?"

"For making me talk about the good times. So often I shut down about her because it hurts. But it's good to remember the best parts of her too."

"Anytime. Besides, maybe I can take notes and come up with my own antics."

He pretended to growl and bare his teeth. "I don't think so."

The waiter came to clear the table and bring the check. "So, I was thinking maybe I could tour some apartments soon." His eyes flicked to mine with no smile behind them. "I have enough saved up for a down payment and feel good about my income. I don't know exactly which school I'm going to, but as long as I stay close to the bus line, I should be fine."

He swallowed and looked down at the table. "You know there's no rush, right?"

"Yeah, I just...I figured that was the plan."

"Speaking of plans, I owe you ten-thousand dollars."

If someone told me a month ago I'd forget about ten-thousand dollars, I'd laugh in their face. But I hadn't even considered it when I thought of apartments and moving out.

"I think I'd rather keep it in savings. Hell, I can open a savings bank account now," I said, giddy at the thought. "I'll use it for school supplies and my new addiction to pizza."

I didn't want to move out—who would when you lived in a place like his, with a man like Erik. But I couldn't stay there forever. The plan had always been for me to get on my feet. But the way he looked at me now, he looked like he liked the idea of my leaving as much as I did.

We were saved from more conversation when the waiter came back and we signed the bill.

"Let's go home, baby," he whispered in my ear. "I'm ready for dessert."

25

ERIK

"Jared," I answered the phone. "What's up, man?"

"Hey, Erik, sorry to bother you on Saturday, but I figure I'll keep you up to date on things."

I froze outside my apartment door. If Jared called on the weekend, it wasn't for work at Bergamo and Brandt.

"Talk to me."

"It's not a sale or anything. I haven't seen anything local since the last extraction we did. But I've seen the name Mr. E brought up a few times."

My muscles tensed, locking the air in my chest.

"I can't figure out where it's coming from and it's pretty vague right now, but it's looking like someone is asking questions about who Mr. E might be. Like I said, very sparse chatter."

"And you can't track it?"

"No. It hasn't popped up long enough and as soon as I start getting a trace on it, it vanishes. Like they're fishing and when no one bites, they reel it back in."

Shit. Closing my eyes, I breathed as deep as my lungs would allow, holding it for five seconds and slowly letting it out. No one had ever asked about Mr. E. Jared and I worked hard to keep it out of the work we did. I had no doubt people could connect the dots, I just tried to be subtle enough to not make waves when we did our work.

"Should we be concerned? Let MacCabe know?"

"No, I don't think we have any concern yet. But I will notify MacCabe for when the next extraction happens."

"Okay. Thanks for letting me know and keep me up to date on this. I don't want it getting too far."

"Will do, Erik. Enjoy your weekend."

I intended to. Taking one more deep inhale, I breathed out the stress and focused on the woman waiting for me.

Walking into the apartment, I tossed my bag aside, ready to rinse off from the gym and wake Alexandra from bed. I'd left right as the sun rose, shining in through the windows onto her pale skin. I'd wanted to wake her then, but I'd kept her up late last night as it was. I tried to give her recovery time since her body wasn't used to so much sex, but when she laid out, her breasts shining like a beacon begging for my lips, it was hard.

Instead of giving in, I threw on some sweats and went to the gym in the basement.

However, when I strode into the room, the bed was empty and the shower was running. Smiling, I began shedding my clothes and heading toward the bathroom. I stopped upon entering. She looked like an angel in heaven. The bathroom was all white with a wall of windows to shine light through the glass shower. The way she carelessly stood under the water, her face turned up and her eyes closed as droplets caressed her skin like I was so desperate to do. She was an angel.

She gasped when I finally made noise opening the shower door.

"Good morning," she said, smiling. Her eyes shined like silver with the light cascading around her.

I didn't say anything, instead stalked toward her until she was backed against the wall. Her smile didn't slip, but the silver of her eyes darkened to a gray, desire glinting in them. All for me.

"Erik," she breathed.

I ate it from her lips. I devoured every word she let slip from her mouth that spoke of the desire I gave her. I fed off it. My hands dug into the curve of her hips and I dipped low to rub my cock against the apex of her thighs. Another gasp where I took advantage and shoved my tongue inside. She met me halfway and tasted me the same as I did her. Her nails dug into my shoulders, scouring their way up my neck into my hair, holding me tight.

I needed her. My body heated beyond the steam of the shower, my want burning me from the inside out until I was sure I'd explode. One of her legs hiked up to my hip so she could rub herself against me. If I thought I was hot before, it was nothing compared to when her cunt met my cock.

"Can't fucking wait," I growled into her skin. Leaning down, I sucked at her breast like a savage whose sole purpose was to have every inch of her in my mouth. I bit her and her cries sank into my skin like a plea for more.

I hoisted her up and she wrapped her other leg around my hip, lining herself up perfectly. Gripping her ass, I eased her down my length, slowly easing in and out until I was all the way and the soft curve of her ass was pressed to my balls.

"Move," she whimpered. "Please."

"Move how? Like this?" I asked into her neck, moving my lips up and down.

"No," she groaned in frustration.

"Tell me. Tell me what you want."

"Move inside me."

I pressed my lips to hers and dipped my tongue inside. She quickly pulled away and nipped my bottom lip and pouted at my smirk.

"Fuck me, Erik. Please."

"God, I love when you talk dirty."

And I did without any more waiting. I thrust my hips hard over and over. I pressed her back to the wall and used one hand to support her so I could move my other to the front and press my thumb to her clit. She arched her back and I almost lost it then and there.

"I love watching these tits bounce for me. So fucking sexy."

"Suck on them."

"Yes, ma'am."

I flicked my tongue against the tip before biting it softly between my teeth, rolling side to side. Her pussy squeezed me and her moan echoed against the tiles and glass.

"What if someone is watching me fuck you against this shower wall? What if they're watching how much you like a bit of pain while I fuck you?"

"They can't," she breathed.

They couldn't. The bathroom was a wall of floor to ceiling windows that were one-hundred percent reflective, but I liked to play the game. I liked the way her eyes widened at the thought.

"Show them how you come. Show them how pretty you are when your whole body flushes and your pussy milks my cock." I pressed on her clit again and didn't hold back. I fucked her hard, racing to my own finish, praying she beat me there.

Her head fell back against the wall and her mouth dropped open, the sweetest, sexiest moans lighting me on fire. The heat raced down my spine and my balls pulled up tight and I pushed in hard, emptying myself. I latched on to her shoulder as I rode the waves of my orgasm, only coming back when her nails dragged across my scalp sending shivers down my body.

I slipped out of her without letting go and moisture followed. "Fuck," I breathed, my lungs still working overtime. Even more so when I realized what I'd done.

"Yeah, that about sums it up." Her soft laugh puffed against my forehead.

"I didn't use a condom."

Her body stiffened, her hands no longer moving through my hair, when she finally caught on.

"Erik. I..."

I could feel her throat move up and down against my head. "I'm so sorry, Alexandra. I-I didn't think."

"Umm...We-we should be okay. I should be starting soon. So, we should be okay."

I nodded, not super confident in her words, no matter how many times she repeated them. I lifted my forehead and cradled her face in my palm. "No matter what happens, I'll take care of you. You know that, right?"

Her eyes were wide and she managed a jerky nod. I placed a soft kiss against her lips offering her comfort. Guilt hit me more than fear. I was thirty-one, a baby wouldn't do damage to my life. It wasn't planned, but it wouldn't hold me back from what I was doing. But Alexandra was only nineteen, getting ready to start her future. I'd played a gamble with her life more than my own. One more kiss and I eased her down to the floor.

"Let me clean you and we can go do breakfast."

"I was already clean before you came in," she said, a small smile tipping her lips. The stress of the moment slipped away if only a little.

"What can I say, I like making you dirty. In fact, after breakfast, I'll do it again."

I grabbed the soap and began running it over her skin. "As much as I'd love that, I have four apartments to look at today and my first appointment is in an hour."

My hands froze on her skin, but I kept my eyes down, pushing through it and continued washing her. I didn't want her to leave. I liked having her with me. I liked waking up to her every day. I never knew I'd so easily fall into a relationship, but I loved it. Somehow I knew it wouldn't feel as easy if it had been with anyone else.

Only Alexandra.

I couldn't be the guy to hold her back. Not when her eyes lit up the way they did when she talked about being on her own. I didn't have to like it, though.

"Okay. I'll drive you."

"You don't have to do that."

"Shut up, Alexandra. I'm taking you."

When I looked up she was making a face and mocking me. I gave a glare that softened into a laugh.

"Don't make me spank you. Although you may like it."

She made the move of zipping her lips but laughed with me.

THE FIRST APARTMENT we didn't even stop at. We drove past. When she argued, I said I was too scared to leave my car for more than a minute in fear it would get stolen. The neighborhood was horrible.

The second apartment we at least made it in the door, but just.

"We haven't even looked at it," she'd argued.

"It isn't safe."

"It's in a better neighborhood."

"Alexandra," I sighed. "Come here." I pulled her into the hall and made sure to lock the door behind us, the confused landlord standing wide-eyed on the other side.

She stood there with her arms crossed, hip out, and foot tapping. "Well?"

I cocked an eyebrow and lifted up on the handle and pushed lightly with my shoulder, easily opening the door. She didn't even say anything, just dropped her arms and rolled her eyes with a disgusted sound.

"Sorry, we won't be looking at this one," I said to the landlord with a smile and happily followed the ball of thunder back to the car.

"I don't want to hear it," she'd argued, her finger in my face at the third apartment. "It's in a great neighborhood and cable and Wi-Fi are included. Cable, Erik. Real, life, cable."

"It's disgusting," I argued back. This landlord followed our argument like a tennis match of words.

"It is not."

"It's a shithole, Alexandra."

"I can clean it."

The landlord opened his lips to interject, but I cut him off.

"I wouldn't even fuck you here, and you know I'd fuck you damn near anywhere."

Red bled into her cheeks and her mouth slammed shut. If she could have burned me down with a look alone, I'd have been another unknown substance sinking into the used-to-be-cream carpet. I managed to hold back my victorious grin until she turned around and rounded the corner to leave.

I gave a nod to the guy, still standing a little slack-jawed, and followed her out again.

I was screwed when we reached the fourth place.

"This place is amazing. The bus stop is right around the corner. It has a workout gym, a pool," she practically squealed. "It's even got a balcony. A freaking balcony, Erik."

Her smile lit up the whole apartment and I did my best to tone it down with a frown. But she was bouncing on her feet and flying from room-to-room just to report back to me with another amazing feature.

"A fucking fireplace," she shouted from the living room.

"What about that other place we passed? The one with the gate," I argued when she met me in the kitchen.

She scoffed. "I can't afford that and you know it."

"I could give you a raise."

"I'm an intern, Erik. I don't get raises. We already know I'm getting more than anyone else as it stands."

"Stop being difficult."

Her eyebrows rose and she gave me a dubious look. "Me? Because I won't take your money?"

Stepping close, I spoke softly to avoid being overheard by the landlord trying to look busy and give us time to talk, but was really trying to eavesdrop. "From what I remember, you wanting my money is what got us here."

She didn't respond. Instead pursed her lips and narrowed her eyes, raising her middle finger for good measure. But she softened quickly and stepped into me, pressing her breasts to my chest. "Think about it. These counters are the perfect height for you to screw me on. We would enjoy every moment christening it."

"I guess it's not that bad."

She beamed up at me. "Okay, then the decision is made."

We both turned to talk to the landlord at once.

"I'll take it."

"We'll think about it."

26

ERIK

"LAURA, can you please send Alexandra in?"

I released the button from my speaker and sat back in my chair, waiting for her to come strolling in. Even though it had been a couple months since she'd first strolled in, she still had my heart stopping in my chest each time she cleared the door. Her clear eyes wide and questioning, a little nervous. At least they used to be a little nervous. Now when she entered, they'd soften to a warm heat that had my dick twitching behind my pants and my heart pounding a little harder.

I'd never felt this way for anyone and I didn't hate it like I thought I would. I'd always associated caring for someone with being vulnerable, setting yourself up to be hurt. But that happiness that filled me to bursting upon just thinking about Alexandra, made it all worth it. I just had to make sure I held on to her tight and didn't let any more harm come her way.

She was making it hard with the whole moving out thing. It'd been two weeks since we viewed the apartment and each time she brought it up, I diverted the conversation to something else. She hadn't taken me to view any others and only talked about that last one, so I know she had her heart set on it. A part of me held out hope that something would happen to force her hand and make her stay.

Pregnancy would not be one of those reasons. She'd finished her period last week and we'd both breathed a sigh of relief when it came.

The door creaked open and my predictable heart thundered at her heated gaze and seductive smile.

"Lock the door, Alexandra."

Her eyes widened. "Erik..."

"Just do it."

She obeyed and then made her way to my side of the desk, coming to sit on my lap. It was where she always sat when we were alone. After asking her to do it only twice, she didn't hesitate to make it a habit.

I wrapped my arms around her and pulled her down for a kiss. "I have something for you. I found it in the mail this morning."

Watching her face for her reaction, I handed her the envelope. She gasped and reached out slowly with shaking hands. Her finger stroked across the University of Cincinnati logo before flipping it over and tearing it open.

"No matter what, you're going to be great," I reassured her when she froze, her hand around the paper but not tugging it free.

She pulled the sheet out and unfolded it. I didn't read it with her, just watched her face. A slow smile pulled at her cheeks as tears glazed over her eyes.

Pride inflated my chest.

She bit her lip and squeezed her eyes closed tight like when she opened them, something else would be there. I brushed my fingers along her cheeks, wiping away the tears that broke free.

"I always knew you could do it."

"Thank you," she whispered.

"I just gave you the possibility. You did this all on your own."

She shook her head and took a shuddering breath, smile still stretching her mouth wider than I'd ever seen. "I'm going to the University of Cincinnati." I laughed when she bounced in my lap. "I'm going to college," she said a little louder.

"How about we celebrate?" I suggested, my hand traveling from her knee up her thigh.

She set aside the letter and faced me, her expression changing from euphoria to a soft heat that shot straight to my cock. "What are you thinking?"

I tapped her bottom. "Stand up and put your hands on the desk."

She complied and I took my time running my palms up the outside of her thighs, lifting her skirt along the way until I could flip it over her hips. I tugged her ass back closer to me, making her bend at the waist and began tugging her panties down her legs. The office was silent except for the sound of her heavy breathing. I knew she was nervous about being caught in the office. I knew she was excited by it too.

She stepped out of her panties and I balled them up, inhaling her sweet scent before stuffing them in my pocket.

"Such a pretty pussy."

She jerked when I finally touched her, slipping my finger between her folds and sliding up and down her slit. I repeated the movement, collecting more moisture on each pass, pressing in a little harder each time. She moaned beautifully when I dipped a second finger inside her opening only to pull back out and circle her clit.

"And already so wet. Do you know what I'm going to do to you, Alexandra?"

She shook her head, but I wanted her words.

"Make a guess."

"Have sex with me?" Her voice was breathy and soft and stroked across my skin like a lover.

"Oh, yes. But first, I'm going to eat your cunt. I'm going to taste every inch of you and you're going to stand there and take it. For however long I want."

"Yes."

Gripping her hips, I rolled my chair forward until I could bury my mouth between her thighs. I'd teased her with my fingers enough. I shoved my tongue inside, swirling to collect every drop. She pushed back against me and tried to muffle her moans. I dipped lower and flicked across her clit before sucking it in my mouth. She rose up and down on her toes, grinding on my face to get more friction.

I moved back to her opening, swirling my tongue around and around as I moved my fingers to brush her clit.

"Erik, oh God. More, please. Harder."

I laughed softly because I knew I was teasing her with soft strokes, but I loved hearing her beg. I rubbed a little harder and moved my tongue from her pussy to her tight little asshole, circling it. She squealed and would have pulled away if I hadn't had a tight grip on her hips.

"What? Oh, God."

I circled it a few more times before pulling back. "I'm going to teach you to take me everywhere." I wanted to play with her more there, but I was ready to fuck her and I needed her to come first. Shoving two fingers deep, I hooked them and stroked inside her. My lips latched on to her swollen bundle of nerves and sucked. She thrust back and must have covered her mouth with her hand to try and hide the way she moaned and cried out through her orgasm. Before she was done pulsing hard around my fingers, I tugged out and wiped my chin, quickly undoing my pants and grabbing a condom.

In the next instant, I was inside her. This wasn't soft lovemaking. This wasn't a tease like I'd done with my hands and mouth. This was me claiming her. Fucking her so hard and deep she never forgot me. Even when she moved out, she would feel me inside her and know she was mine.

Leaning over, I pressed my front to her back and gripped her breasts in my palm, frustrated that they were covered by her blouse and bra. I wanted to rip the damn fabric from her body, but we had the rest of the day at work. I made a mental note to keep extra shirts for her here.

Our skin smacked together each time I thrust inside her. Her wet cunt was loud and mixed with our heavy pants.

"I'm going to take you to dinner tonight to celebrate," I whispered in her ear. "It will have nice long tablecloths and I'm going to want you to climb under the table and suck my cock. I want you to swallow my cum. Will you do that for me? Will you swallow every drop while the waiter stands there and I order our food?"

She whimpered and nodded. I wanted to do everything with her. I wanted to lay her on the conference table and fuck her in front of everyone so they knew she was mine, so they knew I was the only man who'd owned her body. I loved that she loved it—that she loved these scenarios and was willing to play them out.

I dropped my hand to between her legs and slid my fingers around her wet clit. "Will you play with yourself while I stuff my cock down your throat? Will you finger your pretty cunt and come with me?"

"Yes. Anything."

I buried my teeth into her shirt and grunted with each thrust, giving her every ounce of me. Her head shifted and pressed to her shoulder as she came, her pussy fluttering around my cock, squeezing like a vise. I fought to pull out just to have her suck me back in. It was too much. Everything became a white noise with only the thundering of my pulse pounding in my ears as I fucked her harder than I ever had before. Like a man possessed, I claimed her until my world exploded and the air was sucked from my lungs and I emptied everything I had inside her willing body.

My hips moved in small thrusts as I came back to earth. My hand had moved to the desk in front of her to support my limp body and her lips pressed across each of my knuckles.

"I think I blacked out for a minute." I huffed a laugh and rained down kisses where teeth marks marred her shirt. "Did I hurt you?"

"Never."

Groaning, I slipped from her pussy and fell back in my chair. She remained bent over the desk and I stroked her swollen folds, loving the way she jerked.

"Can I have my panties back?"

"Not a chance in hell."

She finally stood and shivered as I got rid of the condom and refastened my pants.

"Well, while I have you and we're sharing good news, I'll share some good news with you." She bit her lip and smiled hard before letting her words fall out in an excited rush. "I accepted the apartment. I move in next month which gives me plenty of time to set up for college."

Any high I'd been riding from being inside her crashed down over me, sucking out every bit of air from my lungs. Somehow I managed to keep a straight face and hide the crushing disappointment. I stared up at her shining eyes and brilliant smile and I knew I couldn't put a damper on her excitement.

It wasn't like her moving out meant I was losing her. I just needed to bide my time until eventually, I moved her back in with me. Forever.

I managed a smile and pulled her hand to my lips. "Good. We can go shopping this weekend for some furniture."

"Just the necessities. I still need to save for everything else."

"We'll at least need a bed that I can fuck you in."

"Do you need a bed for that?" she teased.

"I guess not. I can be pretty creative."

She tugged me to stand and pressed a kiss to my lips. "Thank you, Erik. For everything." One more lingering kiss and she stepped back not letting go of my hand until the last second. "I should get back to work. Wouldn't want the boss to fire me for playing on the job."

"I think he'll understand."

She opened the door and jerked back when she found Jared there with his hand raised to knock.

"Oh, hey Alexandra."

Alexandra dropped her eyes to the floor and tried to run her hand through her rumpled hair. She looked adorable with the blush staining her cheeks. She mumbled a quick hello and bolted.

Jared let the door close and cocked an eyebrow my way. I merely shrugged and sat back down. "What can I do for you?"

"The chatter about Mr. E has increased. Still elusive, but appears more often."

I jerked my eyes to his, my mind quickly running through the implication of people talking specifically about me and what it meant.

"Someone has taken the bait and there's been mention of possibly knowing who you are."

"How?"

My mind scrambled to make a list of enemies. It was endless. I never targeted anyone specifically, we just went after whoever we found. Anyone could be behind this.

"My first instinct is Alex's sister. I didn't want to use your real name with them around and I called you E."

"Shit."

"Now that they are appearing more often I think I can stomp out any fires and delete any traces."

Sighing, I ran my hand through my hair. I needed this taken care of. I didn't want any of it to blow back for a multitude of reasons. One, it would inhibit my ability to continue my work and another was Alexandra. I couldn't risk her getting hurt.

"Keep me updated."

Jared simply nodded and left. I closed my eyes and prayed none of this blew back on Alexandra.

27

ALEXANDRA

"Nothing is catching my eye. Shouldn't furniture shopping be easier than this?"

"All of it's cheap. That's why none of it is appealing," Erik said, his lip curled up in disgust, eyeing another fancy futon.

It *was* cheap, but my expectations had been pretty low. The quality of the furniture wasn't the problem. The fact that my heart wasn't into picking out things for my apartment was the real issue. Part of me didn't want to leave Erik's place. I wasn't nearly as excited as I came off each time I rattled on about all my independence. But I knew it needed to be done. It was my original plan all along: to move out and finally be free of my past. To live on my own and not have to worry about my grocery money being stolen. To not have to sleep in front of my door in fear someone would sneak into my bed in the middle of the night.

My end goal hadn't changed the day Erik came storming into my life—just the way I got there.

But being connected to someone was new to him—to me too, but for different reasons. I hadn't had an opportunity to be in a relationship. Erik actively chose not to be in one. He'd never had a girlfriend. Hell, he'd never even let a woman stay at his place. Until me.

The newness of our situation made it feel unstable.

He could change his mind at any moment. He could decide having a relationship wasn't for him. He could decide I wasn't enough woman for him, that he missed the variety he'd had before. I'd rather move out on my own than be forced to when he was done with me.

I knew leaving was the right decision to make.

But none of it felt right.

I flopped down on an actual couch, not one that could be maneuvered into fifteen different shapes and could double as a bed. "What about this one? Could you see yourself claiming me on this couch?"

He shuddered. "God, no. My sister has that couch."

I laughed and tugged him down with me, curling up against his side. He wrapped his arm around my shoulder and kissed my forehead like we weren't sitting in the middle of a store.

"Maybe I should go see her place. She obviously has great taste if we like the same couch."

"I could arrange that. She lives five floors below me. And don't act like you like it. You hate this couch."

I did hate it.

"How did I not know she lived in the same building?"

My head moved with his shoulder's rise and fall. "She doesn't venture out too much. She lived with my parents until about a year ago and I think moving into my building allowed her some freedom and still feel close to home. I honestly think she forced it because she wanted Ian to see her as an adult and that can be hard to do when you live in a pink room with frills and your mom still packs your lunch."

"That sounds awesome. Will you pack my lunch for me?"

"Not a chance."

"Your mom sounds amazing."

"She is. She wants me to bring you to dinner some time. It's been a while since I've gone to a family dinner and the last one she gave me hell for leaving you at the apartment."

The moisture evaporated from my mouth. *A family dinner?* The thought gave me a mixture of panic and excitement. Would I stand out like a sore thumb, an obvious interloper who had never had a family meal? Would I fall right in line with the laughter and jokes? Each image brought forth a new emotion. I didn't want to focus on either since it probably wouldn't happen and changed the subject.

"How does it feel to have your little sister crushing on your friend?"

He huffed a laugh. "It's fine. I know nothing will happen because she isn't right for Ian and, while she won't admit it, Ian isn't right for her. But he makes her smile, so I never say anything."

"You're a good big brother." I know he didn't believe me since he blamed himself for not finding the twins sooner and saving Sofia, but I wanted to remind him as much as I could that he *was* a good man.

"Speaking of siblings," he segued. I stiffened in his arms and he rubbed his hand along my shoulder to comfort me. He knew I didn't like talking about it, so it must be important if he's bringing it up. "Have you heard from Leah at all?"

"No."

He gave a single nod and left it at that. Part of me wanted to ask more, wanted to ask why he brought it up but was happy enough to let it go when he stood and clapped his hands. "Okay, so no furniture today."

"I guess another day." I stood and walked into his waiting arms, losing myself in his warmth wrapped around me.

"How about we head home. We can order dinner in. You can strip down naked and I can feed you before we watch a movie."

"I need to be naked for this?"

"There may be some sex in between each event."

"I am okay with that plan. Will you be naked too?"

"Definitely."

"Then, what are we waiting for?" I grabbed his hand and started dragging him behind me until we were jogging and laughing the whole way.

We talked about our night on the drive home and by the time we were parked in the garage, I was ready to run upstairs and pounce on him as soon as we were alone.

And then my phone rang.

I pulled it out and my stomach churned at the name on the screen. *Unknown.* No one had my number except Erik and Leah.

Erik saw and a muscle twitched in his jaw. I hit the side button to mute the ringing and was about to shove it in my pocket when he demanded, "Answer it."

My eyebrows shot to my hairline and I hesitated, but he gestured for me to hurry up and I swiped to answer.

"Hello?"

Deja vu hit me when I heard her crying over the line. Unlike last time when I received the call, I didn't immediately panic. It didn't mean that my body didn't seize up and my heart didn't thunder, but there was a veil of doubt covering my reactions, dulling them.

"Alex... I'm sorry. So sor—" She faded off with tears.

"What, Leah?" I didn't hide the annoyance in my tone.

"I need your help." Looking over at Erik, I rolled my eyes expecting him to sympathize, but his face was hard and focused on hearing what he could of the conversation. "When Oscar couldn't sell you, he decided to sell me. I tried to fight, but Bill kidnapped me and sold me. I've been locked in this warehouse for a week and I'm scared. It's by the river, just outside the west side of the city. I think it's an abandoned beer factory. God, Alex, I'm scared."

I could imagine how scared she was all too well and I hated the sympathy that plagued me. I hated that part of me urged to go help her. I hated the voice in my head that reminded me it could all be a setup, too.

"This guy...he jus-just r-raped me and passed out. I managed to grab his phone and sneak off to make a phone call."

"Leah." My voice cracked on her name and I hated the weakness. "I—I don't know what you want me to do."

"That guy, the one who rescued you. You said he saved girls, right? He could save me, can't he?"

I wasn't sure it was possible, but Erik's body hardened more and his usually warm eyes had gone blank and cold.

"Leah," I sighed. "I—"

"What the hell is going on?" a man's voice grumbled over the line. "You dumb bitch."

"No," Leah cried out, piercing the veil and hitting my heart. "Please do—"

The line went dead and I wanted to smash the phone into dust. Tears burned the backs of my eyes and I avoided Erik's gaze, not wanting him to see how stupid I was for being upset for her.

His hand came into view to hold mine.

"Don't panic yet." His tone was soft and calm. "There are... things going on in the background that I haven't talked to you about because I wasn't sure about any of them. But this solidifies a few things. Let me call Jared."

Wiping my tears, I nodded and pulled myself together. He placed the call on speaker phone so I could hear everything going on.

"Erik, I was just getting ready to call you."

"What's up?"

235

"There's been more chatter about Mr. E. These guys have to be amateurs because they're laying everything out online like it's a fucking frat party."

"We just got a phone call from Alexandra's sister claiming she's been kidnapped. Anything on that? Anything over the past couple weeks?"

"Not of her being sold," he hedged.

"Good. Meet me at my place ASAP."

"You want MacCabe in on this?"

"Definitely. Tell him I'll pay extra if he can make it tonight."

TWO HOURS LATER, I sat on the couch with a hardened heart. I was surprised my molars hadn't cracked with how much grinding I'd done as I listened to Jared lay out what had been planned.

Apparently, Bill had heard of Mr. E and had a plan to take him down. Of course not on his own. He had some friends who'd been affected by Erik's takedowns before and wanted revenge. Jared was right, the conversation had been like a frat house chat room. They discussed how I would be a bonus to sell off—but not until Bill finally had what had been denied to him.

If I ever came face-to-face with that asshole again, I was going to deny his right to have a dick. I'd rip it off and make him choke on it.

I imagined the scenario, clutching a couch pillow to my chest and watching the crowd of giants in Erik's dining room hover over their plans on the table.

Jack MacCabe ran a security company and had signed up to help Erik pro bono with all these cases. He was a ridiculously sexy man with ridiculously sexy men that worked for him. Even as Erik stood next to me, I struggled not to stare.

All of them were tall and muscular under their black pants

and shirts, guns strapped to their sides. I wouldn't have assumed that appealed to me, but I guess I was wrong. Erik had cocked a brow and told me to go sit on the couch, but not until he laid a hard and fast kiss on my lips like he was claiming me.

"We're all married, dude. Calm down," the tall blond giant said from the corner with a smirk.

"I'm not." One raised his hand with a smile.

"Shut up, Aarons," Jack said, slapping the young one on the head.

I lifted on my toes and gave Erik another kiss, pulling back to whisper in his ear. "You know I only want you, but I like the caveman act."

"I'll show you more caveman later," he'd growled, slapping my ass.

It turned out, it was going to be much later. The men had their plans and began packing up to head out.

"Are you sure you have to go?" I looked to Erik with hopeful eyes, wanting him to stay back with me.

"I have to go."

"But they're expecting you."

"Yes, but they don't know that I know. I have the upper hand. This is personal. I can't let this go on anymore. It has to do with more than just your sister." His hands framed my face and he pressed his forehead to mine. "Please stay home and wait for me. I need to know you're safe. I promise I will be back."

"You better be."

I didn't care that four other men's eyes were on us, I held him to me and kissed him with all I had. I pressed my tongue to his lips and demanded entrance. He slid his hands down to grip my bottom and pulled me to him so every inch of us touched, his tongue tangling with mine.

"Be good."

And then he was gone.

28

ERIK

"ONCE YOU'RE IN, try to figure out who the lead is. If this is as personal as they made it sound in their chats, he's going to want to confront you," Jack explained, loading a magazine into a gun and passing it off to me.

We sat in a large black SUV in the shadows running through our plan one more time. From our vantage point, we watched a few men stumble in and out of the warehouse. One man stood at the door collecting money and my stomach rolled each time a new male came out.

"We have squad cars a couple blocks away picking up these guys," Shane let us know. His face was dark and showed the same anger each man in this car felt. It was hard to believe that a slave ring had been here for who knew how long, right under our nose. In our own city while we went on about our lives.

"You don't have to do this," Jack reminded me.

"I do. They're expecting me."

He sighed in resignation and nodded. "Ames's crew is already in the back setting up. We'll be planted in the front and trap them in. We have a few men watching any other possible exits, but the main ones are guarded. Go in and try to spot Leah, but something tells me they'll take you right to her eventually."

I had no doubt, but we were going to run this the same we would if it was a rescue. I slipped the black baseball cap on my head and looked to Jack to make sure the camera was working.

He held up the small screen that relayed the feed and currently showed his face. "We'll be able to watch from here."

"You ready?" Jared asked, the blue screen of his laptop illuminating his features.

"As I'll ever be. I'm ready to end this shit."

I left the car and made my way across the street into the light from the front door. I tripped over my feet and fumbled my money to appear clumsy and drunk as I approached the guard at the door.

"How much for a good time?" I slurred and smiled. He studied me up and down with furrowed brows. "Come on man, I just want to get laid and my buddy told me you have the best girls. He even mentioned a new one I'd love to try out."

"Fifty for an hour."

I handed him wadded up bills and held up my fist for a bump like a douchebag. "Gonna use every second."

He tapped his knuckles to mine. "I'll take you to a good one. I fucked her earlier and she's still tight as can be."

I balled my hands into fists and breathed through the rage to keep from sucker punching him right then and there.

We walked into an open factory, the machinery large and imposing in the shadows of the dimly lit room.

A burly man appeared from the double doors we were approaching on the other side. "Hey, Tony. I'll take him from here. We don't want to miss any customers."

Tony turned back after slapping my back. "Enjoy that hour."

I followed the new guy through the doors and entered a long hallway, almost like a shitty hotel. We walked down and I tried to look around as much as possible to give MacCabe's team as much info as I could. We usually went in with blueprints and intensive plans with even more intensive backup plans, but tonight we didn't have that luxury.

Some doors muffled groans and cries, turning my stomach as I tried to focus on the task at hand.

But I almost lost my lunch when we walked past a room with the door partially open. The girl had her hands tied to a pipe on the wall, stretched above, her naked body lying out on a mattress on the floor. Her eyes were glassy and unfocused and quickly looked away when they met mine.

Images of Sofia and Hanna handcuffed to a bed frame and drugged the same way flashed through my mind. I struggled to stay in the present as I was assaulted with memories from the night I rescued them. Hanna had barely been sober enough to remember me, and Sofia...Sofia had been cold with a blank stare.

"Here we are." The man stood back with his arm out like he was welcoming me to his home.

It was the last door at the end of the hall and I prepared myself for what I would find. I slowly opened the door and searched for the bed. Leah was fully dressed—or barely dressed considering she wore a lacy bra-like shirt and tiny shorts—tied to the bed. The door clicked closed, my escort stepping in behind me.

"You came." Leah smiled, not looking fearful at all.

"Hello, Mr. E."

I jerked my head to the corner across from the bed. A short, stout man stepped from the shadows with a smile. I scanned him, making sure the team caught all of him, including the gun he gripped in his hand. This was the head honcho of the organization. He stood there with no fear and arrogance and ease only a leader could have, knowing everyone around him was loyal.

Something tickled at my memory telling me he was familiar, but I couldn't place him.

"Whoa, whoa." I held up my hands and stumbled back, playing dumb. "I paid my money for an hour alone. I'm not into some sausage-fest."

He gave me a patronizing smile before looking over to the bed. "Thank you, my dear, for bringing me Mr. E. You can collect your payment as you go."

Oscar sneered at me as he untied Leah from the bed. She jumped in his arms and gave him a sloppy kiss. "Let's get out of here, babe."

"Asshole," Oscar growled, walking past.

I wanted to trip him just so I could watch him smack into the wall, but I held back—barely.

Bossman focused back on me. "You've ruined quite a few operations for me, Mr. E. So, when a man came to me with such information, I gladly took my chance for some payback."

I kept up my heavy-lidded stare, moving toward the wall to support myself. I wanted to appear too drunk to stand, but really I needed to get my escort from behind my back. "I don't know who you are or who Mr. E is. I just wanted to get laid."

"You're very funny, Mr. E." Bossman took a few more steps into the room. Maybe if he got close enough I could wrestle the gun from him. I didn't know how long I'd have until MacCabe and his team came in. Or if I'd have time to avoid his bullets when they did get here. "I know who you are, Erik. Or should I call you Robin Hood?"

My heart dropped to the floor, my stomach rolled, nausea threatening to take over. I hadn't been Robin Hood in years and not many people had figured it out before I burned it to the ground and created the persona Mr. E.

Only one man had known what I looked like and that I'd been called Robin Hood.

Marco DeVries.

"I thought I'd taken care of you that night. Sure my men had beaten you sufficiently that you wouldn't make it through the night. Yet here you stand."

Only because Jared had found me with enough time to get me to the hospital. I swallowed the bile threatening to rise up my throat. The past was the past. I'd been alone then and I wasn't now. I was trained now. I had more to fight for now.

Thinking of Alexandra helped slow my heart and keep me focused.

"When Mr. E appeared, I assumed it was just another do-gooder I'd squash beneath my shoe." DeVries stuffed one hand in his pocket and paced leisurely across from me. "I've thought of this moment since I knew I'd meet the man who cost me millions of dollars. I thought about torturing you. Making one of the whores suck your cock. I've found most men can't hold back pleasure even when they want to. I thought about keeping you for a while so I could steal the girl's sister and have you watch her get raped by every man I can get. Then I considered maybe just having you tied down as a woman got brutally raped next to you, so close, but unable to help. I've gotten more creative since we last met."

He sighed as though the ideas pleased him. My muscles tightened at every idea he laid out like a screw was pulling them more and more taut until they'd snap. But I needed to wait for the right moment and when that happened, I would crush him. This time I would win and he'd be left for dead.

"In the end, I just want you gone and I'm not cocky enough to keep you around and have a chance to escape. You seem to have gotten smarter over the years and I know you have a team you usually use, but the girl's desperation had you moving too fast to prepare. But your arrogance has reared its ugly head and you came in alone this time, unable to be patient. You came in thinking you'd save the day for all these sluts, but in reality, you'll just die. And this time I won't leave it to chance."

Apparently, he was done talking because, with a serene smile on his face, I realized my time was up. He lifted the gun and aimed for my chest. The time to move was now, whether MacCabe was ready or not, I needed to act.

Taking a deep breath, I slowed my heartbeat and channeled my training in tai chi. I saw Alexandra's smiling face. I needed to get back to her. I needed to tell her how much I cared for her. I needed to tell her I loved her. *I loved her*.

All the tension that had been building in my muscles snapped into action. I lunged and shoved my hand out, knocking the gun off track just as it fired.

My escort groaned behind me and fell to the floor, but I didn't have to focus on him. DeVries was coming at me, his aim realigning for another shot. I reached out and gripped the pistol and twisted, but he kicked out and I took us both down. My bones rattled when we crashed to the floor. I pinned his arm and reared back to land a punch, hoping to knock him out.

He turned his head back with a laugh, blood coating his teeth like a maniacal fucking clown. I went to punch him again, but he thrust up and threw me off balance. He pinned me before landing his own punch and bringing the gun back between us.

I gripped his hands between mine and fought to push the gun off to the side, shoving hard just as the gun went off. Adrenaline flooded my system making me numb to anything other than taking this crazy motherfucker down. The door crashed open and Shane, one of MacCabe's men, landed a solid punch knocking DeVries off me. Another body came in to pin the arm holding the gun to the ground and finally freed the weapon from his fist.

"Holy shit, Erik." Shane stared down at where I laid gasping for air on the floor. "We need to get you to the hospital." I looked down to where he was staring and saw blood seeping out onto the floor under my body, my black shirt dark and wet.

"Oh, fuck. Look at that." The world got a little fuzzy as I realized the bullet had hit me. Too many chemicals flooded my system from the adrenaline rush, allowing me to only feel a light burning pain radiating from my side.

The blond giant of a man leaned down and pulled me upright. I groaned out my pain, the movement causing a raging fire to throb through my body.

"Let's get out of here. We need to get that checked."

He grabbed a sheet and had me press it to my side before wrapping my arm around his shoulder and moving back to the hall where cops were flooding the scene.

People were in handcuffs against the wall and medics rushed to the rooms to help the girls. When we exited, I saw Oscar and Leah in the back of a cop car and despite being shot, the night was a win.

"Is he okay?" one of the medics asked. "He's smiling like he isn't shot."

Shane shook his head. "Yeah, he's fine. Get him taken care of and then bring him to the station." He patted me on the back. "I'll see you later. Good job tonight."

Yeah, it had been a good job.

Now I just needed to get back to Alexandra.

29

ALEXANDRA

Rattling at the front door had me jerking up from the couch. I looked around the apartment trying to figure out what time it was. The city lights sparkled in the dark sky so it was still night. The last time I remembered looking at the clock it had been a little after three in the morning.

Squinting my eyes, I focused on the stove. Four-seventeen.

The door opened and I jumped up and rounded the corner to the foyer. Erik had his back to me as he tried to close the door without making a sound. When he turned, I was already jogging toward him, surprising him when I jumped in his arms.

He still managed to catch me with a pained grunt.

"Oh my God. You're back. It's so late. What happened? Is everything okay? Why did it take so long? I've been so worried."

He buried his head against my neck and huffed a laugh against my skin. He groaned and released me, letting my feet hit the floor. He didn't let me get far, moving his hands to frame my face and held me close to kiss me.

"I missed you," he growled against my lips.

"I missed you too." I returned his kiss like it hadn't been less than twelve hours since I'd seen him, but more like twelve months. I ran my hands over his face, his shoulders, and arms. I touched as much as I could reach. When I skimmed his sides desperate to get under his shirt to his skin, he hissed and jerked back.

"What?" I stepped back and scanned him.

"Nothing, baby."

"It's not nothing." I crossed my arms, giving him my most intimidating stare. "Show me."

"A bullet grazed m—"

"A bullet?" I screeched, lifting up his shirt on my own. A white square was taped to his side covering his injury. "Holy shit, Erik." Tears burned my eyes. "Oh my God."

"Shh, baby. It's okay. It was just a graze and I already got stitches. Barely anything. I'm fine, I promise."

"Erik, you could have been..." I didn't even finish the sentence, not wanting to voice it.

"I wasn't. Now come sit with me on the couch. I'll tell you what happened."

I led him to the living room but left to get a glass of bourbon for the both of us. I knew I could use one and I hadn't even been shot. He downed it in one go.

"This should mix well with the meds." He laughed and tugged me down until I was curled under his arm.

I settled in as he laid out the night for me. I was sure he left things out, like what he saw in the rooms as he walked down the halls. He would start talking about it, then his body would stiffen and he'd start a new sentence skipping the darker parts.

My body heated with shame when he got to how my sister was there waiting. How had she fallen so far from the sister who helped me through my first period? Who held me when the boy I liked had broken my heart by kissing another girl. I rubbed my tears off on his chest, not wanting to admit how much it hurt to know she would be part of something so sinister.

"Come on, it's late," he said when he finished. "Come take a shower with me and we can go to bed."

He tugged me off the couch and held my hand all the way to his bathroom. The city lights sparkled beyond the windows, the beginnings of a sunrise along the horizon behind the tall buildings.

I made him lean against the counter as I got the water started before turning my attention back to him. I took care to help him with his clothes, enjoying each bit of skin I revealed like a Christmas present. I took care to place a plastic cover over his bandage before stripping out of my own clothes.

"Let me wash you." I moved him under the water and began lathering my hands. He groaned when I massaged his shoulders and scrubbed at his scalp. He grew hard as I worked my way down his body, but this wasn't a moment for sex. It was a moment for comfort and being close and being grateful for having each other.

"My turn," he murmured against my neck.

"Not tonight. Let me wash off and we can get to bed."

He sat on the bench and watched me clean myself. When I was done, he tugged me down to his lap and held me, pressing kisses along my shoulder up to my neck, sending chills down my spine.

I gently stroked my fingers along his bandage, hating that I played a part in his injury. "I'm so sorry, Erik." Tears clogged my throat and I swallowed the lump, trying to hold them back. "I'm sorry this happened because of me."

He gripped my chin and made me meet his eyes. They were dark like a forest and pleading for me to hear him. "Don't you dare apologize, Alexandra. This was not your fault. Too many good things came from tonight to be sad about it."

"Tell me," I whispered, leaning down to press my lips against his skin. He told me the details, but I wanted to know more.

"Ten girls were rescued. The trafficker was a powerful one and once the cops are able to question him, more women will be saved." Wet sucking kisses worked up my neck to my ear where he gently bit. His hand smoothed up the outside of my thigh until he cupped my ass. "And one shining realization hit me when he had that gun pointed at me." He whispered the words in my ear and I held still—waiting—needing to know. "I needed to tell you how much I love you."

"Erik." I breathed his name, scared to break the moment between us.

"I've been a stubborn ass and don't deserve you after the way I treated you, but I'm saying it anyway. I love you, Alexandra."

Tears leaked from my eyes mixing with the water from the shower. I couldn't wait a second longer, I pressed my lips to his and held him to me like I could make us one. "I love you too, Erik. So much. You saved me. You're my savior."

"I think it's the other way around. You saved me by showing me how good it feels to love."

Dipping my tongue in his mouth, I brushed my tongue against his. He groaned into my lips but didn't move it any further than making out. We stayed that way until the water ran cold and we were forced to get up.

He dried me off and wrapped me in a robe. "Come sleep with me. I need to hold you and rest."

I couldn't imagine a better way to end the last twenty-four hours. Erik loved me and I wanted to be nowhere else but in his arms.

"Oh God," I groaned, my eyes still closed. My legs were spread wide around shoulders as a mouth moved from my knee down my thigh to my core. I gasped and arched, his fingers pulling my lips apart and his tongue swiping me from my entrance to my clit. "Erik."

"Good morning, baby." The breath from his words brushed against my wet pussy before his mouth went back to work, waking me up.

Two fingers rimmed my opening, playing in my wetness before slowly pushing in, his thumb coming up to replace his mouth. "Play with your tits, baby. Show me how much you want it." I finally opened my eyes, the morning light barely making it through the curtains. Illuminating the room just enough for me to see Erik between my spread legs, staring up at me as I moved my hands to my nipples and twisted them. "When I'm done eating all the sweet cream from this pretty cunt, I'm going to suck on your nipples and fuck you."

"Please."

"You beg so pretty."

He latched onto my clit, fucking me hard with his fingers. I cried out and thrust my hips up against his mouth, clinging to the sheets. My whole body pulled tight and everything started and ended at my core. I twisted my nipples hard just as he pushed in roughly and I came. I cried out, not holding anything back from him. He gave me so much pleasure and I wanted him to know what he did to me.

His fingers slipped from my pussy and he adjusted up the bed, stopping to suck on my pebbled tips as promised.

"Look how red you made these pretty pink tits. I love how much you like a little bite with your kisses." He emphasized his point by nipping at my tender breasts.

"Fuck me, Erik. I need you."

"I need you too, baby. So fucking bad."

He grabbed a condom and sheathed himself before rolling to his back and tugging me atop him.

"Fuck me, Alexandra. Straddle my cock and take me in that tight little cunt."

I held his cock up and positioned myself over him, teasing him with small slides up and down, but not taking him all the way. His hands moved to my thighs and gripped hard. He was right, I did like a little pain with my pleasure and the way his fingers dug into my skin, had me sinking all the way down.

We both groaned, enjoying each other. I was so full with him, being stretched to the max.

"Move, goddammit," he growled.

Laughing, I rolled my hips, sliding up and down his length, watching the muscles in his body tense and relax. The pressure built again and my body flushed hot, like a fire burning me from the inside out. My body almost became possessed as I rode him harder and faster.

"Yes, baby. Take my cock. Ride me."

He sat up, his lips a breath from mine. "I love you."

"I love you, too." His hands controlled my hips, moving me how he wanted me. "Look at you, my little virgin riding my cock like you were made for me. I'm going to fuck you morning, noon, and night. Take every hole you have until it's all mine." One hand moved up to cup my breast, bringing the rosy tip to his lips. "I'll squeeze these tits together and fuck them. Your pretty little lips can suck on the head while your beautiful breasts jack me off."

"Anything. Anything you want." I wanted to do it all with him. "Oh God. I'm gonna come."

"Yeah, baby. Squeeze my dick. Use me."

Sweat dripped down my temples and I held on tight, rocking harder and harder. His thumb slipped between us, rubbing my clit and I exploded. I wrapped my arm around his neck and dug my fingers into his hair, holding tight as wave after wave of pleasure consumed me.

His head pressed between my breasts and he moaned, releasing inside me just as I was floating back to earth.

"Love you. Love you so much," he murmured between kisses.

We rolled to our sides and he slipped out of me, taking a moment to get rid of the condom before sliding right behind me again, his arm pulling me close.

"You wore me out," he mumbled. "Sleep with me until I'm ready to go again."

"Anything for you."

"Anything?"

"You know I'd give you anything."

"Stay with me."

"What?"

"Stay with me. Don't move out."

"Erik, I—"

"Don't answer yet. Just think about it. It's what I want from you."

I swallowed, not sure how to decipher the mix of feelings going through me. I wanted to shout yes without even doubting it, but the fear of it all falling apart held me back.

"Stop thinking. Just sleep in my arms and we'll talk later."

"Okay."

"I love you, Alexandra."

"I love you, too."

30

ALEXANDRA

I woke up deliciously sore and twisted side to side just to feel the ache of the muscles between my legs.

The events of last night came rushing back and I almost burrowed under the covers in shame that my sister had set such a dangerous trap, but then I remembered Erik's words. He loved me. Erik Brandt loved me.

Erik Brandt wanted me to stay.

I hadn't thought I'd be able to fall asleep last night with the way my mind swirled with the possibilities and outcomes, but wrapped in his arms, fighting sleep was a losing battle.

Stretching my arm across the bed, my hand encountered cold sheets. I finally opened my eyes and looked around the dark room. The curtains were still closed, but no light tried to peek through. When I looked at the alarm clock, I was surprised to find it was already after six. No wonder the bed was empty.

I sat up but didn't rush to turn on the lights just yet. My mind had one thought after another chasing the next and most of them weren't making me eager to rush downstairs to face Erik.

If he was even still here.

Life tended to teach me not to trust in a good thing because it will all be pulled out from under you eventually.

What if he changed his mind about me staying and now he was gone again instead of telling me he was wrong? What if he changed his mind later? What if he was high from the pain meds they put him on and he doesn't remember any of it? Sure, he hadn't seemed the slightest bit woozy, but still. What if he did want me to stay, but changed his mind next week, or next month? What would happen to me? Would it be a big fight and he'd kick me out that day?

I dropped my head to my knees and groaned.

I was making a mountain out of a molehill and it wasn't me. I had been dealt a shit-hand, but I faced every day the best I could and now here I was curled up, hiding on a man's bed who told me he loved me, thinking of all the ways it could fall apart.

Finding my resolve, I shook off the doubts and reached over to flick on the lamp and froze.

Rose petals.

There were rose petals all over the sheets, a mixture of reds, pinks, yellows, and oranges. It looked like a sunset had exploded. Warmth radiated through my body, pushing out any negative questions I'd formed. I leaned over and fisted a handful of petals, bringing them to my nose and breathing in the spicy and fruity aroma.

I eased out of bed, happiness making me feel light as a feather as I tip-toed around the petals making a path to the bathroom. Flicking on the light, I looked around at the small notes taped to all the surfaces. I walked to the bathtub first and tugged off the taped piece of paper.

If you stayed, we could fill this with hot water and bubbles and bathe together. I'd hold you in my arms. We'd probably make a mess with all the water we'd splash everywhere when I made love to you. But it would be worth it.

On the shower was another note.

The shower in that apartment wouldn't even be able to hold both of us. How am I supposed to wash you when I stay with you?

I laughed when I turned to look at the mirror. He used my lipstick to write "Stay with me," on the glass. Turning in a circle, I giggled at all the work he'd done. I wasn't sure what my answer would be yet, but I couldn't deny how each thing made me want to be fearless and run to him with a resounding yes.

My feet stopped when I opened the bedroom door to find another trail of rose petals—all various shades of pink—down the hall. I followed the path until I stood outside the media room with another note taped to the door. With trembling fingers and a wide smile, I opened the envelope, becoming desperate for more of his words.

I know what you're thinking. I can't stay here because I'll be a working college girl. How am I supposed to get work done when Erik will be wanting sex with me all the time? How will I fight off such a sexy beast? Don't worry, this door has a key lock just for you.
I love you.
Don't go.

P.S. You sleep like the dead. I don't know how you didn't wake up with all the noise. Must be because I'm such a sexy beast who wears you out.

EXCITED TINGLES RUSHED through my body at what I'd find on the other side of the door. I took a deep breath and slowly opened the door. My eyes burned, tears making the world fuzzy.

"Oh my God," I whispered, my hand moving to my lips.

Everything from the media room was gone, no more gaming systems and extra large couch with an oversized recliner. Instead, there sat a simple white desk and matching white bookshelves on the wall. My laptop was on the desk next to a vase of roses and a picture of Erik and I from the charity gala. On the wall behind the desk was a collage of sayings in frames.

Though she be but little, she is fierce.
I am powerful, beautiful, brilliant, and brave.
Don't be afraid to give up the good to be great.

My eyes moved from one to the next. He chose them all for me. Before I crumbled there on the floor in a mess of happy tears, I turned and followed the path of petals to the stairs, noticing a note taped to the wall before going down.

If you stay, I will add a railing. I know you hate how open they are. But I will miss watching you walk down the steps, pressing your side against the wall.

I laughed and did exactly as he said I did: I pressed my side to the wall and followed the petals down the stairs. But my eyes were glued to the path that led to the kitchen island covered in candles. It was beautiful. My eyes scanned the room, but couldn't find him, meaning he must be waiting for me in the dining room. It was the only place I couldn't see from the stairs.

I wanted to run to him and throw myself in his arms, but I could see another note taped to the edge of the island and I needed more of his words.

I know you want your independence and your pride won't take

handouts. So, you can take care of the groceries and those chick-
flicks you like to watch. Also, maybe the water bill too because,
damn, you like to take some long showers.

Laughing, I wiped at my cheeks, ready to walk to the dining room and see him. I breathed in as deep as my lungs would allow, stretching them to the max, feeling like I could float away any moment. I needed his arms around me to hold me here with him.

When I turned the corner from the kitchen, he stood in the dining room, holding two glasses of wine, a slew of roses and a few candles decorating the table. His green eyes shined even in the dim lighting. I somehow walked slowly toward him and he met me halfway giving me a glass of wine.

"Erik." I breathed his name, not wanting to break the moment. We stood there with dopey smiles on our faces, silence surrounding us like we were our own little bubble the world couldn't touch. He lifted his glass and waited for me to tap mine against his before taking a drink. I went to speak when he held up a hand and began talking, his deep voice washing over me.

"I know you think I'm not a sure thing. But Alexandra, I've never been so sure in my life." He laughed and shook his head. "Which is funny because I started all of this the most unsure I'd ever been about anything. You are my greatest risk." He set our glasses aside and stepped close, framing my face with his strong hands. "You are my light at the end of the tunnel. I love you and no matter what happens—even if you dump my ass—I will always make sure you're okay. I will keep you safe. I will make sure you never know hunger or unnecessary pain." He pressed a soft kiss to my mouth and whispered his plea against my lips. "Stay with me, Alexandra. I love you."

"Erik." My voice cracked on his name and I had to swallow past the lump of tears. "I love you, too. But what do I have to offer you? I'm nineteen years old with a thousand dollars to my name and a shitty past."

He listened to my worries and gave me a smile in return. "We all have pasts, some worse than others. But not everyone can persevere like you can. If I have to be honest, I'm only in this for one thing."

My heart dropped a little, shock hitting me at how wrong I had read the entire situation. Immediately, I began panicking and thinking of where I screwed up, but he laughed and rushed to reassure me.

"Stop right there. God, you have a dirty mind." He gave me a kiss to stop me from saying anything. "I want your brilliant mind."

I shoved his shoulder hard but huffed a laugh with him. "Asshole."

"You are so smart—so fearless. I've never known a woman like you and I love every ounce of it." No one had ever called me smart. No one had ever looked at me past my body and I was back to crying at his sweet words. "I'm hoping maybe I can trap you into staying at my company when all is said and done. I'm ready to offer sex multiple times a day into your benefits package."

"Oh my God. Stop." I hit his shoulder again, laughing. I was a mess of emotions with tears slipping down my cheeks, but laughing at the same time.

"I'm hoping you don't leave me to run off with Carina."

"She is pretty amazing and hot."

He pursed his lips and cocked a brow and I pressed up to my toes to kiss the look away.

"Even if you did want to go with Carina, I would support you. As long as I get to wake up with you in my arms, reminding me of all the good things in life, I'll be more than fine. I'll be better than I've ever felt. You make me a better man."

His hands slipped down my arms, and slid around my hips, pulling me flush against him. I tipped my head back to give him access as he kissed up my neck to my ear.

"Stay, Alexandra."

Tingles raced down my spine to my core and I was unable to come up with a reason to say no. "Okay."

He lifted his head to meet my eyes, a slow smile stretching his lips. "Okay?"

I nodded. "Okay."

The next thing I knew I was lifted off my feet and clinging to him as he twirled us both around, his laughter vibrating against my chest. He sounded so happy I began laughing with him. But then my feet touched the ground and the laughing stopped because our mouths were fused together, sealing our agreement with a kiss. We wrapped ourselves around each other and left no place untouched, no part of our mouths untasted.

He'd done so much for me and I felt more energized and ready for anything than I ever had before. He'd given me that. He'd given me a future I could look into and see something great. He saved me that night from myself and I'd spend the rest of my life loving the man who bought me.

EPILOGUE

IAN

"When's Alexandra coming back with your balls?"

Erik rolled his eyes and gave me a hard stare. "You're just jealous no one is playing with your balls."

He wasn't wrong. Usually, I had no problem playing just as hard as I worked, but the last eight months had me pulling back—being pickier with the women I slept with.

It was that damn woman from the blind date photo shoot. God, she'd been hot as hell. And one of the only women who gave back just as good as she got. She wasn't like other women I'd hung around. She wasn't docile and didn't give into everything I suggested.

No, she argued. It had kind of pissed me off at first, but then it became our unique way of foreplay. Add in the lack of clothes and touching for each photo and I wasn't shocked at all we'd ended up fucking like bunnies.

I'd thought about contacting her again. Even gone so far as to get her contact information from the photographer. But he'd been gone like a ghost, no trace of him anywhere. So, I resigned myself to my fate of never seeing her again. Just remembering her on nights in bed when I jerked my cock. Or in the shower. Or on the couch. Or in the bathroom at work. But that had just been that one time.

"Hey, boys." Alexandra strolled into the office, her eyes solely focused on the man behind the desk.

"Hey, where's my kiss?" I asked when she walked past me to Erik.

Erik glared before shifting Alex onto his lap and kissing the hell out of her. I broke the moment with gagging noises. "Get a room, you two."

"Ignore him," Erik said. Alexandra laughed but pulled back. "How was your first day of school?"

Her whole face lit up with her smile. "Great. It's mostly introductory classes, but it's exciting."

Erik beamed with pride, brushing her hair behind her ear. Even if I was jealous, it was nice to see my best friend happy. He'd closed himself off for so long.

"Hey, everyone." Hanna entered the office next. "We have the meeting with Miss Russo in a few minutes."

"Yes, I get to meet the elusive marketing guru." I'd been in London for every meeting they'd had together.

"I kind of love her," Alex said wistfully.

"Hey, Ian. Glad you're back." Hanna came over to sit on the couch next to me and bumped my shoulder before turning to the overly happy couple. "How was your first day, Alex?"

"Good. I think Astronomy will be my favorite class." Alexandra waggled her brows and Hanna laughed.

"Ah, yes. Dr. Pierce."

"Who the fuck is Dr. Pierce?" Erik growled.

"The hottest professor of all time." Hanna sighed like she was recalling a fond memory.

"Don't worry, babe. You're all I need," Alex reassured Erik.

"Better be," he grumbled. "And how was your sister?"

Alex's smile dimmed. "She's good. Therapy was okay today."

Alex's sister had taken a plea deal for a shorter sentence and going to rehab. It was more than she deserved. After taking part in trying to sell her sister and trap Erik, I'd have let her rot in jail. But Alex was a better person than me, and Erik gave her what she wanted.

"Mr. Brandt?" Laura called over the line. "Miss Russo is here."

Alex hopped off Erik's lap, moving toward the seating area with me and Hanna.

"Send her in, please."

I was flipping through the files for the new London office when the door opened.

"Hey, Carina," Erik greeted her. "Can we get you anything to drink?"

Every muscle in my body froze.

I was going to look up and I wouldn't recognize the woman. She would be an old, spinster who didn't give me the best sex of my life. There was more than one Carina in Cincinnati.

Maybe if I said it enough it would be true. It had to be true.

I slowly looked up and the air was knocked out of me.

"Carina?" Her name escaped on a broken breath, cracking like a boy going through puberty. Not like the man who'd fucked her against a wall and whispered filthy things to her while doing it.

Her eyes snapped to mine and widened. The color drained from her face and I was worried that she was about to collapse. "Ian?"

"You two know each other?" Hanna asked hesitantly beside me.

But I didn't answer. I took in the tall brunette standing in the middle of the office, looking as shocked as I felt. She looked almost exactly the same as she had that day, except now she had a round belly stretching her fitted dress.

I pointed an accusing finger like she had an alien growing inside her. If I had to guess an eight-month along alien.

"What the hell is that?"

ADD CARINA AND IAN'S BOOK TO YOUR GOODREADS TBR, COMING FALL 2019.

THE END

Want to read more in the Voyeur series?

You can meet Callum and Oaklyn in Voyeur.
You can meet Jake, Jackson, and Carina in Lovers.

Each book is a standalone with its own adventure.

Free on Kindle Unlimited.

REVIEW

If you loved, hated, or felt mediocre about Savior, please leave a review. They are so valuable and I cherish every single one, big or small!
Thank you so much!

ACKNOWLEDGMENTS

First and foremost, thank you to my family. You support me when I'm stressed and are more understanding than I deserve. Thank you.

Karla, you save me on a daily basis. You talk me down and talk me up. I honestly don't quite know what I'd do without you.

Serena, you work so hard and I'm so grateful to have you as my PA. You're a group and page queen and kick ass at all things so I can focus on writing.

Thank you to all my beta readers: Michelle Clay, Monica, Graves, Julia Heudorf, and Keri Graves. You ladies gave me the sweetest words and the tough love when I needed it. This story wouldn't be what it was without you.

Virginia, thank you for taking the time to run multiple edits and working with my crazy schedule.

To my proofreaders, Kelly Allenby and Michelle Clay. Thank you for catching all the things I never could.

Linda at Foreword PR. Thank you for always holding my hand and offering a virtual cheers when times are rough. You do amazing work and I'm grateful I was lucky enough to find you.

To all the beautiful authors in this community. Your words and talent always inspire me. The way you take time to offer a kind word and support always blows my mind and makes me giddy to be a part of this community.

To all the bloggers and the beautiful ladies on my ARC team. Thank you for taking time out of your busy schedules to help me achieve my dreams. I couldn't do it without you.

To all the readers and the awesome, dirty, funny ones in my reader group. Thank you from the bottom of my heart. There are endless books to choose from and I don't have words for how much it means that you took a chance on mine.

LIAR

Liar is a FREE newsletter story about Olivia and Kent. Every month in 2019, two chapters of their story will be sent out. Sign up here to not miss a thing about this age-gap romance.

Newsletter Sign Up

He was my uncle's friend, and I was too young for him.

But in the heat of the moment, against the wall in a darkened hallway of an illicit club, none of those things mattered. It was just one night of giving in to what we both wanted.

I never expected to see him two years later, sitting across me during a family dinner, encouraging me to shadow his business for my college project.

On day one we both agree that repeating that night would be a mistake. But it's a mistake we can't help but make again and again.

The rules are simple. We can't tell my uncle. We have to be content with our hotel rendezvous. And we won't fall in love.

But we both know we're liars.

ABOUT FIONA COLE

Fiona Cole is a military wife and a stay at home mom with degrees in biology and chemistry. As much as she loved science, she decided to postpone her career to stay at home with her two little girls, and immersed herself in the world of books until finally deciding to write her own.

Fiona loves hearing from her readers, so be sure to follow her on social media.

Email: authorfionacole@gmail.com
Newsletter: http://eepurl.com/bEvHtL
Reader Group: Books, Wine, and Music with Fiona Cole
https://www.facebook.com/groups/254919681647995/

Printed in Poland
by Amazon Fulfillment
Poland Sp. z o.o., Wrocław

18386405R00167